CW01460652

THE TIGER
AND
THE THIEF

Book 2 in the East Indiaman Saga

By

Griff Hosker

i

The Tiger and the Thief

Published by Griff Hosker 2025
Copyright ©Griff Hosker

Dedication

To Jan, a good friend and a loyal reader. You will not be forgotten.

Contents

Real people in the book

Lord Mornington - Richard Wellesley, Governor of India
James Kirkpatrick - Resident of the Madras Presidency
Arthur Wellesley - Colonel of the 33rd Foot and future Duke of Wellington, brother of Richard
Captain William Barclay - Sir Arthur's Adjutant General
Captain Colin Campbell - Sir Arthur's ADC
Captain John Blakiston - Sir Arthur's Engineering officer
Lieutenant General George Harris - titular head of the Army in India
The Tiger of Mysore - Tipu Sultan, the ruler of Mysore and an ally of the French
Mir Sadiq - 1st Minister of Mysore
Mir Nizam Ali Khan Siddiqi - Nizam of Hyderabad
Colonel Pohlmann - Hanoverian mercenary
Umdat ul-Umara - Nawab of Arcot
Daulat Rao Scindia - Maharajah of Gwalior
Jaswant Rao Holkar - Maharajah of Indore
Baji Rao II - Peshwa
Colonel James Stevenson - East India Cavalry officer
Dhondia Wagh - Mysorean Warlord
Dhondopant Gokhale - Maratha general
Chintamanrao Patwardhan - Maratha General
Nana Farnavis - Maratha politician
Raghoji II Bhosale - Maharajah of Berar
Saadat Ali Khan - Ruler of Oudh (Awadhe)
Balaji Kunjar/Kunjir - Peshwan General

The Section (The Devil's Dozen)

Lieutenant Richard Crozier
Sergeant Walter Grundy
Corporal Ben Neville
Private Albert Wishart
Private George Mainsgill
Private Eddie Lowe
Private Dai Evans
Private Seamus Hogan

2

The Tiger and the Thief

Private Bob Cathcart
Private John Williams
Private Bill (Smudger) Smith
Sepoy Aadyot Ganguly

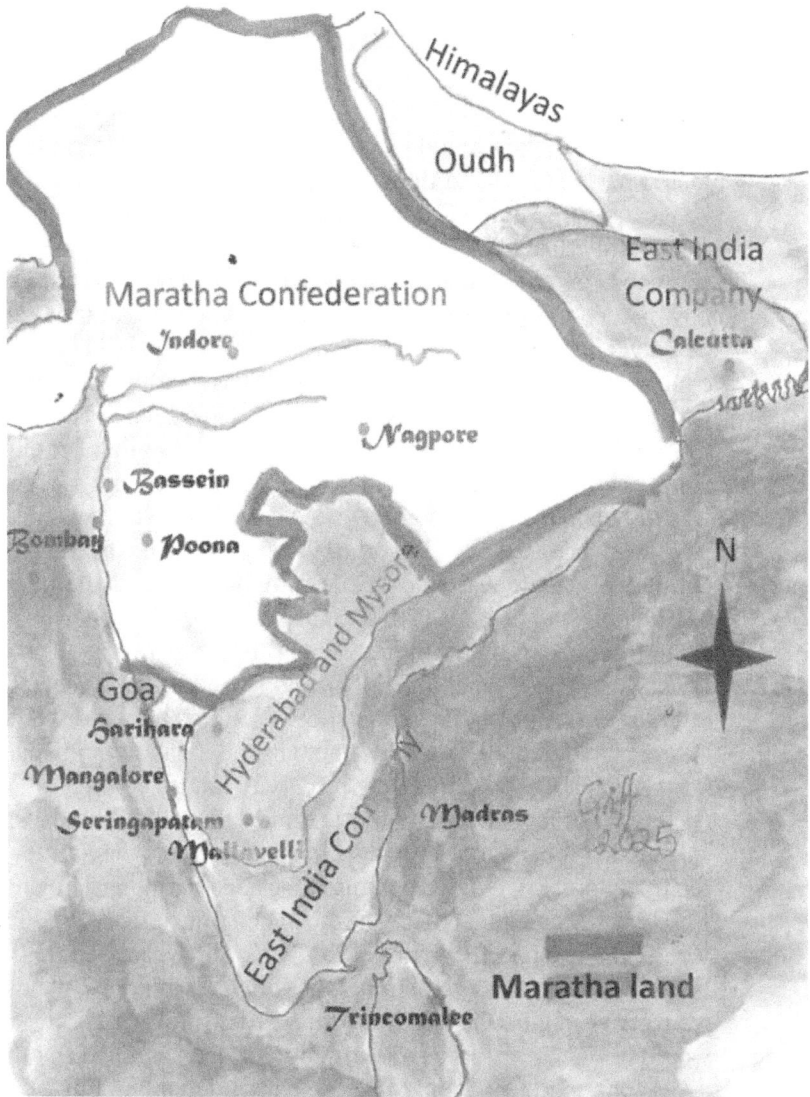

India 1799

Prologue

Men make plans and they plot. I was no different to most men. I had a plan. I had fled my home in England to escape the vengeance of a pirate, Ralph Every, and I thought I had successfully lost myself in the East India Company. Thanks to some luck and more than a little perseverance on my part I was now hidden in a company of East India soldiers. I had, I thought smugly, been so clever and resourceful. I had accumulated enough treasure to disappear, here in the east, and live a life of luxury. I even had the means to escape. I had a French horse, Froggy, and I had learned the language of India so that I could simply ride off in the night and no one would ever find me. That was my plan and it was a good one. The old Bill Smith would have wondered why I did not run. Why wait? That was the old Bill but now there was a new Bill Smith. He was called Smudger and he now had ties. I was tied to the section of soldiers who came from backgrounds little different from my own and I felt a loyalty to them. Worse, I had helped to save the old sergeant after the Battle of Mallavelli and now I felt tied to him. I would still escape but there would be a better time. I had no immediate need to rush off and start a new life.

It was not far from the battlefield of Mallavelli to the river surrounded fortress of Seringapatam and we made the journey relatively quickly. We were going to besiege Seringapatam and from what Lieutenant Crozier and Captain Tucker had said, that would not be a speedy process. The Tiger of Mysore had fled there and the fortress was strongly fortified. I would use the time we were besieging the city and fortress to my advantage. It would be a chance for me to learn more of the language and the geography of the land and to increase my burgeoning fortune. I would wait until an opportunity came up that would let me slip away with my fortune in gold and jewels. I had managed to escape England, the East Indiaman, and the dungeon of Jahan Cholan. The jungle around Seringapatam would be my passage to luxury. I just needed to choose my time.

Chapter 1

The Siege of Seringapatam 1799

Our luck, or rather my luck in discovering the identity of the First Minister of Mysore, had resulted in a benefit for the section. Lord Mornington had rewarded us by giving us a relatively easy duty. We were not camped by the water which was fly and mosquito infested but we were sent to the rocky outcrop above Palahalli. The air was fresher on the higher ground away from the stink of the jungle. We were even given a relatively safe job. We were there to observe the enemy in their fortress across the river. As billets go it was not the worst. The rest of the East India soldiery, mainly the Madra regiments, were with the main army. We were the only European section and that meant we acted independently. We liked that role. We answered just to the lieutenant and Lord Mornington.

While the rest of the army dug trenches and hauled batteries into position we made a cosy camp. We had flattish ground and sufficient grazing for both of our horses, Duchess and Froggy. Duchess was the nag that pulled our cart and Froggy was the French horse I had taken and which carried the sickly Sergeant Grundy. He was getting better, it appeared to us, but we still insisted that he did less physical labour and rode the horse rather than marched. We had a slight trek to fetch water but it was not far to go. Even better, we had a village within spitting distance and Sepoy Aadyot Ganguly quickly established good relations with the villagers which meant we were able to augment our rations. He negotiated for food and milk for our tea. We bartered things we had taken from the battlefield and did not need. When we took from the dead at Mallavelli it had been more than just coins and weapons. The better dressed officers yielded clothes that the villagers needed.

While the tents were being erected I feigned the need to attend to the cart. In reality I was secreting my box of treasures in the bottom of the cart. I had decided that the fine casket I was using attracted too much attention and so I put the coins and jewels in a sack labelled oats. If it was picked up it would fool no one but as it was me who fed the horses and as the bag was

6

below the actual oats, it did not matter overmuch. When that was done I felt relief. My treasure was hidden. I would either sell or trade the casket at some point.

The whole section, including Lieutenant Crozier, made sure that Sergeant Grundy did little actual work. We had tried to stop him working altogether but that had failed. We let him supervise and Lieutenant Crozier put him in charge of the cooking. He was not the best of cooks but we were able to modify his culinary disasters. Our camp was made defensible and secure. The lieutenant had the men clear a good line of fire and we hauled the rocks we had moved from the ground beneath our tents to make a barrier against an attack. We were more than twelve hundred yards from the walls and the cannons we could see but the lieutenant was a careful man. We piled soil around the fortress side of the rocks and then planted stakes to make a redoubt. It kept us busy and meant we avoided having to toil in the thick undergrowth or close to the shallow mosquito ridden rivers. As he allowed us to work in our shirts and wearing straw hats it was not that bad. Seamus and Dai sang songs as we laboured and it seemed to make the work go a little easier.

Five days after we had first set up our camp we were visited. It was not our company that was sought but the view from our position. Lord Mornington, Colonel Wellesley, General Harris and General Baird, along with their aides, appeared. They merely nodded to the lieutenant and then stood behind our barricade.

Captain Tucker, puffing on a cheroot, appeared behind them. I saw the generals take out their telescopes and scan the walls of Seringapatam.

"What is going on, Captain?" This was our position and the lieutenant was curious. We might be used by the general and it was better to be forewarned.

He came over to talk to the lieutenant. The rest of us had begun to don tunics as soon as we had seen them arrive. General Harris did not like us and would find any excuse he could to punish us. We gathered close by, pretending to labour so that we could hear the two officers as they spoke.

"Your little camp is the perfect place to spy out the defences. We have batteries almost in place although the Tipu and his men are doing all they can to disrupt the work."

Lieutenant Crozier nodded, "We have heard their cannons. Damned noisy things."

"That they are and not all of them are ancient pieces. Our friends, the French, have been supplying them with newer weapons. Their guns are manned by locals but they are supervised by French officers and, we believe, mercenaries."

"This won't be a quick job, then?"

"A month or so."

"A brew, Sir?"

The captain looked over at Sergeant Grundy. It had been the captain and I who had found the doctor to diagnose his heart complaint. "Perfect, Sergeant, and you, I hope, are not over taxing yourself."

He sniffed, "Chance would be a fine thing, Sir. These lads won't let me do anything but make tea and stir the pot."

I think it was the memory of that fateful day when we had captured Mir Sadiq that made the captain turn to seek me out, "And you, Smith, still here?" There was a something in his tone that made me shiver.

I went cold, despite the heat. Out of all the men with whom I served the only one who had an inkling of my desire to desert was the captain. The lieutenant gave me a curious look as I answered, "Of course, Sir. It's not like there is anywhere else to go, is there?"

"Quite."

The mug of tea was handed to him and I was glad when the two officers began to talk of other matters. "So what do we do, Captain?"

"You are to protect this little ant hill. It is unlikely that the enemy will try to take it but if a few determined men came at night they might be able to slit the throats of any watchers and could cause havoc. It was a choice of a company of the East Suffolks, the 12th, or your motley crew. It was deemed by those in authority that the 12th could be better employed and your handful of men have shown that they are resourceful."

Corporal Neville sidled up to me as the rest of the section decided to make themselves scarce. Senior officers were seen to be as dangerous as the enemy. "The captain has your card marked, eh, Smudger?"

"What do you mean?"

He laughed, "You didn't really think we were all blind to what you really want."

I tried to brazen it out, "I have no idea what you mean, Corporal."

"Listen we all chose this outfit. It was either this or stay in prison. There was no argument. You, for whatever reason, also joined us but you are looking for a way out." He held up his hand to silence my protests. "We like you, Smudger, and you add something to the section that is, well, different, but if you are unhappy then know this, none of us will stand in your way."

I was so shocked that I opened up, "You all know?"

He laughed, "Of course."

"Well, that might have been true once but I am content now." He fixed me with a baleful stare, "Honest." The truth was that there were simply too many soldiers for me to try to desert. General Harris would make it a personal vendetta to have me brought back in chains and whipped on a gun carriage. When I went it would be when the section was off on its own and far from the army.

"Just so's you know." He nodded to the sergeant, "Make yourself useful and give the sarge a hand. See if you can get him to sit down."

The pot was close to the senior officers and I could hear the buzz of conversation as I neared. Lord Mornington must have sensed the change of pot stirrer and turned. He took in who I was and then returned to the conversation. His brother was saying, "They have trenches protecting the south western corner of the fortress."

General Harris said, "So what, Colonel? We outnumber them. Let us just batter the walls and take this Tiger by the tail."

General Baird said, "General Harris, I have more reason than any to want vengeance. I would give the Tiger the same punishment I endured when I was his prisoner but I will not waste men's lives in a pointless attack against prepared defences."

I did not like General Harris and while Colonel Wellesley was not a likeable man I knew that he was a better soldier. General Baird also seemed to me to be a better officer.

Colonel Wellesley sighed and explained to the officer who was superior to him in rank only, "General Harris, the enemy are giving extra protection to the walls they feel are the weakest. If you would examine that corner you will see that the masonry is not the best. It also looks more ancient than these newer walls to the south. I think that we assault the fortress there." The way he said it made it sound like an order rather than a suggestion.

General Baird said little. That was his way. Lord Mornington drawled, "What about the river, Arthur? Is that not a problem?"

"Look through your telescope, Richard, you will see men wading across it. The Cauvery is not a river that can be forded but that tributary can." I smiled. The use of Christian names excluded General Harris.

General Baird said, "It is a moot point, my lord, until we get the batteries in place."

Colonel Wellesley said, "That is simple, General. We place one there." He pointed, I could see, to the right of us close to where the small stream that ran there took a sharp turn east. "Another two there," he pointed to the left of us, about another five hundred yards away. "They can batter the entrenchments and weaken them. Finally, we need one across the river so that we can weaken the north west corner."

General Baird said, "A good plan."

General Harris just snorted, "Just so long as we do it quickly. I want this fat tiger in my hands."

The colonel said, "It will take at least a week, General, and that is a week when they will have to tighten their belts and this fat tiger may become a little more svelte." He turned, "Come, the smell of this cooking is making me hungry."

I smiled, "There will be enough for you, Colonel."

Before he could answer General Harris snapped, "Eat with thieves and vagabonds! What a suggestion! Know your place!"

Lord Mornington said, "Thank you for the offer, Private. How is that sergeant of yours? I saw you relieved him."

"Sergeant Grundy is being looked after by the lads, Sir. He is a good officer."

It was almost as though my use of the word officer reminded Lord Mornington of something for he shouted, "Lieutenant, Captain, would you join us?"

The two officers hurried over. Lieutenant Crozier had already fastened his tunic and attached his sword and now he jammed his hat upon his head. They both snapped to attention.

"Lieutenant, this observation post must be manned twenty-four hours a day. We need to know what is happening in the fortress and the defences. You have a horse, I believe?"

"Yes, Sir."

"Then send word if there are any changes to the defences. Captain Tucker, you will liaise with these men. We are particularly interested in any strengthening of that northwest corner."

"Sir."

They left to join their aides and horses. The two officers accompanied them and I saw Sergeant Grundy jam his hat on his head and follow them. The rest of the section had been busy feigning to work but now they hurried over. Seamus grinned, "So, Smudger, what did those sharp little ears of yours pick up?"

I used the ladle to point, "They are going to bombard that north western bastion. Artillery there, there and there."

The corporal took in what I had said and then asked, "And us?"

"We watch. At night as well as during the day."

Dai nodded, "That means no digging. I think I could sit and watch quite easily."

Captain Tucker had followed the officers and it was the lieutenant and sergeant who rejoined us. Giving me a knowing look he said, "Now I dare say that Smith has told you his version of the orders but I will give you the official ones."

I gave him an innocent look, "I have no idea what you mean, Sir."

He shook his head and then gave us our orders. They were almost the same but he added, mysteriously, "When the attack happens then our role will change but that won't be for a week or so. Until then we forage for food. We watch for attempts to dislodge us and we try to find out as much as we can about that north west corner."

As duties go that first week was almost idyllic. Captain Tucker would join us not long before noon. He and the lieutenant would look at the fort and then chat while we ate. We watched as the Mysoreans did their best to disrupt the placing of the batteries. Surprisingly it was the bastion north of the river which took the longest to place. I think it was because the enemy had a clearer field of fire and, as Captain Tucker pointed out, the walls on the side facing west were not as strong and could not hold the powerful cannons that made it harder for the northern battery to be established. The generals deduced that it was better to work at night and so our sleep was somewhat disturbed by the sound of muskets as well as the hacking of axes and the lumbering of wheels. I did not envy those troops who had the heat of the day and the noise and stink of guns close by at night. For us they were a rumble. Closer to the ground they would have been a loud crack that would render sleep almost impossible.

Sergeant Grundy, with time to recover, did so. It was gradual but he slowly attained a better colour. The greyness of the moment of the heart attack was long gone and with a regular intake of food, not to mention rum, he was recovering but we were all mindful of the doctor's diagnosis.

I suppose it was inevitable that the movements on the clearly visible mound were seen from the walls. The two officers had commented on the enemy officers who gathered to train their telescopes on our batteries and on us. They identified the Tiger of Mysore, the Tipu Sultan, and Captain Tucker allowed me to see him through the telescope. He did not look like a tiger. He looked like a little fat man although he was well dressed.

It was eight days after we had first established our camp that I was woken by the urgent shaking of my arm. It was Ben Neville, "Rouse yourself, Smith. There are men making their way up the slope."

I was alert in an instant. I did not bother to don my jacket. I slept in my breeches and vest. I just grabbed my musket, powder and ball and hurried to the barricade. I picked up my bayonet. We had placed thorns below the redoubt which was the height of a man's chest. I saw that Dai and Seamus, Lowe, Mainsgill and Albert Wishart were there already. Sergeant Grundy was at one end and the lieutenant at the other. I heard Corporal Neville hiss, "Williams and Cathcart, shift yourselves."

I turned to Albert, "Good luck, Albert." Fighting at night was always a gamble.

"You too, Smudger. Do you think there will be many of them?" Albert had been a thief like me but more of a pickpocket. He had worked during the day and in crowds. I knew his fear. We seemed like a pitifully small number. Being alone never worried me. I had always been alone.

"Just keep firing, Albert, and trust to the lads. We have good brothers in arms."

"Aye, that we do."

The two tardy ones joined us at the barricade. The others had loaded already and I made sure that my ball was well tamped down and my musket ready. My bayonet was rammed into the soft earth behind the barricade. I had no intention of attaching it to the musket for that made it less likely to be accurate and the darkness was a big enough obstacle as it was. It was there in case it came to close quarters. I had not had the time to fetch a pistol. I quite liked the pistol as it was a handy close quarter weapon. As the hammers on Williams' and Cathcart's muskets clicked back, we waited.

There was silence and that alone told us that there were men approaching. The animals of the night were always noisy and we had become used to the sounds of life and death in the night. The presence of men was confirmed when we all heard the distinctive crack as an unfortunate foot found a piece of wood and broke it. Lieutenant Crozier whispered, "No one fires until I give the command."

No one said a word in reply. We knew better. The waiting was hard. The men who were coming would wear dark clothes. Their skin would also help them while our white faces would give them a target. They would know our numbers. The men watching us would have counted us each time they observed our movements. We had no idea if this was a company or a few scouts intent on slitting throats. Captain Tucker had told us that eight sentries down in the trenches had been killed that way in the first ten days. It was not a huge number but for those eight it was the end of their life and that thought had sobered me.

I saw movement but they were mere shadows of men. I could not guess numbers. I had fought enough at nighttime to estimate the height of a man. I chose a shadow and aimed at what I assumed was the middle. When I fired I hoped to hit him there. A wound in the stomach was normally fatal. If he was tall then I would hit him in his manhood and if he was short then it would be his head. I found it easier to fire at a shadow. If it was a man then I would see his face and somehow that was harder. When we volley fired it was at a large number of men. You never knew if it was your ball that had killed a man. When the lieutenant's voice gave the order to fire it almost came as a shock but I squeezed the trigger and there was a flash. Not all of our muskets fired at once. It was a somewhat ragged volley necessitated by the need to find a body to aim at but in the rippling light I saw a half-naked warrior clutch his shoulder. He was shorter than I had expected. I quickly reloaded but I was so practised at this action that I did not need to take my eyes from the slope. There looked to be more than fifty men who were now scrambling as quickly as they could up the slope towards us. This was a determined attempt to rid the fortress of their watchers. Their muskets rippled in reply. I saw that they had bayonets and knew that they would be even more inaccurate for they made the poorer muskets heavier. I aimed my next ball lower as the men would be closer to us. The night was lit up and the air filled with the stink of powder. Most of the balls sent in our direction smacked into the earth rampart and did no damage but two zipped over our heads like angry bees. Firing their muskets had to be done at the halt and that helped us as they came no closer while they did so. I fired a second time.

Suddenly there was a shout from the enemy ranks which might have been an order and this time they did not bother to reload but rushed us. I quickly reloaded. My bayonet was close enough to use if they managed to reach the rampart. The man I hit with my next ball was fast. He had raced up the slope like a mountain goat and his face suddenly loomed up out of the dark just ten feet from me. I still aimed at his chest but in the time it took for the musket to fire he closed even more. My ball tore into his stomach and he screamed. He dropped his musket and grabbed his belly as he fell, dying. I grabbed my bayonet and, after fitting it, took advantage of the fact that the next men had to avoid the bodies of the dead for others had enjoyed the same success as I had. The bayonet that came at my head looked enormous but I think it was an illusion and was the same size as mine. I flicked it to the right and then drove mine at the half naked warrior's head which was just below the parapet. It drove into his eye and thence his brain. He must have died instantly for he made not a sound. Even as I raised the musket to fend off another warrior, I heard a bugle and the attackers began to retreat. I tore the bayonet from the end of my musket and reloaded. The barrel was getting hot. There were few muskets firing in reply and the fleeing men were shadows once more. I fired at one that was thirty yards from me and hit him. It was not a killing wound but I took satisfaction in the fact that he dropped his musket.

"Cease fire."

There was the noise of men now crashing through the undergrowth as they raced to get away from the killing ground.

"Anyone hurt?"

I looked to my left and saw that John Williams was unhurt and Albert, to my right, was reloading. A chorus of voice confirmed that we had escaped unhurt. The lieutenant shouted, "Sergeant?"

"Still in the land of the living, Sir." He sounded cheerful.

We were all relieved.

We stood to until the first light of dawn appeared in the east. The sergeant and Aadyot made a brew and we watched for another attack. When it was light enough to see we were sent to clear the dead and to gather their weapons. Already flies were buzzing around the corpses. The corporal led us while Lieutenant Crozier and the sergeant watched with loaded weapons. General Harris was wrong about us, we were not all criminals but we were opportunists. The dead yielded few coins but some had rings and they had swords. We could sell the swords. There would be soldiers, new to India, who might wish to buy a souvenir and then return to England with extravagant tales of how they had won it.

The bodies were brought back up the slope for we did not want carrion close to our camp. The lieutenant pointed to the east side of the hill, "Pile them there with kindling and when the wind blows from the west we will burn them. Let us spoil our enemies' appetites."

When the captain arrived to observe the camp he was told of the attack. "That tells us that they do not wish us to observe them. It means we will keep on watching and see what it is that they do not wish us to see. I will stay longer today."

It took a few days but we were rewarded, the day after we burned the bodies, when we saw some newer artillery pieces being pulled into place along the north wall. They clearly intended to harass the engineers trying to build the redoubts across the river. The captain hastened to tell the senior officers and we resumed our life of relative luxury. We were able to see smaller guns being brought to fire at the artillery pieces they had pulled into place. It made their fire less effective. The duels were interesting. The guns of the company that were brought up were smaller and sent a smaller ball than the ones used by the men of Mysore but our gunners were faster and more accurate. I did see blue coated officers directing the fire of the enemy guns and deduced that they were French. They might have had the skill but their gunners did not. Our earthworks continued to be built.

My idyllic life ended the day I was summoned to meet Lord Mornington and the senior staff. The captain came with an officer of engineers who stayed with the section when the captain and I left. That I went with just Captain Tucker did not bode well. The last time I had been summoned to meet with Captain Tucker and senior officers I had been sent with him to spy. All the way down the hill and north to the headquarters I ran through my mind everything I might have done that was wrong. I could not think of anything. That meant they needed me and not the rest of the section. I had tried to hide in the East India Company but I now had a notoriety I did not enjoy. I was told that I did not need my weapons but I took my pistol and dagger. I felt naked without any weapons, even in the company of the senior staff. They had taken over a small house and sentries guarded it. I was viewed with interest as we neared the guarded tent and passed the other officers not senior enough to attend the meeting. I could see on their faces the wonder that a private from the East India Company was going to a meeting with the governor and the senior staff.

When we entered Lord Mornington looked up, "Ah Smith, isn't it?"

I had taken off my hat, "Yes, My Lord."

There were five of them in the small room. Captain Tucker was the most junior. General Harris glowered at me, as was normal, and General Baird seemed to be scrutinising me as though he was weighing me up. Lord Mornington and his brother were looking at some documents.

Eventually, Lord Mornington looked up, "Smith, General Harris here, sees you as a thief."

I stiffened, "I won't deny, My Lord, that when I lived in England I did take what I needed to help me to survive, as I did on the ship east, but since I joined the company I am a reformed character." The lie did not stick in my throat and I did not flush.

There was a smile on his lips and his voice as he said, "No, Smith, you misunderstand me for we need a thief and you are in a unique position."

"Unique, My Lord?"

He smiled and lit a cigar, "When you sought the doctor and discovered Mir Sadiq you made yourself so. You know him and he knows you."

General Harris shook his head, "I said, before, that I disapprove of this strategy, My Lord. By his own admission this man is a thief and the last thing we need is for him to…"

For the first time since I had known him Lord Mornington snapped and the smile left his face and voice, "General Harris, let me tell this young man what we wish of him and keep your opinions to yourself." I saw Colonel Wellesley nod his approval as the general nodded in resignation. "As I was saying, you know Mir Sadiq, but what you do not know is the conversation Captain Tucker and I had with him when we were alone." He stared at me, "Are you a loyal Englishman?"

"Of course."

"Then do I have your word, as a loyal Englishman, that you will not divulge what you are about to hear?"

There was no way I would tell anyone. Did they all have such a low opinion of us that they thought we would tell an enemy? I nodded and said, "Yes, My Lord."

"Mir Sadiq is our man. He and some of the others, you do not need to know their names, are willing to help us to overthrow the Tiger of Mysore. Sadly, we were not able to establish a satisfactory means of communication before he returned to Tipu Sultan. As I said, you are unique. You know Mir Sadiq and he knows you but more importantly, you are a thief and can get into and out of buildings unseen. We want you to go into the fortress, find Mir Sadiq, and arrange for a time when he will allow us to enter the fortress without too great a loss of life."

I was stunned. It was impossible. Even if I could get in I would be spotted and arrested. My end would not be a pretty one. Spies were not treated as ordinary prisoners of war.

Captain Tucker was a clever man and he and I had both been behind enemy lines before. The difference was that then he had been in command and I had just heeded his advice. This time I would be alone. He spoke gently to encourage me to agree, "You are good at this sort of thing, Smudger. We will dress you in ragged clothes. There are Europeans inside the walls, mainly Dutch and French but your skin will not necessarily alert those within. I know that you are good at hiding and have a quick wit. You have enough French words to help with the illusion. If any Frenchman speaks to you then you have the words to make them believe you are a local." He had spent some time teaching me French and I appeared, I know not why, to have some skill with languages.

I sighed, "Thank you all for the compliment but how would I find this man?"

Lord Mornington smiled, "That is where I come in. This evening, at dusk, I will parade before the entrenchments. I will ensure that I am well away from the walls. I do not wish to end my life there. I will wait until the Tipu and his advisors come to the walls to spy upon me. When they do and I see that Mir Sadiq is there I will take off my hat and bow. Captain Tucker will be next to me and he will do the same. It will be a signal for he knows us both. The gesture will appear to be provocative to the Tiger but will be a clear message for our man."

This sounded more hopeful, "Then it is prearranged?"

Captain Tucker shook his head, "No, Smudger, but the last thing we said before we let him go was that we would be in touch. This will let him know that we are trying to contact him. He will be in public, at least for a couple of hours, and that is when you will enter and meet with him. That way you could leave the fortress before dawn."

"And the men who are defending the trenches, they will not stop me?"

Lord Mornington said, "You will not be going in that way. Beyond the southern wall and their trenches we have no men and neither do the enemy. The undergrowth there is too thick. In addition, there is open ground before the walls so that if we tried to assault it the men would be cut down from guns on the walls. There is a tributary, the Little Cauvery. Your section is, even now, making a raft for you to use to cross that river and the stream beyond. We will have attracted their attention to the west and you can use darkness to make your entry. How you escape..." he shrugged, "we will not tie your hands. When you do escape then return to your section. Captain Tucker will be there."

General Harris said, "Men like this have no honour. He will refuse."

Any thoughts I might have had about refusing disappeared, "Very well, My Lord. I do not think I will survive but I will do as asked, if only to show General Harris that titles and breeding alone do not make Englishmen. It is what is in their hearts." I held the gaze of the general. I would show him.

Lord Mornington beamed, "Well said, Smith. Now, Captain, we have little time. Get him to the hilltop and prepare him."

Chapter 2

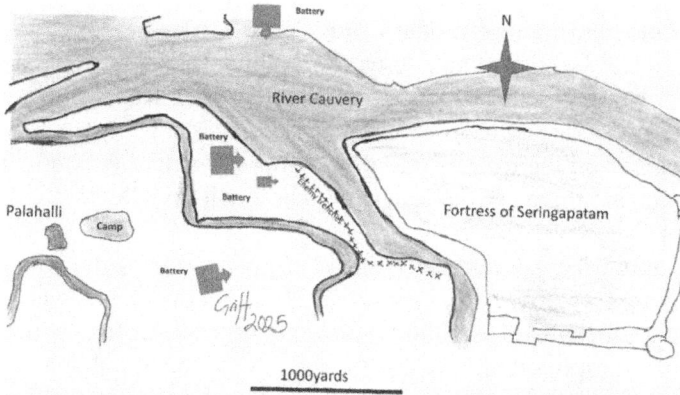

The fortress of Seringapatam and the siege lines

as of April 1799

As we hurried up the hill I was silent. If I was back to being a thief again then I would need all my old skills. I knew that they were all wrong. They thought it would be an easy task to get to meet the First Minister inside the fortress but I knew that they were wrong. I was a thief and a good one but in England I had known the land and the people. I knew how to move and where to hide. Here it was as different as it could be. I would be amongst enemies and my face would mark me as different. I would not be able to blend into the background. I forced myself to think about the cities and places I had visited. There would be sentries but they were, in many ways, predictable. They walked the same routes. I had observed how some sentries seemed not to see what was in front of them. They expected to see what they always saw. The men on the walls would be looking for an attack by a number of men. A single shadow would not be a threat. I knew how to avoid their attention and if their eyes were on the west wall then it would be easier. My problem was that I did not know the fortress. Once I was inside the walls I might waste time and risk capture by searching the wrong places. Getting in was possible but finding the man would be far harder.

We had left the camp and were walking along the trail that led to our camp. It was becoming more well-worn. "Captain, where will I find Mir Sadiq?" I stopped for we had just begun to ascend the slope and the fortress was a little more visible. I pointed. "It is huge and there are thousands of people within it. Where will he be?"

Captain Tucker nodded, "You are right but Mir Sadiq will know that we are sending someone. He just won't know who. That is why we are sending you. He knows you. He saw you when we captured him. In the fortress he will be in public but, knowing we are sending someone, he will try to be alone. The fortress is also a palace and there will be a garden with fountains and ornamental trees. I would begin there. You could use the cover of shrubs and bushes. The First Minister might well use such a place for contemplation."

It was a start but that was all. "And if he is not there?"

"Then seek those who are well dressed but not warriors. He will be in their company. If you fail to see him then seek the grander quarters. Remember what we did when we were behind the lines. Find yourself something to carry and pretend you are a servant with a message."

I sighed, "His lordship has set me a challenge which is impossible. I will die or at best be as General Baird and spend years in gaol."

"It is a hard task, I confess, but our hand was forced. We assumed that Mir Sadiq and the others who support our cause would have persuaded the Tipu to surrender. He has not."

"Then I am to make up for Lord Mornington's error of judgement."

"His lordship is doing what he is doing for Britain. You are also serving both the country and the East India Company," We were nearing the camp and Captain Tucker paused, his hand on my arm, "This could be the making of you, Smith. With a friend like Lord Mornington, your star could rise."

"And what good would that do if I were dead?" I gave him a shrewd look, "And you, Captain, will you also have a future set on an astral trajectory?" I paused, "Without the risk to either your life or your freedom?" He flushed and I knew that he had been promised something. Before he could speak I shook my head, "It matters not. To benefit from this association I need to survive and, at the moment I think that is unlikely but I did not flee London to die without a fight. I will do my best, not for his lordship but for Bill Smith."

When we entered the camp Lieutenant Crozier approached. Captain Tucker said, "I will tell the lieutenant what we are to do although the engineering officer will have given him more than a clue. You had better prepare."

I nodded and went, not to my tent, but to the pot where Aadyot and the sergeant were talking as they watched it bubble and blip. There was no time for pleasantries. "Aadyot, I am being sent inside the fortress as a spy. If I am to survive then I need your help."

Sergeant Grundy's mouth dropped open. Aadyot shook his head, "Smudger, I will come with you."

"No, it is bad enough that one of the section is being put at risk. Just tell me all you can to help me to evade discovery. What should I wear? Are there any words that I do not use that might aid me?"

I think that I was Aadyot's best friend in the section and he was desperate to help me. He led me to my tent and spoke non-stop while helping me to ready myself for the ordeal ahead. The section had been issued new clothes at Calcutta but we had not discarded any of the old ones. We found the dirtiest shirt and the breeches that had been so dirty that they were now a sort of pale brown. The red from my tunic had seeped in the white and with an accumulation of dirt and the detritus of travail in the jungle looked nothing like the uniform of an English soldier. When I was dressed he looked satisfied. The lieutenant must have told the rest of the section for they were busy hammering and chopping as they made a raft under the supervision of the officer of engineers. I knew that they would all be desperate to speak to me but they would also want me to succeed and play their part.

The lieutenant and the captain appeared, having briefed the men. The captain nodded, "Better, Smith."

Aadyot shook his head, "Not yet good enough." He untied the queue in my hair and ruffled it so that it looked wild. "Wait here, I have not yet finished."

Left alone with the two officers I laid my weapons on my bed. I would be guided by Aadyot and let him decide which ones I should take. Lieutenant Crozier, more for something to say than anything else said, "We will wait for you where we drop you off."

I shook my head, "I cannot be tied to the place I will leave. I will make my own way back." I gave a wry laugh. "Getting out appears to be a little unrealistic at the moment. First, I have to find this man and trust that he has not decided to remain loyal to the Tipu."

I saw from the captain's face that it was a possibility. He shook his head, "I do not think he will do so. Promises were made by Lord Mornington and Mir Sadiq is a survivor. He knows that against the might of Britain and the company then the Tiger is doomed. He may well have a way to get you out. I think you are right not to be tied to a particular place you will use."

Lieutenant Crozier did not look convinced. "Is there a watchword, Captain Tucker?"

"Dublin."

I smiled, "The horse."

Captain Tucker nodded.

Aadyot appeared and tossed me a pair of sandals. "These were mine and they should fit but do not put them on yet." He had a bowl and in it were some berries. I did not know the name of them but I had seen them and we had used them in our cooking. He mashed them with his fingers and said, "Take off your shirt."

I did so and he began to smear the concoction on my face, neck and exposed arms. He finished up by putting the last on my feet.

"Now you look better. You do not look like one of us but you no longer look European. You look like a bastard born of a white father and an Indian woman. There are many such beggars who live in our land. You will be treated with scorn if you are noticed at all. There are some words you should know." All the time he was talking he was cleaning the bowl out with my shirt. He handed me the shirt and said, "Put it back on." The berry stains had added to the look of a beggar. He fastened the sandals and then gave me the bowl. "Hold this out and adopt a pleading look on your face." I knew how to do that. When I had been a young thief I had learned that a wide-eyed look often allayed suspicion. "Good. Now here are the words you will need." The words he taught me I had heard from beggars. He ensured that I had the right inflection. I knew what the words meant. I was asking for food, alms, shelter.

"What about weapons, Aadyot?"

He looked at the array on the bed and said, "No pistols. The bayonet marks you as a soldier." He selected a long thin stiletto and a wicked looking native dagger. The stiletto had come from England but the dagger had been acquired on my travels. "Put the dagger in your belt, it will not look out of place."

Captain Tucker said, "The stiletto should be hidden. Drop your breeches." I did so and he took a length of leather thong that was with the weapons and he tied the weapon to my right thigh.

"How do I get to it, Sir?"

"If they have taken your other weapon it means that you are a prisoner. When you ask to empty your bowels…"

I nodded, "Thank you, Sir."

He glanced at his time piece, "We had better go. I want to be in place well before the signal." He turned to the lieutenant, "You know the place?"

The lieutenant's voice was harsh as he said, "We will look after our own, Captain. You just look after yourself."

"Harsh, Richard."

He gave the captain a wry smile, "Oh, we are used to being used, it is not just you."

He left to hurry back to Lord Mornington. The last thing I did was to secrete my lockpicks in my breeches. They had been the tools of my trade in England and I might well need them again. We went outside and I saw that the simple raft was finished.

The engineer said, "It will get you across and, if you need it, back. Good luck." He saluted and turned. He would return to his men and tell them about the young soldier being sent across the river. He would not know the reason and speculation would be rife in the camp.

The raft was just big enough for one person. That was good. I would be able to hide it easily. I was touched by the looks of concern on the faces of the others.

Sergeant Grundy handed me a bowl of food and some bread, "Here y'are, Smudger, get something in your belly."

"Thanks."

"There is some rum too."

I had a mouthful of the hot food and I shook my head before swallowing, "If they smell rum they will know I am not a native." I saw Aadyot nodding. "Just a cup of tea will do." I smiled, "Of course, a double ration of rum when I come back will not go amiss."

The section looked uncomfortable as they waited for me to eat. I was gobbling it for I knew we had to be by the small tributary well before dark so that I could identify where the sentries would be found as well as finding a good place to enter.

Seamus joked to lighten the mood, "Sure, and now that you are a friend of the general's we can expect an easy life, eh, Smudger?"

Dai shook his head, "It is never a good thing to be too cosy with the nobs and the like. We are always better off with our own kind."

I finished the food and swallowed the tea in one. I would not make water as that might be something I could do inside the fortress. It would help me to blend in for I intended to seek out the poorer quarters first. That way I would be able to disappear more easily.

I was the one without a job as we headed down the trail to the tributary of the Cauvery. Sergeant Grundy was remaining at the camp and he said, "I will keep my eye on your things."

"And Duchess?"

"And Duchess."

We passed the two twelve pounders of Number 8 battery manned by British gunners. They were too concerned with the walls to worry about a section of East India soldiers who were probably going to collect kindling or hunt for food. We had to

skirt the deep ravine that lay to the south of us and that took us
closer to the entrenchments than I would have liked. The most
difficult section was as we crossed the Little Cauvery by the
stone bridge. We were somewhat exposed and just four hundred
yards to the north west lay the trenches and they were manned.
The red uniforms were spotted and muskets popped from both
the walls and the trenches. There were plenty of musket balls but
they were all wasted as the range was too far to be effective. It
meant, however, that they knew soldiers were down by the river.
That was not unusual. There were regular patrols and probing.
Perhaps the timing was different, the patrols were normally at
dawn but it would not be seen as something of note.

Once we crossed the bridge we disappeared through the
undergrowth. The men on the walls could not see us and the men
at the trenches would be watching for us to reappear. We would
not. We were heading for the water course we had seen from the
hill. It joined the river close to the fortress and that was a good
place to watch. It was nerve wracking as we could not see the
tops of the walls. Were we being observed? Red uniforms would
stand out against the green undergrowth. I would be the one who
would be invisible. Aadyot, who was now my shadow, had done
a good job. The lieutenant halted us when he saw the large
rectangular tower loom up. There was a round tower at the south
eastern end but here the large tower guarded the gate. The gate
would be barred. Leaving the raft on the trail under the watch of
the corporal, Lowe and Mainsgill, the rest of us crept through the
undergrowth. We did it carefully to avoid any snakes that might
hang down and prematurely end the expedition and also to make
as little disturbance of the undergrowth as possible. We reached
the edge of the water and hid behind the boles of the trees that
had profited from the open aspect and presence of water.

The first thing I discovered was that I could see rocks in the
river and that it did not look deep. It was moving relatively
quickly and that meant there would be no crocodiles. I said
nothing but I was already thinking of wading across. It was not
far and I could swim. Better that than taking a raft I had to hide. I
next examined the walls. My heart sank. I could climb and there
were enough handholds to enable me to do so but the men in the
round tower would easily see me. I would be like a spider

exposed by a sudden light. I looked at another means of egress from the fortress. I saw a door and the disappointment of the walls vanished. I had my lock picks and, as I had discovered when we had rescued the Hardcastles, even a barred door could be opened.

The lieutenant had said nothing but when I squatted he said, "Satisfied?"

I nodded, "Yes, Sir. I think I will wade the river rather use the raft and have to find somewhere to hide it and that door yonder looks a promising place. However, I may need a bayonet."

"Wishart, give Smith your bayonet."

I stuffed the bayonet in the back of my belt. We waited. I found myself smiling for when I had been a thief in England I had learned patience through waiting for owners to vacate their shops and homes. I found it easier than the others. I could hear them swatting the flies and mosquitoes from the water. Only Aadyot and I did not for we were not bothered. I wondered if the juice he had used was effective against the beasts. If so then when I returned I would ask him to make me a batch. Inside my head I laughed. The chances of me surviving were slim. I studied the water. There did not appear to be anything in it but as it was a murky brown it was hard to tell.

We knew as soon as Lord Mornington and Captain Tucker arrived at the trenches. We could not see them but we saw the reaction of the men on the walls. Albert Wishart was up a tree and watching the men in the trenches he said, "The men in the trenches are acting like something is up."

I just said, "See you soon, lads."

I slipped in the water. It was surprisingly warm but as I waded to the middle, avoiding the rocks, it became a little cooler. I could not watch the walls and the water. I chose to keep my eye on the latter so that I did not fall in. A splash would draw attention to me. If I was seen the first I would know would be the report of a musket shot. I reached the other side and then looked up. There was no one ahead and, mercifully, no one watching from the round tower. Perhaps Lord Mornington's act had intrigued them. I had to cross the road before I could sprint to the door. I breathed a sigh of relief when I reached the wall and I was not seen. I turned with my back to the wall. I could see

Seamus' face but his was the only one. I held up my thumb to show him I was safe and then turned.

I would not need my lock picks. There was no lock and that meant it had to be barred from inside. I put my ear to the gap and listened. It was silent. There was still enough light from the west for me to see the door jamb and I put the bayonet between the door and the frame. I slowly lifted it. When we had rescued the Hardcastle family, the lieutenant and I had been forced to move it together to ensure silence. This time I might make a noise but I hoped that the other side was devoid of humans. I slowly raised the bayonet. When I felt resistance I prayed that it was a simple mechanism and just a piece of wood to stop the door being forced. When the wood moved I found myself smiling. I slightly leaned my left shoulder into the door as I lifted the wood. When I felt the door move I stopped moving the bayonet and eased open the door which led, I could see, by the last light shining from my left to a dark lightless corridor. I dropped the bayonet outside the door and entered. I closed the door by feel and then turned. I did not put the bar back in case I needed to leave in a hurry.

I had learned, when I had broken into English houses, that your eyes gradually adjusted to the dark and what appeared to be impenetrable blackness took on form and shape. So it did and I could see that it was a little lighter at the far end of the low corridor. I gingerly moved along the narrow passage. I kept my head bowed as I was not sure the distance to the low roof. I almost stumbled on the steps that took me to a slightly higher level. I climbed them slowly. The presence of the steps made sense to me for the door I had used was at ground level and places that were inhabited would be higher. This was India and there was often flooding. The corridor might be flooded but the stairs would keep the rest drier. I remembered the cellars from the houses I had robbed in England. When I reached what I had thought was the end I saw that it simply joined a longer corridor that was lit and therefore lighter and led to the left and right. As the door I had used was close to the west wall I headed to my right which I hoped would take me closer to somewhere the First Minister might use. As I moved down I became aware of noises ahead. There was a buzz of conversation and the sound of pots and pans. I also caught the smell of woodsmoke and food. They all suggested a kitchen. When I began to make out actual words I slowed. If I had been in England the voices would have made me turn around and flee. Here I had to stay. When I could hear the conversation and spied the door, I paused. I looked beyond the door and saw an opening to the left. The shaft of light told me that it led outside. I took a deep breath and darted my head forward to look to my right. There was a kitchen and inside were about a dozen sweaty cooks. They appeared to be engrossed in their work and so I boldly walked past the open door. There was no shout. I still had the bowl given to me by Aadyot and I held it before me ready to adopt the role of beggar.

When I reached the opening I saw that it led to a garden. This was not, however, the garden where a First Minister might wander to be reflective or to seek a spy. It was a kitchen garden with rows of salad crops and vegetables. Flowery herbs and bushes lined the beds. There was a path but before I took it I saw a basket on the floor and I picked it up, leaving the bowl there. If anyone saw me in the gloom of twilight they might think I worked in the kitchen and that I was collecting food for the cooks. To add to the illusion I did not hurry but feigned the picking of beans and the red and green fruits that I knew were hot. I saw a gate at the end of the garden and when I reached it I turned. The garden was enclosed and was not overlooked. I laid down the basket and then went to the door. This was a good door made of fine hardwood; I think it was mahogany. I doubted that it would be locked or barred. I lifted the latch and peered within. I could hear the tinkling of water. The sun had set but the garden was still lit by the residual light from the setting sun as well as a couple of lamps hanging from trees. I slipped inside and when I pushed the door closed its fine workmanship manifested itself. The door, on this side, was carved.

I could smell the lemons and oranges. This was a garden in which to reflect. I pressed myself into the carved door and remained still. That was the best way to remain invisible. I then scanned the inside of the garden. There were lights ahead but they were from lamps hung from the trees. I waited and then heard voices. I did not recognise them but then why would I?

The voices could belong to anyone. I still did not move and trusted that my shadow would be seen as the carving on the door.

When the voice was raised my ears pricked up. Whoever spoke, whilst not shouting was making his voice clearly heard. "I will wander alone, Daulat. I must ponder the gestures made by the British. They are up to something that is clear. A walk in the garden alone will focus my mind. Make sure I am not disturbed." I thought I recognised his voice but I was not sure and I would make no assumptions. Such mistakes could cost me my life. There was a reply but I could not make it out. What I did see was a turbaned figure walking past the lights. Having spotted the man I was able to follow his movements. He took a hidden path I could not see. There were neat little paths before me and they were lined with some sort of topiary, little clipped hedges. The trees stood against them. The man then turned and as he walked I made out the flicker of water reflected from the fountain. There was clearly some light I could not see and the man halted near to it. I saw him bend down and lift a lamp which he held, as though to examine the water. It was Mir Sadiq.

Unlikely as though it had seemed when given this task, I had found my contact. It begged the question was he an ally or had he been turned? The fact that he had come to the garden, as had been predicted, did nothing to allay my fears for this could be a trap. The old Bill Smith came to the fore. I had to speak to him. If nothing else I knew that, if it was some kind of trap, I could reach the carved door, make my way through the kitchen garden and be in the corridor leading to the gate before Mir Sadiq could catch me. I was still careful and I used the hedges and trees for cover as I made my way to the sound of the water. It had been clever of Mir Sadiq to use the water for its sound would disguise any words we might speak.

I stopped just ten feet from him and crouched next to the huge rosemary bush. It was in flower and the smell filled the air. His back was to me. I waited for a moment or two to ensure that we were alone and then, when I was satisfied, said, "Mir Sadiq."

He did not turn but stiffened.

I said, "I have been sent by Lord Mornington to make contact with you."

"And how do I know that?"

"We have met."

"Where?"

"At the house of the doctor where you were hiding."

There was a pause and then he said, "Where did you find me?"

"In the toilet."

I heard what I took to be a sigh. "And what does Lord Mornington want?" He turned and moved the lamp briefly so that he could see my face. No doubt he was confirming my identity. He then put the lamp down. It was hidden by the bushes and our faces were, once more, hidden.

"He needs to know when and where to attack."

There was silence. I saw the First Minister do a little play acting and he leaned forward as though studying the water. "The where is obvious. He has chosen the best place to attack. The walls at the north western side of the fort are the weakest and his cannons can destroy them. The when is more difficult." There was silence. "You are not an officer as I remember. Why were you chosen?"

"I am a thief."

"Then you will not know what is in the general's mind." Silence filled the night. The tinkling water made me want to make water. "We will use the taking of the trenches as a starting point. When they are taken I want the general to make his attack at noon two weeks exactly after the trenches are taken. I will be at the north western tower and will ensure that the men who attack will do so where there are no defenders. Do you have that?"

"I do."

"You should tell the general to attack at midday when the defenders will be having a meal break and so that I can identify who is attacking, I will wave a white handkerchief."

"I will tell him." Hope rose within my chest. There was a chance I might get back and report this to his lordship.

"One more thing, you must be with them for I need someone that I recognise and I do not think that Lord Mornington will wish to risk himself. If I do not see you and the captain I also spoke with at the house, then I will not take men from the walls. The two of you must accompany the Forlorn Hope. I cannot risk being killed and your presence or that captain I met will ensure that. Do not wear a hat."

I now saw why it had to be noon and as only the captain and I would recognise the man waving the white handkerchief, we had to be there. I nodded in the dark although I knew he could not see me, "Then the captain and I will be with the Forlorn Hope and one of us should survive."

"And now I must go. I will wait until you leave and when I hear the door close I will go."

I turned. I had managed to do what I had thought was impossible. I opened the door and slipped through. The latch clicked as I closed it. I waited, once more, in the dark and then, picking up the basket, headed for the door at the end of the kitchen garden.

I had just reached it when two men appeared. They saw me and started. One said, "Who are you?"

I tried to bluff my way out, "I was sent to pick some vegetables, look."

"Bring a light!" The man shouted to someone in the kitchen and a light was brought. "I do not know you and I am the chief cook in this kitchen. You are a liar!"

There were now three of them and while I might have been able to take on one, perhaps two, three was impossible and I did not want them to know my escape route.

"Guard!" I was suddenly pinioned by the cook and his men. I had no chance to escape. After a few minutes, the carved door behind me opened and two sentries with swords in their hands stood there. The cook said, "We have found an intruder. Take him to the Tipu Sultan!"

I was dragged through the gate. Mir Sadiq had disappeared. I had failed. Mir Sadiq had made contact but neither Lord Mornington nor Captain Tucker would know. When the attack was made men would die and their deaths would be the result of my failure.

Chapter 3

I did not see Mir Sadiq when I was dragged from the garden and into the palace. The First Minister was a survivor. He would be as far away from the spy as possible. My dagger had been taken and two guards held my arms while the original two followed with levelled swords that threatened to hack me down at any attempt to escape. All the way through the palace side of the fortress I kept my eyes open. I was memorising what I saw so that, in the unlikely event that I escaped, I could make my way back to the gardens. Despite my capture it would still be my best means of escaping. I was a survivor. I would not simply accept my fate. I would do everything I could to escape.

We reached some double doors and while three of the guards waited with me one knocked and then entered. There was a delay and then the doors opened and I was thrown by two of the men to abase myself before a raised throne upon which was perched a short man. I recognised him from the walls. It was the Tiger. Next to him stood two half naked warriors with drawn swords and at the foot of the steps leading to the throne was a European dressed in a blue uniform. I tried to raise myself up to get a better view but a foot was pushed against my back. I could see the man on the throne and the European but little else.

The European spoke to me and he did so in English. I could speak some Bengali but not enough to convince anyone that I was other than what I was, English. The man's English was accented and I guessed that he was either Dutch or German. He was not a French officer. Captain Tucker had made me into a spy. I had gathered that information without even thinking about it.

"Who are you and who sent you here?" He spoke calmly, almost kindly.

I feigned innocence, "I am a street beggar and no one sent me for I know no one."

The man spoke but not to me. I understood half of what the European said. He told the man, who, from the officer's address was Sher-e-Mysore or Tiger of Mysore, what I had said. I recognised the title; it was Tipu Sultan himself. I had been right.

I picked out the words that they were saying. While the Tiger asked the officer why he thought I was here I craned my neck so that I could study the man we had been sent to oust. He was short and very fat. He had large eyes but few whiskers. He was dressed in a fine white linen jacket, with chintz drawers, a crimson cloth round his waist with a red silk belt and pouch across his body and head. He did not look like a tiger to me. Perhaps the name was a joke. Mir Sadiq was not present and, as far as I could make out, there were no other advisors with him. The European had to be an important man. Mir Sadiq had abandoned me. He would not risk me identifying him by word or look. I was alone.

"My master is not happy with your answer and, to be frank, neither am I." The tone was still calm but, it seemed he was adopting a more interrogatory tone.

I was learning about this European too. His English had phrases that meant he had learned his English through service with the British Army. I gave him the story I had embroidered before I entered the palace. "I can only speak the truth. I am a beggar and, yes, I have stolen if only to stop myself from dying of starvation. Your men found me in the kitchen garden for I needed food."

He laughed, "Come, there are easier places to steal than the kitchen garden of Tipu Sultan."

I adopted an outraged tone, "How do you know? Have you ever tried to steal food? Men guard it. I took a risk getting to the garden but I thought that because it was dark no one would be there and I intended to be well away before I was found. I could have gathered enough food for a week."

My story was plausible enough and my clothes were so tattered and torn that I looked like a real beggar. I could tell, from the silence, that I had put doubt in the mind of the officer. He spoke again to Tipu Sultan and this time I listened for the way he was addressed. I learned his name was Colonel Pohlmann. I stored that in my head but I doubted that I would ever be in a position to tell anyone about it. The Tiger of Mysore also appeared to be ready to dismiss me. His tone had changed. My story had an air of authenticity about it. My heart soared when he waved a hand for the man with his foot on my neck to remove it and the colonel said, "You may stand."

I stood. I peered around the room. There were few people there. I saw the colonel, the Tipu, two servants and two bodyguards. I assumed the four guards were still behind me. Tipu Sultan spoke. He spoke English but it was very heavily accented, "You are English."

There was no point in denying it, "Yes, Tipu Sultan."

"What are you doing in Seringapatam?" It was as though he had discovered a new problem with my presence.

I lied. I said the lie confidently for that often works, "I live here. I have done for five years." I knew it was a large place and there were many people. I doubted that the Tiger left the lair that was his palace to walk the streets of Seringapatam.

"Why?"

"My Lord?"

"Why live here in Seringapatam? We have no love for the English."

I had learned that any lie you told needed a complete history to it. Even as I had been coming up with the lie I had been adapting the story of my life to fit this street beggar I had become. "My father was an English soldier of the East India Company. After he had fathered me he left. My mother tried to make a living but could not and she pined for her home. After ten years, she brought us from Calcutta to here for her father was born here and she hoped we had family who would care for us. It took a long time to make the journey and often she was ill. She died just five miles from the city and I buried her. I sought her father but could not find him. I did not wish to make the journey back to Calcutta and so I stayed. You are right, My Lord, life has not been easy but the thought of walking back to Calcutta would have been just as hard. I tried to exist and I was desperate enough to risk stealing food from your kitchen garden."

I saw Colonel Pohlmann nod and he said, "Sounds like a reasonable story."

Tippu Sultan's eyes narrowed until they were like a cobra's slits. He did not believe me, "Too reasonable. Have him confined. We will speak to him tomorrow. Perhaps a night without food and water will make him tell us the truth."

I put my hands together and pleaded, "Please, I am sorry for breaking in but…"

One of the guards smacked me so hard on the side of the head that I saw stars. The colonel said, not in an unkindly tone, "Just go with the guards. If you speak the truth then I am sure all will be well."

I was dragged away. I expected a dungeon but, instead, I was taken to a windowless room two corridors away from the fountain garden. My observations now came to my aid. I recognised the corridor. An oil lamp burned but it was cheap oil and it sputtered and smoked. There was a pot in the corner, obviously for me to make water. The guards threw me against the wall and then the door was slammed shut and I heard a key turn in the lock. They had not searched me and I still had my stiletto and my lock picks. I was not dead and I still had the means to escape. I went to the keyhole and peered through. If the key had been left in the lock then I was done for. They had not. I put my eye to it and saw people moving up and down the corridor. I heard the guards talking. If there was more than one guard then I would not be able to escape and I would have to rely on my ability to lie convincingly in the morning. I planned on escaping but I would have to time my escape attempt well. I knew I would only have one chance to do so. If I failed they would execute me. That thought made me realise that I needed to make water and so I went to the pot and emptied my bladder. That done I lay down and closed my eyes. I was not trying to sleep but by closing my eyes I could hear the noises from the corridor better. As I lay in the darkness I began to think about the position I was in. I had not thought we would succeed and it seemed that I was right. When I did not return the generals would come up with another plan. I knew from the number of eighteen pounders I had seen pulled into position that the attack would succeed. When they began pounding the walls the ancient masonry would crumble. My death was an irrelevancy. This was all a waste, however, as I sat in the darkness I realised that my attempt was necessary. If I had succeeded then British soldiers, perhaps the Devil's Dozen amongst them, might not be slaughtered as they attempted a breach. Mir Sadiq would have been able to allow the attack to take place without hindrance.

Now no one would know. This was no longer about me. I hoped to survive but if I did then more British soldiers might also survive. It steeled my resolve. I told myself that I had to escape and get back. It was not about me but saving British lives. I had no idea of the time but gradually the noises from the corridor diminished to the point where I counted up to one hundred and had heard no noise.

I risked going to the door. What I did not know was if there was one guard or two outside. I decided to risk opening the door and looking out. I knew how to pick a lock silently. Often I had stolen from houses with people asleep within. I took out my tools and then darkened the lamp. I did not need the light to pick the lock and I did not want the flare of light to alert a guard, if there was one. Picking a lock was done by feel and sound. It took longer than I had expected. I knew why. I had not used my skills for some time but, luckily, it was a simple lock and when I turned the last tumbler I gave the slightest tug to the door and it moved. I replaced my picks and then took out my stiletto. I did not want to kill anyone for the simple reason that I did not want to be delayed but I needed to protect myself.

I opened the door by fractions. It opened inwards and, peering around the edge, I saw the guard. He was on a chair next to the door jamb. I pulled the door open a little more and realised, from his regular breathing and his lolling head, that the man was asleep. I slipped outside and seeing no one in the corridor, silently, closed the door. To all intents and purposes it would still appear to be locked. Without disturbing the guard, who was now snoring, I moved swiftly down the corridor. I could hear some noise but it was so far away as to be inconsequential. At each turn I stopped and peered around before I risked going further. When I saw that the corridor was empty I moved on. I finally found the door to the fountain garden and slipped through. The lights had been doused but I could see the distinctively carved door in the shadows at the far end and I headed for it. I made it through without discovery as there were no guards there, and I moved quickly down through the kitchen garden. The door to the corridor I needed to use was closed but, mercifully, it was not locked. There was no reason for it to be. I opened it and listened. There was not a sound to be heard. I slipped down the corridor.

As I passed the kitchen I felt the warmth from the ovens and it was then I heard snoring. The cooks must sleep close to the kitchens. The sandals were wonderfully silent. I found the corridor leading to the passage with the steps that led to the outside door. It was pitch black from this end. I found the steps and, gingerly, I made my way down, using my hands to feel for the roof and sides. When I reached the door I discovered, to my amazement, that the bar was not in place. It was where I had left it. That meant no one had been down since I had entered. I stepped outside and picked up Albert's bayonet. I put the two weapons in my belt. I did not run to the river. Instead I turned to peer at the round tower. I saw nothing. There was no movement from the parapets. If there were guards there then I would wait to see them. I had got this far and better to take my time than to rush and risk a musket ball. I waited until I saw the shadow of a sentry move and then I set off, at a crouch, to the water. I crossed the road and flung myself behind a bush. I waited. If I had been seen then there would be a shout. There was none. I looked at the water. The teeth of the rocks now looked threatening and I feared stepping into it. I looked back at the fortress. The choice was clear. Either I tried to find another route or I risked the water. I had crossed in twilight but at night it seemed somehow more sinister. If I stayed there until dawn then I would be found. I steeled myself and taking the bayonet from my belt held it before me. I entered the water and moved across as quickly as I could. I climbed the bank and left the water. I hurried to the safety of the undergrowth. I was still in danger. To my right I could hear the sentries at the enemy trenches as they chattered away to one another. The soldier in me smiled. Sergeant Charlton and his ilk would have torn a strip off them. A chattering sentry could not watch. The problem I had was that it was dark and I could not see the path. We had descended in daylight and it was now pitch black and the hill of our camp was hidden by trees. I just knew that the fortress was behind me. I realised that the longer I procrastinated the more danger I would be in. What if someone decided to check up on me? If they found I was gone there would be a hue and cry. The unbarred door would tell them my escape route. I hacked with the bayonet at the undergrowth. I would have to carve my way to safety. I worried that the noise might attract attention. The trenches were still relatively close to me.

Suddenly a hand grasped my shoulder and I whipped my head around, the blade ready to stab the guard who had caught me. I saw a surprised Dai take a step back. Next to him stood Corporal Neville. He was peering at the fortress to see if I was followed. Dai grinned and whispered, "Steady on, butty."

I almost wept with relief, "Dai what…?"

Corporal Neville said, "The section has been taking watches to keep an eye open for you. We saw you cross the water but could not shout for fear of waking everyone. Follow me; there is a safe path to the camp."

He turned and headed away from the trenches. After thirty yards or so we found the path and headed up it. We crossed the stone bridge and were halfway up the path to the camp before the corporal spoke again, "We were all worried when you hadn't returned after a couple of hours. Lieutenant Crozier had the first watch. Private Evans and I had the third. Scamus and Bob are waiting to relieve us."

"Thanks."

We moved along the path and then the corporal said, "Did you get it done, Smudger?"

"I did."

Dai said, "Well there is an extra ration of rum for us all. Well done, Smudger."

He was happy but I was not. I knew that it was not all good news. I would have to storm the breach with the Forlorn Hope. My life was still in danger. I found that I was both ravenous and my throat felt raw from lack of water. I could smell the fire beneath the pot as we ascended and hoped that the night watch had food on the go.

Albert and George had their muskets at the ready but they recognised Dai and George Mainsgill said, as we passed, "The prodigal returns. Well done, Smudger. Eddie owes me a shilling." I could not help smiling. The section would gamble on anything, even the life and death of one of their own.

His words alerted the camp and by the time we reached the fire, heads were appearing from the tents. Lieutenant Crozier, wearing just his breeches, emerged, "Well?"

"I met him, Sir, Mir Sadiq." I wondered if I ought to tell all and then realised that if I could not trust the section then I was in the wrong army, "We are to attack two weeks exactly after the trenches are taken."

He smiled, "Then there is no rush. We can report to the general tomorrow. Well done." He pointed at our tent, "You need your rest."

I nodded, "Any tea, Sir? And my stomach thinks that my throat has been cut."

"Of course. Ganguly."

"Yes, Lieutenant. Good to have you back, Smudger." Aadyot materialised from close to the fire. He had been waiting for my return.

"And you can tell us what delayed you, while you eat." Lieutenant Crozier said.

"That is an easy, not to mention short, story. I was captured."

I had rarely surprised men like Seamus and Dai but my words made their faces freeze. Seamus said, "The Tiger had you?"

Aadyot handed me a mug of sea and I drank half of it before I spoke again, "Aye, and I met him. There was a European with him, Lieutenant, a Colonel Pohlmann." He nodded as Aadyot handed me a flatbread wrapped around some meat. I bit into it. Aadyot knew my tastes and the meat had been slavered with mustard. It was just how I liked it. I saw the faces eager for the story to continue but I ate the meat filled treat and finished the tea before I did so. "I told them a story about how I was a beggar. The colonel believed me but I think the Tiger was suspicious. They locked me up. I used my lock picks and escaped as soon as the palace part of the fortress was quiet."

Seamus nodded, "A grand story, Smudger. You have the luck of the devil."

The lieutenant said, "Right, Smith. When you have eaten, you had better get some rest. The general and his staff will be desperate to know if you are dead or alive."

"Yes, Sir."

My bed was more than welcome. I laid my two weapons on the floor and stripped off. I noticed the other three men, my tent mates, watching me. What I saw in their eyes was concern. I was the youngest of the section and I think that they genuinely liked me. "Night lads."

"Night, Smudger."

I covered myself in my sheet and buried my head. It was the best way to keep the insects away. My sleep was almost instant and I found myself in a black hole. It seemed like moments before I was being roused by Ben Neville, "Right, Smith, rise and shine. We gave you a bit of a lie in but Captain Tucker was here at dawn. Lord Mornington is keen to talk to you."

I rose and went outside. I made water and then went to the strung canvas that was filled with water and washed myself. The fact that I was naked meant I could use the soap and wash my whole body. I said to Albert who was nearby, "Just empty the water over me, Albert. I need to get some of this berry juice off me." He tipped the water filled canvas over me and I began to towel myself dry.

I went back to the tent and attempted to comb my wild hair into a queue. Aadyot came in and said, "You dress yourself. The captain is impatient. I will comb your hair."

As I pulled on my underwear I said, "They can wait." I was a little angry. I had almost been dumped in the fortress. I had been caught and had I been executed, as was likely, then they would have lost little sleep over it. I had reflected on this when I had lain on the mattress in the palace of the Tiger of Mysore. When I was dressed I felt more like a soldier. I did not don my tunic. I would be too hot.

I went outside and the rest of the section whistled and commented, "Where is the little fellow we saw last night?"

"Who's a smart boy then?"

Lieutenant Crozier said, "That's enough. Ganguly, saddle the French horse for Smith. That should give you the time to eat some food."

Captain Tucker said, "There is no time for food, Lieutenant Crozier, the generals are keen to speak to him."

Lieutenant Crozier eyed his superior officer, "Private Smith is in my section. He will eat, Captain."

He emphasised the rank and the captain nodded and gave a wry smile, "I am beginning to see what General Harris means when he calls you the Devil's Dozen. You are unlike the rest of the army, that is for certain."

Sergeant Grundy had been stirring the pot, "Aye, Captain. We may be the Devil's Dozen but we are the best dozen soldiers fighting for his lordship."

I had managed to eat and drink enough by the time that Aadyot brought my horse. The captain mounted Dublin and, after donning my tunic, I hauled myself onto the back of Froggy. I waved to the others as we headed towards the main camp.

He began his questions as soon as we moved. "Well, Smith, what did you discover?"

When I had been behind the lines with Captain Tucker I had quite liked the officer but his recent actions suggested to me that he was now keen for promotion and Private Smudger Smith was a stepping stone. "I was told to tell the general, Sir, and I don't want to repeat myself." The captain was silent. He could not force me to speak. He was not happy. I knew that if I told him he would tell his lordship and it would appear, especially to General Harris, as though Captain Tucker had managed to gather the information and not the thief. For the first time since I had donned the red coat I felt as though I was in control of my own destiny.

It was Sergeant Charlton who was on duty and he nodded as I dismounted, "Like a bad penny you keep on turning up, Smith." There was a smile on his face. "You do have some adventures. What have you been up to this time?" I might have told the sergeant for he was a proper soldier.

The captain handed his reins to the sergeant and said, stiffly, "Thank you, Sergeant, but gossip only aids the enemy."

"Yes, Sir, they are waiting for you." I saw the sergeant roll his eyes as we entered, "Hat off, Smith."

I took off my hat and, holding it under my arm, entered the building they were using as a headquarters. The four officers were there but they had been joined by a richly dressed prince. Lord Mornington introduced him, "This is Mir Nizam Ali Khan Siddiqi, and he commands half the army, the men of Hyderabad. He needs to know what you learned." He added, "Well, did you succeed?"

Their obvious lack of concern at the risks I had taken made me delay delivering the news. I knew it would irritate them all, especially General Harris. I also knew that five minutes here or there would not affect the outcome of this siege. "Yes, Sir, I managed to get into Seringapatam and although I was taken I effected an escape." I paused and smiled.

General Harris banged his hand on the table, "Well, out with your news, Smith, or I will have the skin taken from your back. This amounts to insubordination."

I returned the stare and remained silent. Lord Mornington lit a cheroot. He drawled, "I think that Private Smith has good news to deliver and he is enjoying keeping us on tenterhooks." He smiled, "You have our attention, Smith. Tell us what happened and how you managed to escape the Tiger's claws."

I told them the story as a tale. I described getting into the garden through the kitchen garden and the meeting. I told them of the arrangements and the timeline. I gave them the details of my capture and my escape and my return to the camp. I saw Sir Arthur's eyes widen when I mentioned Colonel Pohlmann.

Lord Mornington had finished his cheroot by the time I had finished and he turned to smile at General Harris, "There you are, General, that was news that was worth waiting for was it not? Well done, Smith."

Colonel Wellesley said, "I have heard of this Colonel Pohlmann. He is a good soldier, a mercenary but a good one."

General Baird asked, "Did you get a chance to examine their defences?"

My mouth must have dropped open for I saw the smile on Lord Mornington's face, "No, General. I was just trying to get in and out unseen."

Colonel Wellesley said, "And you have to go in with the Forlorn Hope?"

"Yes, Sir, along with Captain Tucker. Mir Sadiq says he knows us and we are the only ones he trusts."

General Harris snorted, "Damned nonsense. We are all Englishmen."

The Nizam spoke for the first time. He had a measured voice with barely an accent and he was quietly spoken, "Not all of us,

General, and Mir Sadiq is just being careful. In his position I would be as cautious."

Lord Mornington nodded, "Quite. Well, Smith, I think you can return to your section. We have an assault to plan and then an escalade into the fortress. You have done well." He paused, "If you wish you can have a transfer to a regular regiment in the British Army."

I shook my head and held the glare from General Harris, "No, Sir, I am quite happy being part of the Devil's Dozen."

For some reason that made General Baird, Lord Mornington and his brother laugh. Colonel Wellesley shook his head, "You have wit, Smith, as well as daring. If you ever change your mind then the 33rd has a place for a man like you."

Captain Tucker said, "You can make your own way back, eh, Smith?"

"Of course, Captain Tucker."

Outside Sergeant Charlton was stroking Dublin's mane. He held out Froggy's reins for me, "I hear you have been sneaking around for his lordship."

I tapped my nose and hauled myself up into the saddle, "I might have, Sergeant, but that information is for those above the rank of lieutenant."

He laughed, "You are a game 'un I will give you that." His face became serious, "I am an old soldier, Smith, and I can tell you that a soldier only has so much luck. You may have used all of yours up. Keep your head down, eh?"

"I will do, Sergeant." As I rode back to the camp I reflected that in a Forlorn Hope I would need all the luck I could get.

Chapter 4

"But what is a Forlorn Hope, Lieutenant?"

I was glad that Aadyot asked the question for I was unsure. From the looks on the faces of the others, Sergeant Grundy apart, the rest of the section were as much in the dark as we were. We were chatting after what was one of the best meals we had enjoyed. Lord Mornington had sent up some beef, not salted but fresh. How it came to be in a land where the cow was sacred I do not know but we did not complain. He also sent up two bottles, not of rum as we had expected, but whisky and they were more than welcome. The corporal who had led the men bringing them also gave us half a pound of tobacco. "From General Baird, I think."

Those who smoked enjoyed the tobacco and we each had a quarter of a mug of whisky. While for those like Seamus, Dai and Bob, the heavy drinkers, it was just what Lieutenant Crozier called an aperitif, for me it was enough to be nursed until time for sleep. I was ready for sleep but I did want to know what I would be doing once we attacked.

Sergeant Grundy tapped out the ash from his pipe and began to refill it with some of the new tobacco, "They are not Chosen Men as some may believe but volunteers. The generals will ask for men to put their names forward and volunteer to be the first to attack the defences. General Baird will lead them. The corporal told me."

Dai shook his head, "Proper daft is that. Why volunteer to climb defences where men are waiting to kill you?"

The sergeant smiled, "Rewards, Dai. The men who lead it, the officers and non-commissioned officers can all expect promotion. Some of the rank and file will be promoted too but their main motivation will be to be the first inside the fortress."

I asked, "Why?"

He laughed, "You should know better than anyone, Smudger. Loot! They can thieve to their hearts' desire and they won't be stopped. By the time the rest of the army get inside then there will be provosts to stop them."

Seamus looked at me, "And you, you poor bugger, don't even get the chance to volunteer. You have to go."

I nodded and gave a weak smile, "But if Sergeant Grundy is right, I might make my fortune, eh?"

Eddie Lowe shook his head, "There's little to spend it on in a grave, Smudger."

Silence fell and the mood changed. Lieutenant Crozier said, "Smith has no choice in the matter but as we have all witnessed, he has a remarkable capacity for survival. Not that I am a gambling man, Private Lowe, but if I was I would bet a guinea on Smith here being one of those who do survive. But as that is not likely until two weeks after the trenches are taken we needn't worry too much now, eh?"

I did sleep that night but it was a mixture of the whisky and the lack of sleep the previous night that sent me to the arms of Morpheus. I was now scared witless at the thought of being at the fore as our army broke into the fortress.

The next day we had a fine view of the attack for Lord Mornington had wasted no time. He assembled the 33rd, the Suffolks and the Swiss mercenaries. The batteries we had seen assembled began to pound the northern end of their trenches.

Sergeant Grundy nodded his approval, "Clever, he is not attacking along the whole line but has three battalions facing two companies. His guns can batter them and when he attacks he outnumbers them so much that they have to win. Then he can roll up their line. It is not defence in depth, see. The river is at their backs."

Strategy was new to me but as the British infantry fixed bayonets and raced forward I began to see what he meant. The two companies of defenders, or the ones who survived the bombardment and the bayonet charge, turned and fled across the Little Cauvery. I saw that it only came to their ankles. The battalions then turned and worked their way down the line. It was not even a fight. Each company they attacked was attacked in the flank and were well outnumbered by men who knew how to use a bayonet. By noon the trenches were in our hands. More men were lost when the enemy guns began to fire at them than had been lost in the attack. When the eighteen pounders switched their guns to fire at the ramparts, they were able to begin to repair trenches and defences they had wrecked in their attack.

I wondered why Mir Sadiq had asked for a two-week grace. I could see no reason for it but the man had struck me as someone who liked to plot and plan. It would be to his advantage, whatever the reason. However, it became clear that a quick assault could not be made for with just one battery firing at the bastion it was obvious that we needed more guns. A second battery was moved close to the walls but the most important battery, the one to the north of the river, took almost eight days to be in a position to open fire. The Mysorean guns were all switched to the north wall and while their gunners were not as good as ours, they were all ready on the walls and harassed the men trying to get the guns in a place where they could pound the walls.

Sergeant Grundy nodded, "If they can hit the walls from two angles then the whole corner will fall and the Forlorn Hope will have a much easier time."

Albert said, "Yes Sarge, but if Smudger is right then it doesn't matter. There will be no defenders."

The sergeant sighed, "Wishart, the Forlorn Hope has to get up the wall. They can't do that until the walls are reduced. It will take time. Why are you worried? It is Smith who will be taking the chances."

Albert looked up to me a little. He had been a thief but nowhere near as successful as I had been, "I don't want any of the lads to die, especially not Smudger."

We used the time to make ourselves as comfortable as we could. Captain Tucker still came up but not as frequently. During the quiet times Sergeant Grundy, who had the most experience of such things, gave me advice about the attack. "Don't take your musket, it will be too cumbersome. Get as many pistols as you can and hang them from your neck. Take my hanger. It is razor sharp and short enough to use in the confined area you will be attacking."

"Confined area?"

"Aye, the guns will make a breach and, if the gunners are any good then the debris will fall and make a slope over which you can climb." He smiled, "You should be alright. You were good at

47

The Tiger and the Thief

climbing the rigging on the ship and you have a good sense of balance. You keep low and try to get to the top without injury."

"But," interjected Lieutenant Crozier, "you will be at the front so that Mir Sadiq can tell the men to stop fighting."

That was the biggest doubt I had. This could all be a giant trap to ingratiate himself back into the Tiger's good books and a way to kill a large number of men. The defenders would know, once the Forlorn Hopes formed up, exactly where the attack would take place and the only thing in doubt would be the time. I did not like it.

It took until the first day of May for the northern battery to be finished and the bombardment was set for the next day. I was summoned to the breach for I would have to be visible from the walls along with Captain Tucker. The rest of the section had all offered to come with me but I had refused their offers. I think that the lieutenant and the sergeant were grateful as they only wanted to lose one man and not the whole section. I thought Aadyot was going to burst into tears. He had listened to Sergeant Grundy describe an attack up a breach and he feared he would never see me again.

"Do not worry, Aadyot. I am tougher than I look and I will do nothing that is heroic. I leave that to Captain Tucker." The captain, who was stood close by, flushed. I did not ride, for the section did not want to lose its spare horse. When we moved the horse would ensure the survival of the sergeant.

"No musket?"

"No, Sir, the lads reckoned these four pistols would do."

"They may be right."

I was given a bedroll with the 33rd but I had the luxury of a tent to myself. I had brought my own bowl and cup and I ate alone. I was viewed with suspicion. None of the 33rd were going with the two groups of Forlorn Hopes which were made up mainly of Highlanders from the 73rd and 74th regiments. The 33rd would make a third reserve column in case the first two failed to take the breach. General Baird was being clever by using two attacks. It would keep the defenders guessing but, if Mir Sadiq kept his word, then the two groups would make the walls without being hurt. Once we were in the fortress then it would be a different matter. We would have the whole garrison to contend

with. General Baird hoped that they would be confused. I had to agree.

with. I watched the walls crumble as I ate my food. The bombardment ceased at dark. I wondered why for the guns were already aimed at the breach and could continue to pound them.

"Why have they stopped, Sir?"

Captain Tucker pointed to some engineers. They had barrels of something. "They probably have barrels of gunpowder and they are going to sneak over there tonight and plant them."

"Ah."

There was a pause and he said, "You and I are to go with them."

"What?"

"There is next to no risk and General Baird will be with us. He wants to inspect the glacis."

"But why do you need me?" I was going to refuse. I had agreed to meet Mir Sadiq and to go with the Forlorn Hopes but this seemed ridiculously unnecessary.

He sighed, "Lord Mornington spotted Mir Sadiq not far from the breach. He was far enough away to be safe. General Baird does not wish to be shot. You and I are insurance."

Once more I was given no choice.

When darkness fell four Highlanders, with blackened faces and without headgear, advanced from the trenches. The engineers followed and then, while Colonel Wellesley, Lord Mornington, General Harris and the Nizam watched, the captain and I went with General Baird. The general had been held prisoner by the Tipu for more than three years. He had revenge on his mind. Captain Tucker sought promotion and me, I was just the poor fool forced to follow.

We waded across the stream. It held no fears for me for I had waded through a much deeper one already. Once on the other side the four Highlanders stopped. It seemed to me that they were sniffing. The sergeant waved forward the engineers who made their way up the glacis. General Baird headed up and Captain Tucker put his hand in my back. We passed the engineers who halted just forty paces from the top. The Highlanders stopped but the general, like us, hatless, made his way to the top. He wanted to see what the terrain was like. When we reached the top I braced myself for a flurry of musket balls but all was silent. There were no sentries or, if there were, then they were ignoring us. Suddenly I saw a movement to my right and when I turned I saw, on the top of a small tower, eighty paces from us, Mir Sadiq. I grabbed Captain Tucker's arm and pointed. He saw Mir Sadiq and waved. The First Minister of Mysore waved back and when General Baird saw the movement he looked up. He turned to me and smiled and then nodded down the slope. I had never been so relieved in my life as when we waded through the water. No one spoke until the Highlanders and engineers had returned and we reached Lord Mornington and the others.

"Happy, General Baird?"

He smiled, "I am indeed. It is not too bad and when we explode the mine it will ensure that any defenders who are close to the breach will die. We saw Mir Sadiq."

"And?"

"He saw us. I think that Private Smith reported accurately."

"Well done, Smith."

The next day the guns bombarded again but disaster struck. The powder we had planted was hit by a ball which fell short. The glacis was no longer as smooth as it should have been. I know that it caused consternation for the generals immediately held a meeting. I wondered if the attack would be called off and that night, I enjoyed my food a little more than I had the previous night. I thought that I had another day of grace and I would not be ascending the breach. I enjoyed the breakfast, too, as it was fried ham and fresh eggs. I was living a life of luxury.

At eleven in the morning my hopes were dashed. We were ordered to form up. The attacks would go ahead as planned. I loaded my pistols and hung them about my neck. I went, reluctantly, with the captain to the place where we would form up into the two columns. I had been briefed the day before but as I had thought the attack was going to be cancelled I had been less than attentive. The two columns would advance up the glacis together and when we reached the top we would go right and the other column left. We were given whisky to drink along with some biscuits. They were shortbread and I think the choice of beverage and treat was guided by the fact that the ones attacking were Scottish. I drank the whisky and ate the biscuit but both tasted like sawdust and vinegar in my mouth.

The waiting was worse than anything. I needed to make water and I went to the Little Cauvery and emptied my bladder. Some of the Scottish soldiers jeered as I did so. I didn't care. I felt much more comfortable once I had relieved myself. I looked at the ramparts and saw, as the hour of noon came and went, that the sentries and guards appeared to be disappearing. It made sense for I was baking in the sun. The Scottish soldiers had their hats but I was bareheaded. It was so hot that two soldiers passed out. I hoped, as they were taken to the medical tents, that they had been two who jeered at me.

The artillery opened up twenty minutes before we were to attack. If there was anyone waiting in ambush they would have had to endure a terrible and unrelenting fifteen minutes of balls and bombs. When it stopped my ears were hurting from the din and the air was thick with the acrid smell of powder. General Baird raised his sword and pointed forward and we raced through the water. The Scots were cheering wildly. Captain Tucker had set us off a heartbeat before the Highlanders. We were not as heavily armed as they were and moved faster. We were ahead of General Baird.

I heard a Scottish soldier shout, "Bloody heroes!"

If he only knew. The slope sapped the air from my lungs and by the time I reached the top I could barely move, let alone speak. As we recovered I saw a white handkerchief being waved and Mir Sadiq and his co-conspirators stood there.

General Baird went to stand before them and Captain Tucker pushed me to join him. We were the human protection in case any wild Scotsman saw easy plunder. The officers of the two columns pointed their swords and the columns ran, left and right. When it was clear and as Colonel Wellesley brought his men up we led the traitors down the glacis. Lord Mornington and the others had left the camp and were by the trenches.

"Welcome Mir Sadiq." The general bowed, "Captain, you and Smith go and see if you can find Tipu Sultan. I would like him as a prisoner."

It was an order and the captain tugged my arm to lead me back up the slope. "Why me, Sir?"

"Because you met him."

"Sir, he is not hard to spot. He is a little fat man with lots of rings."

"Smith, it is an order from the general."

It was at that precise moment I decided that I had endured enough of this army. Despite the friendship I felt for the section, when we moved from Seringapatam, I would find a way to run.

"Yes, Sir."

This time I made sure I had a cocked pistol as we ran. There would be no white handkerchief waved and no guarantee of survival. When we found the defenders then they would try to kill me.

The glacis might have been undefended but once we headed to the right and followed the path of General Baird, we saw dead Highlanders and others having their wounds tended. We could hear gunshots from the fortress and saw men falling from the ramparts. They were both attackers and defenders. There were cries and shouts as men fought to the death. Guns, large and small cracked and spouted smoke. It was like moving through a fog. Bob Cathcart was our Scotsman and the others often teased about the way his countrymen screamed and shouted as they went into battle. I had never heard the sound of charging Scotsmen and it terrified me. I took comfort from that as I knew it would have the same effect on the defenders.

We reached a staircase leading from the fighting platform and there was only one dead defender. We could hear the noise from our left where the right-hand Forlorn Hope was charging around the perimeter to meet up with the other Forlorn Hope. Captain Tucker said, "Smith, you have been inside this place before. Where should we go?"

I shook my head, "To be fair, Captain, I entered at the bottom and saw just the lower corridors, kitchen, and gardens."

"What about when you were taken to meet Tipu Sultan?"

He was right, "Well, yes, Sir, it was along from the garden."

"And these stairs go down. I am betting that the Tiger will be somewhere he knows. Lead on."

The 33rd had followed us and as we headed down the stairs I was aware that a section of red coats was close behind us. We had support. It was all very well the captain saying that we would find Tipu Sultan. I did not doubt that it was a possibility but a certainty was that he would be guarded. I remembered those half naked guards with the huge swords. I did not want to meet those in a dark corridor. It might be daylight beyond the walls but the staircase we were descending was pitch black.

We turned a corner and a bayonet darted out. The bayonet lunged at the captain who was unprotected. I was leading with a pistol that was already cocked and my reactions were sharp. I raised and fired it in one. The blast in the stairwell was deafening and the flash from the muzzle lit it up. The warrior's head disappeared in a mess of blood and bone as his body tumbled down the stairs.

"Sir, let me and my men lead." We turned and saw the sergeant of the 33rd. "We want to earn our pay today." I knew it was not heroism that drove the sergeant, it was the thought of loot.

The captain was shaken at his brush with death and he nodded, "Thank you, Sergeant."

I saw one of his men searching the body. I might have objected but I did not think the man had much to offer.

The hobnails of the soldiers' boots thundered down the steps. It was useful to have a wall of red before us but that wall was a noisy one and heralded our approach like a bugle. When the sergeant and his men reached the bottom of the stairs they just turned to head along the next stairs, throwing caution to the wind. They paid for their haste when there was the crack of muskets and I saw men falling. The sergeant shouted, "Back! They are waiting."

It was too late for four of his men. Three were killed instantly but one writhed in agony for a few moments until he was still.

"How many, Sergeant?"

The sergeant was shaken, "Not sure, Sir."

I said, "It takes time to reload, Sir. If we can make them fire prematurely then we can return fire."

"And how do you suggest we do that, Smith?"

I gestured with my thumb, "The man I shot back there. If we use his body we throw it down the stairs. It is black as Hades in here and all they will see will be the movement."

The sergeant nodded, "Worth a try, Sir. Atkins, Bowes, fetch the body from the stairs." He said to his men, "The rest of you," there were now just six left, "make sure your muskets are primed and ready. When they fire we step out and give them a taste of their own medicine."

The two men brought the body. Captain Tucker said, "Start to swing it. I want you to hit the wall at the bottom. On three." They began to swing. "One, two, three." The body flew through the air and even before it had hit the wall there was a ripple of flashes and the echo of muskets in the confined space of the corridor.

"Now!"

We all stepped out and I pointed my pistol down the corridor. We fired and were blinded by the flashes. The noise hurt my ears and while I could see nothing I heard the cries as men were hurt.

"Reload and be quick about it."

I reached down and took the musket from the hands of a dead soldier. It was primed and I raised it and fired. There was a bayonet on the end and I was unsure if I had hit anything.

The sergeant was clearly fired up by the loss of his men and the heat of battle, "Charge the bastards!"

We all ran into the darkness. The flashes from the muskets had rendered us all partly blinded but that was true of our enemies too. The bayonet which lunged at me was too high for I had run crouched. However it was close enough for me to realise how near I had come to death and I stabbed at the man's middle. When Sergeant Grundy had taught me to use a musket with a bayonet, back on the ship, he had told me to twist the end and pull. This was the first time I had used a bayonet in this manner but the sergeant had been right. The bayonet came out with a sucking sound. The soldier next to me did not twist and as he tried to pull the bayonet from the man's shoulder his victim slashed across his neck with a sword. I drove my bayonet up and under the outstretched arm. I did not save the soldier but I ensured that his killer was dead. As I twisted the blade out of the wound I saw the sparkle from his hands. The man was a noble. My eyes were adjusting to the darkness. The rest of the men who had tried to stop us were all dead.

"Reload. Atkins, see to the wounded."

The man said, dully, "They are all dead." I saw that two of his men had died in the vicious fight in the darkness. That we had slain ten was immaterial to those who had lost tentmates. I reloaded the musket. I still had one loaded pistol festooned around my neck but the bayonet had saved my life. I noticed that the captain had his sword in his hand and it was bloodied. He said, "Recognise anything, Smith?" As he spoke another couple of the 33rd appeared behind us.

"Not yet, Sir, but this is a plain corridor. The ones near to the Tipu Sultan's quarters were richly decorated and had lights in the sconces. This is a servants corridor." I knew to recognise such things from my time as a thief in England.

The sergeant said, "You have been here before?" I nodded. "Then you stay just behind me." He chuckled, "I took you for an officer's servant." He looked to see that his men were ready and then turned to Captain Tucker, "You ready, Sir?"

"I am, Sergeant, but you should know that we are seeking Tipu Sultan, the Tiger of Mysore, and Lord Mornington wishes us to take him as a prisoner."

"With due respect, Sir, Lord Mornington can wish all he likes but we shoot first and ask questions later."

I knew that no matter what the captain said the soldiers' sense of self-preservation would take over. I worked out that the corridor we were on was part of the south wall. It was the one with the door and corridor I had used to enter. That meant the Sultan's quarters lay to our left and the door I had used to our right. As we moved down I wondered if there would be any more ambushes ahead. If there were then as I was just behind the sergeant I would be amongst the first to know about them.

Suddenly, from ahead came the sound of muskets and shouts. There was a volley and then, after some cries, single shots. Captain Tucker shouted, "Hurry. Someone has found enemies."

We ran down the corridor, the hobnails sparking from the rough paving intended for the sandals of servants and not the boots of British soldiers.

"Sir, I recognise this corridor. It leads to the kitchens and there is a corridor that leads to the outside door that I used."

There were more cracks and flashes from ahead. I saw the light from the open door that led to the kitchen garden and it confirmed where we were. I saw eight dead Highlanders and I put my arm out to stop the sergeant. He turned and glared at me.

I shook my head and pointed, "There is a corridor down there. It is black as night and those lads have paid the price for their eagerness."

The captain said, "He is right, Sergeant. Smith, shout and ask them to surrender."

I moved closer to the wall and called, "We outnumber you. Surrender and be treated as prisoners."

I recognised the voice that shouted, in English, "If you try then you will all die like your foolish comrades."

I turned, "That is Colonel Pohlmann, Sir. There is a good chance that he is with Tipu Sultan."

The captain nodded and called out, "Captain Pohlmann, if we send for grenades then all of you will die. Surrender." I knew that the captain would not use a grenade. If he did it would guarantee the death of the Tiger and while it was still likely that our prey would elude us, Captain Tucker would do all he could to try to take him alive.

There was silence and I said, "Sir, they are just fifty or so paces from a door. They can escape and as far as I know the only ones who could stop them are our lads and they are on the top of the hill."

The sergeant had clearly had enough and he said, "Right lads, on three we step out and blast the corridor." Before Captain Tucker could do or say anything the sergeant said, "One, two, three." His men stepped out and fired. Even as they fired there were gunshots from within and the sergeant fell clutching his leg. Atkins' face disappeared as a ball ploughed into it.

Captain Tucker said, "Smith, with me. Let us end this."

We turned and ran down the corridor. I braced myself for the flash of a musket and the slamming of a ball into my body but when I saw the light at the end of the corridor I knew that they had escaped because the door to the outside was now open. It was the captain who found the bodies when we tripped over them. It was the Tiger of Mysore and he was dead. Around him were the bodies of his servants. It was clear to me what had happened. He had made his last stand here where the steps ascended and the sergeant's last volley had done for him. There were empty muskets and it was obvious to me that the Tiger had lived up to his name and fought to the end.

"I can't see a European. Smith, see if he is in the corridor."

I made my way down the corridor to the door that I had used, it seemed like weeks ago now. I pulled it open but kept in the shadows. Peering out I saw three Europeans and recognised one as Colonel Pohlmann. The other two wore blue as well and I guessed that they were Frenchmen. The colonel was rushing and I watched as he tripped and dropped a bag. They were about to cross the Little Cauvery. Even as I raised my musket to fire, two of the men with him raised their muskets. I switched to fire at the closest of them. My ball hit him in the shoulder and he spun around. Splinters from the striking of the balls next to my head told me how close I had come to death.

"Captain!"

The colonel and his companion were wading across the river and I dropped the musket and cocked my last pistol. I ran after them. I would not waste a ball until I was closer. I reached the river and pointed to direct the captain, "They are across the river, Sir."

I heard horses and saw some of the Nizam's men. Captain Tucker shouted, "Stay here, I will go and see if they can get after them."

As I went back I found the bag dropped by the colonel. In it was a purse with some coins. I took them. There were also some items of clothes and some bottles and some papers. I would examine them later. I rolled him over and saw that it was not my ball that had done for him. I had merely wounded him. The man had drowned in six inches of water. He was a French officer and I took his sword and his purse. When I opened it I saw that there were not only coins but also jewels. The officer had been a thief too.

By the time the captain had returned I had secreted the purse and hung the sword from my belt. It was a good one and I could sell it. "They will chase him. Perhaps if they capture him it might be compensation for the loss of the Tiger."

I slung the bag over my shoulder and headed back into the passage. Captain Tucker followed me. I left the door open to allow in light. I went to the body. Tipu Sultan, the Tiger of Mysore, was dead. By the time we reached the body of Tipu Sultan, the soldiers from the 33rd had gone. They had stripped the body of anything of value. The rings from his fingers were gone as were his weapons. It was a sad end for the man who had defied the British Empire.

Chapter 5

The killing of the Tiger of Mysore, Tipu Sultan, annoyed Lord Mornington. Sir Arthur was also less than pleased that his men had done the deed. Neither Captain Tucker nor I identified the culprits. In my case it was because I chose not to. I felt more affiliation to the sergeant and his men than any senior officer. I was not sure why the captain feigned ignorance of their identity. The annoyance was aggravated by the failure of the cavalry of the Nizam of Hyderabad to capture Colonel Pohlmann who, along with one of the French officers, evaded them. The only good news, apart from the capture of the fortress, was the discovery of papers implicating the Nawab of Arcot, Umdat ul-Umara, in a plot to support the Tiger. I learned from Captain Tucker that Lord Mornington, on behalf of the British government, sought to take over the Carnatic Sultanate. The papers gave him the opportunity to do so. That he did not do so straightaway showed the politics of the land.

I learned all this because we gained control of the palace and I accompanied the captain as he searched the fortress and we awaited the arrival of my section. I was there when Colonel Wellesley arrived and viewed the body of the Tiger.

He turned to the captain, "Who did this? I gave orders that he was to be taken alive."

I said nothing but kept my head down. The captain said, "It was dark and confusing, Colonel. We found him hidden in a corridor. In fact, until we had light we did not even know that it was Tipu Sultan."

The brother of Lord Mornington suddenly whipped his head around, "Was it you?"

I was not about to become a scapegoat and I shook my head, "I was chasing Colonel Pohlmann, Sir."

"Hmm. Well, we cannot bring him back. We could have used him as a figurehead." He turned to his aide, "Let us go and secure this fortress." He walked back a little way and then said, "Well done, you two. My faith in you was, it seems, justified."

There were still places where the defenders held out but the soldiers of the Nawab were winkling them out. The ones who held out and took time to eradicate were in the town, for the palace and fortress had been taken early on. It proved to be a rewarding time for me. While Captain Tucker sought papers, I sought treasure. I was even more determined than ever to flee. My only worry was that when they loaded the cart someone would discover my treasure trove. If they did then that would be a disaster. The rest of the section might know I was going to run but they did not know of my treasure trove. As well as any coins and jewels I managed to pick up I also gathered as much food as I could. That was for the benefit of the others rather than me. Knowing where the kitchens were helped. I also secured a room for us. While the Highlanders and the English battalions sought quarters in the more luxurious parts of the town and the palace, I commandeered the servants' chambers near to the kitchens. I reasoned that we could tether our animals just outside and when we were evicted, as I knew we would be, we could camp there and enjoy the kitchen garden and the supplies I had purloined.

It was dark when the section arrived. Captain Tucker had taken his finds to the Tiger's great hall which Lord Mornington had made his new headquarters. I had watched the section leave the hill and when they were crossing the stone bridge I left the ramparts where I had watched for them and went down to wave to them, "Over here."

They saw me and made their way, first to the Little Cauvery and then across the shallow water that I had crossed in the night. The lieutenant was smiling as were the rest of the section, "You survived. Well done."

I could not help grinning. I liked these men. They were more like family to me than my family had ever been, "Even better, Sir. The animals can graze here for there is water and if you would follow me I will show you the quarters I have taken. It might well be that we have to move but it will not be tonight."

Lieutenant Crozier nodded, "Aadyot, watch the animals and the cart. Do not unpack yet. Let us see what Private Smith has discovered." The lieutenant was wary and quite rightly. The army and the East India Company had rules and regulations that took no account of common sense.

I led them to the door I had used to enter and Seamus said, "This is where you went in?"

"It is. Watch your step, it is dark and there are uneven places as well as some steps."

When we reached the corridor Sergeant Grundy shook his head, "I will say this for you, Smudger, you have plenty of nerve."

I shrugged, "I had little choice." Like a conjuror revealing a trick I spread my arms when we entered the kitchen, "Ta-da!" I pointed to the door that led off the kitchen. "The staff slept in there. There are a dozen beds. I have stored some food in there too and as no one else has discovered this treasure trove we have it to ourselves, at least for a while."

The lieutenant nodded his approval, "You have excelled yourself, Smith. Go and help Aadyot empty the cart and see to the animals. Bring the tents in here. They will be safer. Sergeant, make a rota for duties. We need a couple of men to do two hours on and six hours off. They can watch the animals. Evans and Hogan, get some food on the go."

I went back outside. It was getting dark. "We can start to unpack, Aadyot. The tents and supplies are to go inside. It is down the corridor, up the steps and turn right. While you get the tents out I will water the horses."

"They are already watered, Smudger."

"Good, then I will tether them." I took out the sledgehammer and the metal pole from the cart and hammered it into the ground. I tied the two halters to it. The horses had room to graze. The tents were on the ground and while Aadyot began to take them inside I sought my treasure. Although it was safe I could see that it had been moved. I stuffed the sack inside my tunic.

When Aadyot came out he said, "Smudger, when I packed the cart I found some things that I did not expect." I looked at him and saw, from the expression on his face, that he had found my sack. "That sack which is in your tunic had more than oats in it."

I was a liar and one who could do so adeptly but I could not lie to Aadyot. I nodded and resigned myself to telling the truth, "It is my nest egg, Aadyot."

"Nest egg?"

"It is for when I leave the army. It is the coins I have gathered from the battlefield. You have some too, do you not?"

"Yes, Smudger, but not as many as you. You are clearly skilled."

"Aadyot, we are friends are we not?"

"I think so." He smiled.

"Then if you keep my little secret I will share it with you."

I did not get the reaction I had hoped. He stiffened and the smile left his face, "We are friends, Smudger, and you do not need to buy that friendship. I will keep your secret because we are friends."

I had offended him and I felt awful about that. I thought everyone was like me and looking out for themselves but I saw that I was wrong. "Forgive me, Aadyot, I learned bad habits in England. I must learn from you."

The smile returned, "I am a simple man, Smudger, you are complicated. You cannot be me and I cannot be you. We are what we are but I am happy that we are friends."

The air was cleared and I felt a sense of relief I had rarely enjoyed. Honesty felt good and I did not expect that.

I was given the first watch along with Aadyot. It was not a punishment but rather the reverse. We watched at sunset for two hours. The rest of the section were preparing our beds and cooking the food. I had secured my treasures, old and new, in my knapsack. Our knapsacks were safe. No one, even a thief, would steal from a man's knapsack. Aadyot and I sat outside and listened to the sounds of the night. Animals were hunting and life and death struggles took place just a few yards from us. It was the same as our world. I did not understand why we had assaulted and taken the fortress but men like Lord Mornington were different to me and the section. The duck ate the worms and the fox took the duck. Here in India the wolf and the tiger would take the fox. We were at the duck end of our world. We killed because we were ordered to and to survive. When we had searched the fortress for Tipu Sultan the defenders were trying to kill us. They managed to kill four of the 33rd and wounded four others. They had paid for the taking of a fortress that would, eventually, be given back to the men of Mysore, with their lives. The difference was that the ruler would be someone chosen by Lord Mornington. That was the reality of life in India.

"Is this like your home, Aadyot?"

"No, Smudger. I live in a city. These palaces are in the hills in my land and my family eke out a living raising whatever crops we can. I have not seen many fields here. There must be some but this is a rocky party of the world."

"I, too, come from a city. I would not survive in the countryside. I do not know how to raise crops."

"But you are good with animals, Smudger. Duchess and Froggy are better when you are here. The rest of us do our best but they like you and you understand them."

I shrugged for it puzzled me, too, "I don't know how. Until I came to India I had never even seen a horse that wasn't pulling a cart."

Aadyot tapped his chest, "Then perhaps it is in here. Sometime in the past one of your ancestors was a horseman and he is reborn in you."

"You believe in that sort of thing do you?"

He nodded, "If I am good in this life then when I am next reborn I will have a better life."

It did not seem the right thing to suggest that; as men like the Tipu Sultan and the Nizam of Hyderabad were the ones with the best life, then it begged the question how they had achieved that feat. It seemed to me that they had become what they were, not through being good in a former life, but by being as ruthless as they could be in this one.

We were relieved by John Williams and Eddie Lowe. They seemed content. The lieutenant had given them all a double rum ration and they had all eaten more in one meal than we normally consumed in a day. "We ate well. Plenty left for you lads, though. Any problems?"

I shook my head, "The animals are happy. They are watered and they have grass. Plenty of animals across the river but none have come close."

Eddie said, "I think we will light a fire. It will keep the creepies away and stop the midges biting."

Aadyot went into the corridor which now seemed almost familiar. The smell of the food drew us to the kitchen along with the noise of good humour and banter. Life was good and despite my brush with death, I was happy. Even Sergeant Grundy seemed to have benefitted from the relatively restful time since the battle of Mallavelli. We settled into a pleasant routine. We took the items from the stores that would last a long time and hid them. Sergeant Grundy knew what we were doing but not the lieutenant. We enjoyed three hot meals a day and that was luxury. The tea we found was good quality, as one would expect in a palace and we took and hid half of that, too. We found smaller cooking pots that would augment our own. In short, we scavenged all that we could so that when senior officers decided they wanted the kitchen to be used again, we would be more comfortable than we had been.

It took three days for us to be evicted and it was not Lord Mornington who did so. He left and took with him Captain Tucker. His brother, much to the obvious chagrin of General Harris, was given command of Seringapatam and when he discovered there were kitchens he could use and we occupied them, we were sent to camp outside the walls. It was not a punishment but we were not his regiment. Until we had a senior officer from the East India Company in command then we could expect short shrift. By the time we left we had purloined the best of the food, acquired more pots and taken all the kindling. The cooks from the 33rd who took over from us, cast hateful glances at us as they passed us on the way to collect more wood. Ours was dry and seasoned. The kindling they collected would make more smoke.

That first night back under canvas, George Mainsgill asked, "What about us, Lieutenant? It seems to me we are neither fish nor fowl. We are not part of the army and they clearly do not want any part of us."

The lieutenant was unhappy too. I had seen him and the sergeant in deep discussions at night. The lieutenant sighed, "We are paid, Mainsgill. We have food and life is not too unpleasant. Let us just bide our time." He did not sound convinced.

John Williams said, "The last pay we had was well before the battle where we lost Byers. When will we get paid again?"

Sergeant Grundy chuckled, "Then you can't spend it, can you? Don't worry, it will be mounting up and when you get it, well, even you won't be able to spend it quickly." He began to fill his pipe, "One thing about the army and the company is that they do pay, eventually. You will get your back pay and then you can waste it, eh?"

"And it is better than prison, me bucko. Sure, and I quite like this life. We are in the open and as the lieutenant said, fed. A bit more action would be good but let us see." Seamus was a real optimist.

The British soldiers were sent to march across the land of Mysore where they evicted the last supporters of the Tiger of Mysore. The Highlanders and the 33rd left the city and headed out to have the thankless task of seeking enemies who vanished at the approach of the red coated soldiers. We were, surprisingly, left out of it. I think that we were forgotten. The local sepoy regiments of the East India Company were used but not us. Thus it was that life settled into a pleasant routine. We explored the land around Seringapatam. We even received the back pay. It came when Colonel Stevenson brought some East India cavalry to the fort. They escorted the payroll wagon from the port of Mangalore. It was a laden wagon as it had the pay for all the soldiers: British and East India Company. We were no longer isolated. The colonel met with both the lieutenant and the newly promoted General Wellesley. When Lieutenant Crozier returned he had mixed feelings. We had been paid and not only had Colonel Stevenson brought us our money but we also had an officer who could give us direct commands. Colonel Stevenson was not an infantryman and both the sergeant and the lieutenant viewed him with suspicion.

Some of the others immediately spent their money. They bought drink and trinkets. The drink was an obvious purchase but the trinkets were hard to explain. They would have to carry them around in their knapsacks and as there was little likelihood of returning to England any time soon, it begged the question of when would the trinkets be given as gifts? I kept my pay with my treasure. What I did do, however, when we were given the chance to go into the town and spend our money, was to take my jewels to exchange them for coins. I needed less bulk. As Aadyot now knew my secret the two of us went to a man whom Aadyot suggested we use.

"Do you know this man, Aadyot?"

"No, Smudger, but when I met with the other sepoys, on the day we were paid, they told me that he was an honest man who was happy, for a fee, to exchange coins. He might rob others but if I am with you then I do not think that you will be robbed."

The man had a small house with no obvious shop front but he had an enormous bodyguard and the door looked like it would withstand a battering ram. The man frowned when he saw I was a European but Aadyot explained that I was a friend and when I spoke to him in his own language then he became less suspicious. When I emptied the bag of jewels his eyes widened and I saw that even the bodyguard was impressed. Aadyot cast me a questioning glance but he said nothing. He had seen some of my treasure but, clearly, not all of it.

"You have done well. There is enough here to buy yourself a small army. Will you leave your East India Company now?" The money lender asked.

I did not like the question for it sparked my hidden secret. I still planned on leaving and my consolidation of my finances was the first stage but Aadyot was with me. I shook my head, "I have been lucky so far but I still have some years to serve."

My answer seemed to satisfy him and besides, he would profit from the arrangement. He might be trustworthy but he was not doing this out of the goodness of his own heart. He would make a profit. He had a counting frame with beads upon it. I had seen them before. Some merchants used them and Aadyot had told me they were Chinese in origin. The beads flew along the racks as he examined each jewel and placed it down. He made marks on a blackboard with chalk. It took some time but we were going nowhere. When he was satisfied he turned over the blackboard to a new side and wrote a figure down. I expected this. It was a test to see if I could read and also to present me with a derisory offer. I shook my head and asked for a greater number of coins. The man smiled and rubbed out the figure. So it went on until we agreed on a number that was about three times as much as he had first suggested. We were both happy; I had coins that would be easier to hide and he had made a profit. We left and I took Aadyot to treat him. As we headed for a place that served beer and food he asked, "Where did you get all the jewels from, Smudger?"

"Battlefields, the rooms we searched…I have sharp eyes, Aadyot. The rest of you were looking for other things but I knew which were valuable items and which were not."

He smiled, "Then when we next battle I shall watch you, Smudger. I need to make my own fortune."

We made a few more purchases. I invested in a money belt to wear beneath my tunic. I could now do so for the treasure was not as bulky. Aadyot had found my sack and I did not want someone who was not from my section discovering the fortune I held.

It was when we were enjoying the food that we heard of another enemy of Britain. There were men at the next table and they were speaking of a warlord who was raising an army. The term warlord seemed strange to me but Aadyot was familiar with it. "There are many such men. The land of the Marathas is one with princes and rulers who command a small area. Often a warlord raises an army and takes over those places. They are like bandits."

While we ate we listened to the sepoys talking about a man who was a warlord to the north of us. I learned that the warlord, Dhondia Wagh, had been a prisoner of Tipu Sultan and that he had been released by the British after the Tiger's death. He had gone to a place called Shikaripur where he raised an army, mainly from those who had fought for the Tiger. He clearly had delusions of grandeur for he gave himself the titles of Ubhaya-Lokadheeshwara and Nayaka of Bidnur. The sepoys wondered why Sir Arthur did not destroy the man for he seemed to be a threat. I think that General Wellesley wanted Mysore and Hyderabad free from men like the Tiger before he took on a warlord. Especially one who had, according to the sepoys, the largest army in India. I stored the information. If we went to war again and it was further north then I would be able to put into place my plan to escape.

When we returned to the camp the others were in a good mood. Seamus and Dai had the contented looks of men who have had a sufficient quantity of drink to make them happy. The lieutenant and sergeant had found some fellow officers who had also been paid and, in their own circles, had enjoyed a pleasant day. When I told them about this man, Dhondia Wagh, it interested them all. If we went to war again then there would be a chance for more profit and, in Seamus' case, the chance for some action. He liked drink and singing but his favourite occupation was fighting.

It was May when that prospect became a reality. Orders were sent and we were told that we would be moving in the next days, north to Chitradurga. I was delighted that General Harris would not be with us. Colonel Stevenson commanded the East India soldiers while General Wellesley took the 25th Light Dragoons, 73rd Foot, and the 77th Foot. His own regiment would stay at Seringapatam. I wondered if they were being punished for the actions of the sergeant and his men.

The East India Company moved out first. The cavalry led, we followed and then the rest of the army. We saw strange looks cast in our direction, especially from the cavalry when it was Sergeant Grundy who mounted Froggy and not the lieutenant. No one said a word but we could all see the questions on their faces. We had more than a hundred and twenty miles to travel and we wanted Sergeant Grundy to continue his recuperation. He had survived a long time since the doctor had advised him to leave the army. The sergeant was a realist and knew how close he had come to dying. He was obliged to me for, in his words, '*saving his life.*' I had done little enough.

On the third night of our travels we heard a story from one of the Madras regiment about the man we would face. Dhondopant Gokhale had raided and plundered the camp of Dhondia Wagh when the warlord had first raised his army. We heard that the warlord, when he escaped, swore he would *'dye his moustache in the blood of Gokhale's heart'*. It chilled even the toughest of our men. It was one thing to fight an enemy but to battle with one who could cut out a heart and smear the blood on his moustache was somehow, terrifying. The other rumour we heard was that this warlord had an army of ninety thousand men. The number seemed ridiculous to me but as Ben Neville pointed out, it had to be an enormous army and even if exaggerated would suggest an army of at least fifty thousand. Even with the three British regiments as well as the East India battalions we would number less than five thousand. The odds were not in our favour.

We got to know the other regiments as we marched north but their officers, all Englishmen, shunned us. They shared General Harris' view that we were thieves and vagabonds. The privates quickly realised we were neither of those things and they shared with us.

As I led Duchess I reflected that once a man had a label or a title, it was hard to shift it. We were viewed as useful but also expendable by officers like General Wellesley. The way I had been thrown into danger with little regard for my safety illustrated that. I had survived but not thanks to them. It had been my own wits that had managed to extricate me from probable death. To most of the army I was just a thief. Captain Tucker was held in higher regard because he was a gentleman from a good family.

Our fortune in having been the first ones to the kitchens in Seringapatam helped to make the journey north that much easier. We still had the spices we had taken and the dried beans and pulses. They would not last much longer for we used them at every meal but they did help to enliven the dull diet we endured. We ate better than the others. We had also taken some gin. That had come courtesy, I think, from Colonel Pohlmann. The bag I had recovered from the side of the stream contained three bottles. I was not a gin drinker but men like Seamus and Dai would drink anything and they were still eking out the treasure which we kept hidden from Lieutenant Crozier.

The horses had also benefitted from both the grazing and the leisure that they had enjoyed. Duchess needed all her energy for the cart was laden. I knew we were lucky to have our own cart. The wagons, pulled by bullocks for the rest of the East India Company soldiers, were heavily laden and always pulled into camp at least half an hour after the last of the soldiers. The camps we made had to be well guarded. This was Maratha land and they were suspicious of the East India Company and Great Britain. They would steal from us if they could. We were allowed in the land for the simple reason that the warlord was as much as threat to them as to us. They had sent General Chintamanrao Patwardhan with their own army to deal with him. It was hoped that between us Dhondia Wagh would be cracked like a walnut.

The Tiger and the Thief

The warlord had taken a series of forts in the Haveri region and we knew, as we left Chitradurga, that if he held them then we would have to assault them. I still had nightmares about the Forlorn Hope. It had turned out well but I still remembered my legs feeling like jelly and my guts complaining as I crested the top of the glacis. I hoped it would be like the battle in which I had fought alongside my tent mates. There was security in their red coats.

Chapter 6

We marched through the heat of a hot June. We marched in our uniforms but wearing the straw hats helped. We undid our top buttons and whenever we could we took off the tunics. Some of us chose to march without boots, wearing sandals like the locals and with our breeches rolled up. It kept us marginally cooler and meant that our boots would be saved. We wore our shirts but most men had their jackets open or carried. Lieutenant Crozier dressed in the full uniform and melted. I felt sorry for him.

I began to believe that the rumours about the numbers facing us were just that, exaggerated numbers, for the enemy ran at our approach. We marched, ready to fight, but Dhondia Wagh seemed unwilling to face us in battle. Sir Arthur was keen to bring him to the field and so we split up when we reached Harihara. I think he was tempting the enemy to pick off one of our armies which, if the numbers were correct, would outnumber us by ten to one. We camped overnight in the city that the warlord had left when he heard of our approach. He had taken all that he could but we still found enough to augment our supplies. A fleeing army often leaves forgotten items to be taken by good scavengers. Colonel Stevenson was to lead the East India soldiers to take the Rennebennur fort while General Wellesley took the British troops under his command and took another nearby one. We left our cart and tents at Harihara and marched to the fort. It was thirteen miles and Colonel Stevenson wanted a quick strike. The bullocks pulling the wagons used by the other units would have slowed us. We were annoyed because having our horses meant we would not have been slowed. I now wore my treasure safely secure in the money belt I had bought in Seringapatam. If I fell on the battlefield and the others survived then they would share in the bounty. There were men left to guard the wagons and our cart. We had come to know them on the march and knew that they would be safe. It meant that both the sergeant and the lieutenant could ride to war and we marched behind them.

The cavalry were new to the region and had yet to fight. They had been spectators at Seringapatam. While their officers did not think much of us, their troopers did for we were battle hardened. Those at the rear of the regiment spoke to us to ask us about our enemies. They had heard terrible stories and feared them. Ben Neville gave them sage advice, "It is not their muskets you should fear but their long swords and axes." They were grateful for the information.

The Madras infantry marching with us with us had light artillery pieces that were small enough to be carried on mules and then assembled. Their ten guns would be our only cannons but, as we were attacking a fort, they would be necessary. We learned, from the scouts, that the forts guarded strategic routes. They were there to slow us down and make us bleed to take them. They were made of stone and had cannons. It would not be easy. A few men could delay an army and make them lose men in an attack.

The cavalry left us four miles from the fort and we became the advance guard. We marched behind Colonel Stevenson and the colonels of the Madras infantry. The cavalry would take no part in the assault. Their task was to ensure that no one escaped when we did attack. Sir Arthur wanted to eliminate as many of the enemy as he could before he faced them in open battle. The warlord thought to decimate us but Sir Arthur had different ideas. When we reached the fort I saw that it was not as big an obstacle as I had expected. It was no Seringapatam. The walls were solid enough and there were a couple of artillery pieces on the wall but it looked to me that it held less than eight hundred men, although the walls bristled with muskets, bayonets and what looked like old fashioned spears. For some reason the spears looked more terrifying than the bayonets. The walls would need ladders to escalade and we had no time for ladders. It was clear to me that our leaders planned to use our small artillery pieces to punch holes in the wall and then simply charge and rely on cold steel and the resolve of the Madras battalions to climb over the fallen rubble.

The walls erupted in musket and artillery fire as soon as we were seen. The weapons were fired prematurely for we were in open order and too far away for them to hurt us. The balls bounced like stones thrown across a pond and we were able to avoid them. It showed the nerves of the enemy gunners. The balls struck trees and scythed through the undergrowth but no one was injured, at least not in their first bombardment. The light companies from the Madras regiments quickly went into action. While the cannons were taken from the mules and assembled they scampered ahead of us, using whatever cover they could find and then peppered the walls and defenders with ball. The cannons stopped their firing while the defenders duelled with the skirmishers. Our muskets were hitting the gunners and they were more important than the men with muskets. It meant that our better trained gunners were able to ready their weapons without balls and canister being sent in their direction. Our gunners would aim them at particular targets and they would choose the best balls. I had seen that skill when I had been a sailor. A good gunner chose the smoothest balls to use first. Once the battle raged then any ball would be used but the first shots would be well chosen.

Colonel Stevenson waved his sword and the officers marshalled their men into the lines ready for the assault. We were to be part of the force attacking the main gate. Despite all of our efforts Sergeant Grundy insisted on accompanying us. Seamus and Dai decided, without telling him, to flank him and be ready to assist should he need it. As soon as our guns began to fire, aiming not at the pieces on the wall, but the masonry next to the gate, the enemy guns fired back at them. Although they had larger balls to send at our guns, they were neither as accurate nor as fast as our guns. The Madras gunners prided themselves on their skill and speed of reloading. Although one of our guns was upended during the fierce and noisy battle of the guns, the rest continued to fire. They struck targets and we saw the walls and gates visibly weakened. Hunks of masonry fell and small cracks began to appear in the walls. The enemy fire became desultory. We had bayonets fitted and we waited with primed muskets. I had not returned all the pistols to the quartermaster of the 33rd and two loaded ones hung around my neck.

We watched as the balls struck at the base of the wall. When they first hit, the balls appeared to be failing to damage them but when a huge fissure suddenly appeared and then a section of the wall dramatically crumbled down revealing the interior, we knew we were winning. The accurate fire weakened a section of the masonry and ensured it would fall. As soon as the wall fell half of our guns were switched to fire at the gatepost next to the crumbled wall. The rest continued to bombard the walls. Within half a dozen balls the post collapsed taking the gate with it. I expected the order to charge to be given but Colonel Stevenson knew his business and he switched the guns to fire at the wall closest to the hole they had made. As with the gatepost it quickly fell. There was rubble to clamber over but there were no longer any guns or muskets firing from the walls. The fighting platform had collapsed and men and guns had fallen. The order was given to charge. We had a large enough gap and the rubble made an easy ramp for men to scramble over.

This was not a Forlorn Hope. There were no volunteers but as in any battle there were men who raced ahead of their comrades. They did not have a death wish but, instead, a need for glory or perhaps the treasure that they might find on the corpses of those that they slew. There were others who might enjoy that moment when, after the battle, their comrades would comment on their courage. Our section did not seek glory, we craved survival. Others ran ahead of us and they were the ones blasted by the smaller artillery pieces the enemy had brought from the other walls to cover the gap. They fired guns that were filled with stones, grapeshot or canister. They scythed down twenty men in an instant. The muskets of the defenders, brought to cover the gaps, all fired at once, too, and the effect was to make a hole in our line. The ones awaiting our charge all cheered but their elation was short lived. As they hurried to reload we raced across the open ground. Seamus, Dai and the sergeant were a few steps behind us but that was a good thing, our bodies protected them. Lieutenant Crozier found a gap near the gates where there was no rubble, just the ramp made by the fallen gate. We cheered and the cheers made the men reloading panic even more. Men like that make mistakes. They leave ramrods in muskets, they forget to swab out their cannons. There are many things that can go wrong if you are not well trained and these men were not real soldiers. They made mistakes that sent ramrods flying and caused muskets to misfire. When a cannon that was not swabbed out exploded in a riot of flames, flying metal and screams, we knew that poorly trained men had paid the price for their mistakes.

Lieutenant Crozier levelled his pistol and shouted, "Fire."

We did not bother to aim. There were so many men before us and they were just forty paces from us, that even a ball fired from the hip would hit something. We fired and I saw that one of us had been lucky. The gunner with the linstock fell and in that instant their fate was sealed. There were no cannons filled with grapeshot to thin our ranks. We were joined by the men of Madras who were out for vengeance as they had seen their comrades butchered. Our bayonets reaped a fine harvest. The defenders had unloaded muskets without the advantage of a blade at the end and the gun crews and the muskets that defended them died. We raced on.

The fort was not large and we could see at the other end of it, the gates opening as some of the surviving defenders fled. They were in for a shock. The sabres of our cavalry awaited them and their joy would be short lived.

The lieutenant shouted, "Reload and find shelter."

Bob Cathcart began to reload but said, "Shelter from who, Sir?"

The lieutenant had reloaded and he pointed the pistol at the far gate, "From the men who will come running as fast as they can to get away from the cavalry."

Sergeant Grundy, the old soldier with an eye for such things, shouted, "There are two stone water troughs over there, Sir. They will do nicely."

We dropped behind them and levelled our muskets which we had quickly reloaded. Many of the Madras infantry had raced after the fleeing men and the lieutenant proved prophetic when the two hundred or so men who had fled now ran back wielding swords and muskets. The Madras infantry were a safer option than the cavalry. The first fifteen East India Company soldiers fell, wounded or dead, and the rest found cover.

"Fire!"

The Devil's Dozen only had twelve firearms but they were handled by men who knew their business and even as the first volley smacked into the enemy, we were reloading and we fired again. In less than one minute we had fired four times and almost fifty lead balls can do serious damage.

It was an East India major, leading his cavalrymen through the open gate who shouted, "Cease fire."

As the smoke cleared we saw that the enemy had their hands raised in surrender or were abasing themselves before the horsemen. Before us lay a wall of bodies.

Colonel Stevenson appeared and raised his sword in salute to us, "Well done, Lieutenant Crozier. I am pleased to see that at least one officer kept his head." He was chastising the Madra officers who had not controlled their men.

As we cleared the bodies from the fort we took any treasure that we found. General Wellesley did not want the fort but he wished it rendered defenceless and so we took the guns with us and broke the doors. We levered broken masonry and made it tumble into the ditch. We made the walls so that they could not be used by a defender. They could be repaired but it would be the work of half a year to do so. While we sought treasure we also sought food. We ate well, using the stores in the fort. We enjoyed a roof over our heads and the two water troughs provided water for our horses. We left, the next day, to continue our march north. The cavalry kept us in touch with the rest of the army. With General Wellesley commanding I felt safer than had General Harris been our leader.

We joined up with the other column and headed for the British held fort at Haliyal. Messengers from our allies had ridden in to say that Dhondopant Gokhale and his nephew Appaji, along with Patwardhan, intended to fight the warlord not far from Kittur. I knew it would annoy the general. He wanted our allies to fight with us. That way we had a chance to defeat this warlord. He had split his army to catch the enemy between us. Dhondopant Gokhale had isolated his army. We were setting up our camp when the riders spoke to our commander and I had seen enough of him to be able to gauge his mood. None of us knew what the message was about until the next day after General Wellesley had spoken to Colonel Stevenson and he had told Lieutenant Crozier. Our officer confirmed that the general was less than happy.

George was puzzled, "Why should it matter if they fight this warlord or us?"

Sergeant Grundy took his pipe from his mouth so that he could use it to point to the north, "Simple, Private Mainsgill, this warlord has the numbers and as he has survived this long then he must possess the skill to defeat our allies. Now if we were there, while we don't have the numbers, we have the men and the resolve to beat him and this General Wellesley knows how to soldier. We could join with our allies and guarantee victory and an end to this campaign. We could go back to the fortress and enjoy our little camp by the river." Sergeant Grundy brought with him a lifetime of experience and we benefitted.

We were told that we would be marching the next day but when we saw the survivors of the battle, led by the Maratha general, Patwardhan himself, we knew the outcome of the battle. The men were bloody and hung their heads. They had been bested. We knew exactly what had happened quickly for the men who came into our camp and were tended were more than happy to tell us of the disaster. Dhondopant Gokhale and his nephew Appaji had been away from the army and ambushed. The warlord, it seemed, knew his business and both men were killed. Sickeningly the warlord had kept his word and his moustache was now stained with the blood of his enemy. Patwardhan and Bapuji Gokhale had been badly beaten by the warlord and fled the field. We had the battered survivors of the battle and our enemy now had the confidence amongst his men of victory. The loss of small forts was nothing. Their victory was everything. We had now lost a large number of men and those numbers might have guaranteed victory. We had just the British troops and the men of the East India Company to fight a much larger and victorious army. The Maratha survivors would be with us but they would need a victory to give them confidence. That victory would have to come from our muskets.

Surprisingly Sergeant Grundy seemed happier about that than I had expected. As we cooked the meal I said, "Sergeant, you don't seem worried that our allies have been defeated, why?"

"Because they now need us and General Wellesley and Colonel Stevenson have a larger army. The Marathas thought to show the British that they could beat the warlord and they were wrong. It is not as large an army as it would have been if they had obeyed the general's instructions but they will listen to him. They have to. We have slightly greater numbers now and when we start to hunt this warlord he will run. We have more men to make a net. It might take time but the general will win." He dipped a spoon in the pot to taste the stew. He added a little more salt and a spoonful of pepper. He chuckled, "Britain and the company will benefit because we will control more land. Men like this Patwardhan will be grateful to the general and happily let us be their bodyguards. Lord Mornington was clever to promote his brother."

"It doesn't help us, Sergeant."

"Ah, there you are wrong. We will benefit because we will be there when we win the battles. The men we are fighting have been looting this part of the world for almost six months. They have treasure and where will that treasure be?"

I knew the answer because I was a thief and my money belt held my treasure, "Either on their bodies or with the baggage train."

"Clever lad, Smudger, and when we win we make sure that we are close enough to be the first to reap the reward." He handed the ladle to me and went to sit down on a barrel we had emptied. He intended to light his pipe. "It won't be for me." He held up his pipe, "You lads can have my share of any treasure. So long as I have my baccy, then I have enough. Mallavelli was a warning, Smudger. If I see the year out then I will be surprised. I now enjoy each day as it comes." He laughed in a dry sort of way, "Just waking up is a relief." He lit the pipe from a twig lit from the fire and puffed contentedly, "I am proud of what we have done with you lads, all of you. General Harris calls us the Devil's Dozen and thinks it is an insult. I take that as a badge of honour because all of you were villains. I know the change the lieutenant and I have made to all of you and take pleasure from that knowledge. The lieutenant and I were lumped in with you but between us we have made a body of men that has, in my view, no equal here." He jabbed the stem of the pipe in my direction, "You and the captain showed that when you hunted the Tiger in Seringapatam. The sergeant from the 33rd and his men let down their colonel. Our lads wouldn't have." He took a brand from the fire to relight the pipe that had gone out during his speech and when he had it going again he said, "You lads are my legacy. I am happy with that."

His words made me feel guilty. I was still planning on fleeing. We were now close enough to the Dutch colony of Goa for me to make a move but the sergeant had called us his pride and joy. How could I leave? As I served up the food for the section I decided to wait until the sergeant was no longer with us before leaving. The sergeant had said he would be lucky to see the year our but I was not so sure. I was more hopeful. Aadyot had tried to incorporate foods that his people said helped men to live for longer. We added the grated yellow root of plants to the food. It gave it an interesting taste but Aadyot was confident that it would help with the health of the sergeant. The garlic, onions, spices and lentils we used now represented more than half of the food we ate. That was partly because, as we marched, the supply of meat diminished. Perhaps the sergeant wouldn't die, at least not soon.

The next day the chase began. Neither army could move quickly. The terrain and the animals we used to pull the guns slowed us. The warlord tried to slow us by sacrificing some of his men at the forts which littered the road. Every river crossing was contested. General Wellesley showed his skill by using the horsemen of our allies to cut off the retreat of the defenders before using our guns, including the captured ones, to blast them into submission. They began to surrender quickly and, as we stopped him from heading for the safety of Kittur, his men began to desert. His huge numbers began to dwindle. He had attracted men because he was a successful warlord. Once he began to lose then many men chose to leave him.

We had still to fight the battle that Sergeant Grundy had said promised treasure but we were relatively well fed and the Devil's Dozen were happy. It was at Manoli on the Malpurba River that we finally caught up with him and his, now greatly reduced, army.

River crossings were always tricky affairs and our scouts had found the enemy strung out as they tried to cross the river with their laden wagons. We were ordered to move under cover of darkness. Our horses and cart were left so that we just took our

muskets and we went with the other East India soldiers. Colonel
Stevenson had delegated command of his cavalry who were
already fording the river further west, to the colonel of the 25th
Light Dragoons. The brigades of cavalry would close the doors
to escape. We were in open formation moving in a long line
through the undergrowth. The enemy had camped by the river
and half of them had crossed to camp on the other side. We
waited. I wondered why we did not attack in the dark and said so
to Lieutenant Crozier when he came to ensure we were all
awake.

"Simple, Smith, we have allies who look and fight the same
way as our enemy. The last thing we need is for someone to
make a mistake in the dark. The general will wait until dawn.
That way there should be no mistakes. We see the enemy and we
kill them."

He might have been right but the insects that bit us were more
annoying than anything else. The sound of men slapping them
was stopped by the sergeants who used their swagger sticks
rather than their voices. No one wanted the noise to be heard by
our enemies. Sergeant Grundy just put his hand on our arms and
shook his head. We obeyed.

Dawn seemed to take an age to manifest itself. When it did,
the order to stand to was given, not by a bugle but by a command
hissed down the line. It sounded like the surf on a beach. We
loaded and primed our weapons. We fixed our bayonets and
waited for the command. Lieutenant Crozier waved us forward
and we moved with muskets at the ready. Seamus and Dai were
either side of the sergeant. Corporal Neville was at one end of
our line and Aadyot and I were at the other. We moved until we
neared the clearing at the edge of the trees. We could see the
unsuspecting enemy as they moved around their camp and
prepared to leave. It was not us who alerted the enemy but one of
the men from the allied forces. He prematurely discharged his
musket. It happened, especially to nervous men whose fingers
slipped onto triggers. Immediately we were ordered to present
and fire for surprise was now gone. The smoke erupted all along
our line masking our targets but as the enemy camp held
thousands of men it did not matter. The wall of balls would find
flesh. We fired five volleys and then we heard the bugle that

sounded the charge. We ran through the smoke. I know that I braced myself for the musket volleys that would be returned but there were none. We had caught them unawares.

The men we had killed were almost our undoing. There were so many that we were in danger of tripping over their bodies. We barely needed our bayonets for the ones who survived just ran for the water. I saw men hurl themselves in. This was not the shallow water of the Little Cauvery. This was deeper and men drowned. We lined up on the bank to open fire at the ones scrambling to safety on the other side. When we heard the sound of the bugle and the thunder of hooves we knew that the cavalry had arrived. The East India cavalry and the 25th came from one flank and the native cavalry came from the other. The men on foot were surrounded and they began to surrender. We had won and that meant we could reap the rewards.

We moved back from the river searching the strewn bodies for signs of life and treasure. I found four daggers, two of them bejewelled. I found some money belts and the coins augmented my own treasure. By the time General Wellesley arrived and ordered the bodies to be burned there was little left to be taken.

That night, as we camped by the river, the bodies having been burned downwind of us, we asked the lieutenant if the campaign was over. He shook his head, "Dhondia Wagh and his horsemen escaped. It was his infantry that we slew and destroyed. He can move faster than we can now."

It was disappointing but Sergeant Grundy had been proved right and as we had not a scratch between us then all was well. We had all taken treasure. We had captured food and enjoyed horsemeat from the dead animals. That was all good for a soldier on campaign.

The next day the general divided us into three columns. He led one with the Highlanders and the 25th Light Dragoons. The largest, our allies, was led by the Maratha general, Patwardhan, and the East India soldiers were led by Colonel Stevenson. It became clear that this was like the game of fox and geese. The three columns would try to anticipate the warlord's moves and negate his mobility. There would always be a blade in his back and if he turned left or right then there were more blades awaiting him. It was slow work but the result was inevitable as the net grew tighter around him and we closed his avenues of escape. We spent August in the unbearable heat of India marching through jungle and sometimes more open woodland. I think if we had not had Froggy then even with the better diet he enjoyed and the lack of fighting, Sergeant Grundy would have succumbed to his illness. He rode and we marched. I had long ago given up on the boots and taken to wearing the sandals I had in Seringapatam. Our uniforms were tattered and torn for the thorns and undergrowth through which we marched took their toll.

It was not an incident free pursuit. We almost caught him twice. The first time it was our horsemen who discovered his camp and they attacked prematurely, perhaps too eager to end the campaign. The warlord and his men escaped when they heard the approach of the horses. The horsemen were rebuffed by musket fire and troopers were lost. The second time was four days later. The swathe cut by the enemy made their trail obvious but Colonel Stevenson was wary of losing his horsemen again and so we plodded on at the speed of the infantry. The trail we followed veered south and that meant they would meet the general if they continued their course. It was our section and a company of Madras infantry who were at the fore that discovered them. This time they were not at camp but crossing our line of march. The English captain who commanded the company of sepoys outranked Lieutenant Crozier and it was he, perhaps eager for glory, who alerted the enemy. He shouted, "Charge!" It meant that instead of forming a line and discharging our muskets he ordered his men to charge and take the warlord. The warlord's men were mounted and they simply charged us. Our section had their muskets raised already and we fired on the lieutenant's command. It saved us as we loaded and reloaded so quickly that our muskets sounded like forty. The Madras infantry, even though there were a hundred of them were slow to raise their muskets and even slower to reload. The horsemen were fast and while we made a hole in their line that kept us safe, they did not. The captain paid for his mistake with his life as a sabre hacked his skull in two. When Colonel Stevenson brought up the rest of the battalions it prevented a slaughter of the Madras company but Dhondia Wagh escaped with enough men to outnumber our cavalry.

There was no point in having a debate about the disaster. The colonel ordered our section to search the dead for papers while the Madras battalion buried their own dead and burned the enemy. We found few papers but some of the men we had killed yielded jewels and coins. We took them as payment for having done our job well.

We trekked after him again and August drew to a close. We looked more like a ragged band of bandits than soldiers but we were closing in on the warlord. Our bayonets in his back had stopped him from resupplying and he was in a bad way. When the remains of his army crossed the Malapurba River at the end of August we sought a glimmer of hope that he was heading south and our allies, the Nizam of Hyderabad and his men, would bar their way to safety. We found him on the 9th of September or rather he found us for in trying to avoid one of the other columns he ran into us and this time Colonel Stevenson was in the fore. He ordered us into lines when the scouts reported the approach of a large body of horsemen. By the time the warlord and his men saw us it was too late for them. We gave five volleys and unhorsed almost a quarter of his men. Although he fled Colonel Stevenson sent riders to warn General Wellesley of the proximity of our prey.

We camped at the battlefield and enjoyed horsemeat. When the subaltern from the 25th Light Dragoons rode in the next day we knew our hunt was over for after he reported to the colonel we were told that Dhondia Wagh was dead and General Wellesley had his four-year-old son in his charge. We could go back to civilisation and be given new uniforms and equipment. We had earned them.

Chapter 7

We reached Madras by January. It was the depot for the battalions with whom we had fought and although we were based in Calcutta we did not mind as we had grown to know the Madras sepoys and got on with them. We knew no one in Calcutta. When we had first arrived there we had been made less than welcome by everyone at the barracks. General Wellesley had left us in October to take command in Ceylon. He had been promoted to senior general in India. Even Lieutenant Crozier and Sergeant Grundy were surprised at his rapid promotion. To go from being a colonel to a general in a couple of years was remarkable. When we reached Madras, Colonel Stevenson showed that he liked and appreciated us by making sure that we not only had a building in which to sleep rather than tents as well as providing new uniforms, boots and muskets, but also by taking us off the rigours of guard duty. While that pleased most of the men Sergeant Grundy was a natural sceptic. He feared that being left off duties meant that some other fate awaited us.

Lord Mornington had medals cast for the British soldiers who had taken part in the attack and they were presented to us at a formal ceremony by Colonel Stevenson. Aadyot was also given one and he was almost moved to tears by the gesture. We did not see him as a sepoy but as part of our section. I put my medal with my other treasure. Its value was in what it represented rather than the weight of metal but I found myself oddly proud to have won a medal.

Madras was the chance to flee but it was not a port in the regular sense. As I had discovered when we had landed horses here, there was no convenient quayside. Boats were rowed out to the ships and that meant a nautical escape was out of the question. However, as I was close to the sea I was ever hopeful. The sea lay to the east as did the dream of a home on some island where I would not be known and my fortune would enable me to live like an eastern potentate. I saw the little boats rowing out the Indiamen waiting to sail east and felt envious. My money belt was full and I was rich yet marching around India I could not spend it.

We were also rewarded with the promotion of Lieutenant Crozier to Captain. He was summoned to headquarters and came back with the new uniform. That night he celebrated with a bottle of whisky and after we put him to bed Sergeant Grundy explained the timing of it.

"When we caught the warlord and that captain of infantry almost cost us our lives it must have been clear to the colonel that Mr Crozier needed more rank. He is a damned good officer and far better than the ones they normally have in the company. It backs up what I was saying, the colonel has plans for us. Now, Captain Crozier can only be out ranked by a major and even in the East India Company if they have earned that rank then they have skill."

With the title came a new one for our section. We were now called a platoon. While, as Sergeant Grundy said, we were undersized for such a unit, it suggested that more men might join us.

A month later we began to believe him for another twelve men with a second corporal arrived to join us. They came from a ship that landed men in the surging surf and they marched to the barracks to be presented to the captain. We all had new uniforms but, somehow, we wore ours differently. It was hard to explain to an outsider but we stood at attention in a unique manner. We were the Devil's Dozen and enjoyed the accolade. When we lined up the captain addressed us. "Welcome to the thirteen of you." He smiled, "I hope that is not an unlucky number. As you can see you double the number of our platoon. This is not our normal home so do not become too comfortable here. We have been based in Calcutta, Mallavelli and Seringapatam. This platoon is well thought of. We have a reputation and that means that we are used by Lord Mornington and the East India Company to do specialised work. While we are here Sergeant Grundy and I will improve on the training you enjoyed in England and get rid of the rust you acquired at sea. Work starts tomorrow. For now, get to know the old hands."

As much as we tried to do as the captain asked there were problems from the start as the new men did not get on with us. Perhaps, to be generous to them, it was the other way around. Perhaps we were the arrogant ones. I am not sure but within a day of us sharing the barracks Seamus and Zebediah Thompson came to blows. There was only ever one winner for Seamus was the toughest man I had ever met. The flurry of blows meted out by the burly new man were easily fended off by Seamus who then landed four blows in rapid succession that laid the new man unconscious. The new corporal, Edward Teach, sided with the new man, of course. He came in and saw Thompson on the floor and our huge Irishman towering over him. It did not help that the old hands stood behind Seamus while the new men faced us. It threatened to sour the section which, until that moment, had all worked together and had a spirit that others envied. Captain Crozier decided the matter. He came into the barracks as Thompson was being brought around. The only signs of damage to Seamus were his grazed knuckles.

He glared at Seamus, "Hogan, you are a man who does not know his own strength. Poor Thompson here thought he was coming to a platoon made up of footmen and servants. He did not know this is a fighting unit. Until we have trained them," he whipped his head around and stared at the corporal, "all of them, then we must be considerate. After all they have not fought in four or five battles. They have not marched across India, twice, they are new from England and have still to recover from that sea voyage. Let us give them time to adjust."

Seamus and the rest of the section, the Devil's Dozen were all grinning and Seamus said, "Quite right, Sir, and from now on we will be gentle with them."

Corporal Teach said, "But, Captain Crozier..."

"We will have an officer's call, now. To the office!"

The two corporals and sergeant all saluted and followed the captain out. When they had gone there was silence and the new men looked sullen. Dai smiled, "Now, boys, we have got off on the wrong foot. Thompson, I can see from your size that you are used to throwing your weight around and getting your own way. Perhaps these lads are a bit frightened of you. I don't care. Here you lads are the new boys who fit in with us. Clear?" His eyes moved around them and none, not even Thompson could hold his gaze. Dai was not as big as Seamus but he had a real power and authority to him. "As far as I am concerned until you have stood in the line and fought alongside us then none of us will

trust you. Any respect you get you will earn. You know what
General Harris calls us?" Three of them, the younger ones, shook
their heads. "I will tell you, the Devil's Dozen, and we quite like
that name. If I were you I would keep my head down and try to
avoid annoying any of us. Walk gently and all will be well."

The captain must have said something similar to the corporal
for he looked quite chastened when he returned.

Sergeant Grundy was an old soldier and the problems we had
did not surprise him. When we sat in the barracks after our
evening meal he and Ben would sit and talk with us. The new
men occupied the far end of the barracks. Walter was not
bothered by the divide. He saw it as inevitable. "They will
become part of the section, but it will take some time. It happens
in every regiment. New men arrive and do not know the pecking
order. You have men who are like Zebediah Thompson, men who
see the chance to be cock of the walk. It won't last for we will be
needed again and see further action. I have got a feeling that the
arrival of the men means that someone has another little job for
us and we know what that means."

The sergeant was prophetic. In June Captain Crozier was
summoned to headquarters and when he returned it was with the
news that we had our orders. General Baird had replaced General
Wellesley in Trincomalee and General Wellesley was now in
Bombay. He was on his way to take command in Seringapatam.
We were ordered to join him. This time we would have to march
there from Madras. We would be returning to the lair of the tiger
and I confess I was quite looking forward to it. We had enjoyed
our billet there and our camp by the river. I hoped that we would
be given the same freedom we had enjoyed the first time we had
served there. However, before we got there we had a long march
from Madras, west to Hyderabad and Mysore.

One cart was not enough and so a pair of mules and a new
cart were acquired. That was the doing of Colonel Stevenson. He
was a good officer and he had seen that we were good soldiers.
The cart we were provided with was bigger and the two mules
were not at the end of their working lives. We set off in a longer
column than we were used to. We had a bigger cart and three
draught animals and there were twice as many of us. When the
captain had spoken to the NCOs they had devised a plan. He and

the sergeant would be at the fore. The two corporals would march in the middle where it was hoped, I think, that Ben could make Teach into a proper corporal. That left me at the rear with the cart and the two mule men, Tom Finn and Jack Grey along with Aadyot. The two men had been lumbered with the mules for they were the youngest. Each led one of the mules and the mules were loaded with tents as well as the muskets of the two men. Both were younger than I was and neither of them were happy about their new role. That helped me to get to know them. On that first day as we trekked from Madras and took the road west, I tried to teach them how to be good mule men. I spoke to Duchess and stroked her.

After a mile or so, when the two mules had done what mules do and stopped cooperating, Jack picked up a stick. I shook my head, "That is the worst thing to do with mules. Talk to them."

He snorted his reply, "Talk! They are both dumb animals and the only way to change them is to beat them."

I sighed, "We have a long way to go and you need your mule more than she needs you. She carries your tent and your cooking pot. She even has your pack and your rifle. Would you rather carry them?" I stared at him, "Because, believe me, that is the alternative."

Aadyot smiled and added, gently, "Listen to Smudger. He knows what he is doing. This is a good duty. See how the others have to carry their knapsacks and muskets. Yours lie on the mule."

It might have been Aadyot explaining it in even simpler terms than I did but I saw Tom nod. He was quicker on the uptake and he began to adopt the same sort of tone as I had. It worked and he grinned when the mule he spoke to seemed to cooperate. Jack's mule was still obstinate when he urged the mule to move. I think it was his tone. He was not trying.

"No good. Mine is a bad 'un."

I laughed, "I have seen men fit that description but never animals. Try singing."

"What?"

I led Duchess with my right hand and I held out my left and said, "Give me the tether." He gave it to me and I began to sing.
Farewell and adieu to you, Spanish ladies,

Farewell and adieu to you, ladies of Spain.
For we have received orders
For to sail to old England
But we hope in a short time to see you again.
We'll rant and we'll roar, like true British sailors,
We'll rant and we'll roar across the salt seas

It was a song they had sung on the Indiaman and helped the men to work. The mule responded and walked a little quicker. When I sang it a second time, Seamus and Dai, further ahead joined in with the chorus. I saw the look of surprise on Jack's face as I handed him the tether without stopping my singing. I nodded and he began, self-consciously, to sing as did Tom.

We did not need to sing for long but we sang another two songs, this time chosen by Seamus and Dai before we stopped and by then the mules were happy to be led by their new masters.

Jack said, when we stopped for a break in the small village and we watered our animals, "It's Smudger, isn't it?"

I nodded as Duchess drank, "Bill Smith."

"You are alright."

"We all are." I lowered my voice so that only the two of them could hear, "Listen, lads, you seem like you have something about you. We all got off on the wrong foot back in the barracks but when we fight, and trust me, we will, then you will need us more than we need you. Have either of you ever put a musket ball in a man and seen its effect?"

They shook their heads and Tom said, "Just at a target." He paused, "We missed."

"And that was because your life didn't depend on it. The men we will fight are brave. God knows their weapons aren't as good as ours but they will try to kill you. The bayonet you carry needs to be razor sharp because, and I can't stress this enough, their weapons will be. You can trust us but you have to work with us. When we stand in a line and raise our muskets we have to be of one mind. Captain Crozier and Sergeant Grundy aren't like the rest of us, they are real soldiers. We listen to them and look after them."

"Why does the sergeant ride and the officer walk?"

We had set off again and the two young soldiers flanked me. I told them the tale of the Battle of Mallavelli.

"Why doesn't he leave then? If he is sick…"

"Because he is a soldier and this is his life. He doesn't want to live here and the voyage back to England…you took the voyage out here, was it enjoyable?" They shook their heads. "And that is why he rides and we look after him because as long as he lives, we have more chance of surviving. He will die out here. He will be one of the many British red coats who served their country and their only reward was a piece of earth in this land. Most are forgotten men but we will make sure that Sergeant Grundy is not. We will do everything we can to ensure that he survives. The longer he does then the more of us will live. It is as simple as that."

That was the moment when, for at least two of them, their view of the platoon changed. By the end of the first week Corporal Teach had clearly listened to the same stories from Ben and he smiled at the Devil's Dozen and spoke to them in a friendlier tone than he had before. We seemed to be winning for just Thompson and three others, who hung around with him, remained distant. The others were warming to the camaraderie of the platoon. Thompson still resented the beating he had endured when he had provoked Seamus and tried to be cock of the walk. He seemed to have an influence over the other three, McKenzie, Talbot and Watts or perhaps they were all cut from the same cloth.

It took ten days to reach Seringapatam by which time the new uniforms had become as tattered and torn as the old ones. The Devil's Dozen had all worn their old uniforms on the march so that when we arrived we simply put the rags away and wore, as we marched into Seringapatam, our new ones. In contrast the new men were the ones who looked like beggars. The captain presented himself and the platoon to General Wellesley who nodded approvingly.

"You have made good time, Captain Crozier. You have a week to rest and then you and your cut throats will be marching again."

We were all close enough to hear his words and, like the captain, curious for as far as we knew the land of Mysore and the Maratha Princedoms were peaceful.

"War, General?"

"Not yet. We are waiting for some papers from the Lieutenant Governor. Until then you can camp where you did the last time." He was being enigmatic and that did not bode well for our section. He had called us cutthroats and that suggested more work for the Devil's Dozen.

We left the city and walked to the camp by the river. It looked familiar. The walls no longer seemed threatening but reassuring. The small river would give us water and, by using fishing lines, fish and crayfish. It would be home. The door to the fortress was closed but, once we had pitched our tents, Sergeant Grundy and I went inside to ensure it could be opened. We walked back around the walls and I said, "How are you feeling, Sergeant? Did the trip take it out of you?"

He smiled, "You know, I never thought I would say it but I quite like riding. Froggy is a gentle animal and my backside must be getting harder or accustomed to the saddle. I feel fine, Smudger, and my chest doesn't hurt like it did at the battle. I take each day at a time." He smiled, "I know you and the lads look after me but trust me, I am getting stronger."

We didn't recognise many of the sentries. The regiments were East India Company but they were not the Madras ones. Walter's rank helped us to pass through the native sentries. We walked through the fountain garden and I saw some British officers enjoying the shade, the aroma from the trees and the tinkling sound of the water. When their heads were raised Sergeant Grundy called, cheerily, "Just taking a short cut, sirs, to the kitchens." We passed through the kitchen garden and into the corridor where the smell of cooking greeted us. We took off our hats and peered in at the steamy kitchen. I was still the best at speaking to the ones who were not English and that was why the sergeant had brought me. He nodded to me and I said, "We are camped beyond the door that leads to the river. We just want you to know that we will require the door to be open but we will ensure that it is guarded."

The havildar cook narrowed his eyes. He seemed to recognise me but I did not know him, "You are the one who was there when Tipu Sultan was killed. You witnessed the death of the Tiger."

I bowed my head, "Yes, I was there."

He looked at the sergeant and said, in accented English, "Then you are the leader of the Devil's Dozen."

The sergeant said, "I am the sergeant, yes, but Captain Crozier commands."

He smiled, "And that is like our Lieutenant Harris who we never see unless he wishes to complain about the food we cook. You and I know who really leads, Sergeant."

It was not true for Captain Crozier was a good officer but we nodded our agreement for we wanted to be on the good side of the havildar.

The havildar turned to one of his men, "Fill a pot with food. These are friends."

"Thank you."

The havildar smiled, "Just return the pot. We have plenty of food but pots are valuable."

And so began a pleasant time. Our reputation helped us. The stories of our conduct in the various battles were well known and we benefitted from food left over from the officers' mess. The cooks preferred their own food and the British officers liked English food. As more was cooked than they could consume, we enjoyed a good diet.

That we were marked for something became clear when more new uniforms were issued. It was mainly for the benefit of the new men but the quartermaster allowed all of us to be given one. More worrying was the issue of flints, ball and powder. The general had said that we were not going to war but we had enough ball and powder to fight a campaign. The new men did not understand that but, as we got on with most of them better, we were patient as we explained. "When you have more than fifty balls in your pouch then it means you will need to fire them. Someone needs us to be ready to fight and as we are the only ones being issued the extra powder and ball we are all suspicious." Ben Neville made sure that all of them, even Thompson and his cronies, heard his words.

It was the arrival of officers from the west that told us a little more for we recognised one. It was Captain Tucker but now, we saw, he had been promoted to major. There were also civilians with him. We did not get to speak to them but we saw them as we fished in the river.

Captain Crozier was invited to dine with the general and after he had departed, with polished boots and new uniform, we speculated about our future.

The new men listened although Thompson and his cronies sat apart and glowered. They were unhappy men.

"Sounds to me like war, Sergeant."

Sighing, Walter took his pipe from his mouth to point at George Mainsgill, "Have you seen any other men preparing to go on campaign?"

"Well, no but they have been here some time. Perhaps they were waiting for us to come."

The sergeant laughed, a heavy rolling laugh for the words had clearly amused him, "You have a high opinion of yourself, George! This sounds like the Hardcastle thing all over."

Tom Finn asked, "The Hardcastle thing?" The rest of the platoon looked at me as I had been the most involved and I told him the tale. When I had finished he said, "You mean we have to go and rescue someone?"

Sergeant Grundy said, patiently, "No, son, but when you lads arrived we became a larger unit and we were sent all the way across India. There has to be a reason and as there is no campaign planned I think that means we will be going with Mr Tucker again, or perhaps it will be just Smudger."

Every eye swivelled to me. As soon as I had seen the newly promoted officer my heart sank. He did jobs for Lord Mornington and the general that were not the usual ones of a serving officer. The last time had seen us operating behind enemy lines. The difference now was that we were not at war with anyone so what would we be doing?

The captain did not dine with us that night. He ate with the generals and Tucker. I was not on duty that night and so I missed his return. I was on breakfast duty and that meant I rose before dawn. It was not a hardship as the air was marginally cooler. I watered all four animals and fetched a pail of water. Boiling it would kill any wildlife. The two new lads, Jack and Tom, were also on duty and I said, "Watch the water and when it boils then make a pot of tea." I pointed to the sky, "Don't wait for reveille, when the sun rises then wake the lads and give them a cup of tea."

They nodded and Tom said, "Where are you off to, Smudger?"

I tapped my nose, "See what the kitchens have for us."

We had been there long enough for us to be known and the fact that I showed them respect and spoke in their own language helped to make me welcome. I managed to get some fresh bread, bacon and half a dozen eggs. I took my treasure back to the camp. There would be porridge, there always was, and with the bread, bacon, some sliced salted beef and the eggs we would dine well. Aadyot had begun to make a sauce which was spicy and sweet. Some of the men liked it with their bacon. When we could get it we used honey in the porridge but, failing that, we had plenty of sugar. The sun was not yet up when I got back and so I began to fry the bacon and salted beef. The sizzling sound of the bacon and beef, not to mention the smell, worked better than any bugle. Men were roused from their sleep by the anticipation of a good breakfast.

I nodded to the two new men, "The water is boiling, make the tea. Remember a spoon of tea for all of us, two for the sergeant and two for the pot."

I had learned how the lads liked their tea. It took some time to get used to goat's milk in it but it was better than nothing. As with all food, the first to get there had the best choice. I made a plate up for the captain and told Tom Finn to take it to him and a cup of tea. The rest of the Devil's Dozen had risen already and having made water were ready for food. As the sun came up they were tucking in. The last ones to rise, it was Thompson and his friends, had just porridge and bread left for them. I saw them looking ruefully as Seamus and Dai mopped up the last of the egg yolk with their bread. The four of them had yet to learn how to be soldiers.

Captain Crozier came from his tent and handed Aadyot the plate to be washed, "Good breakfast, Smith. It sets a man up for the day."

"Thank you, Sir."

"Animals watered?"

"Sir. They are happily grazing."

"And are there any problems with the four of them?"

Something in his voice made me stiffen a little, "No ill effects from the journey here, Sir, why?"

He didn't answer but said, instead, "Sergeant Grundy, gather the men around."

Some of us sat on boxes while others stood. Sergeant Grundy always sat when he could. Before he sat he said, "Right lads, gather round, stand easy. Can we smoke, Sir?"

"Yes, Sergeant."

The smokers took out pipes and used twigs lit from the fire to get them going. Captain Crozier waited until those who wished to smoke were doing so.

"First, the good news. Despite the rumours running around our little camp we are not going to war." I smiled as I saw Eddie hand money to Bob. A bet had been lost. "Now the bad news or, should I say, the slightly more unwelcome news. We are to escort two officials sent by Lord Mornington to Oudh to meet with the Nawab there. Our job is to take them safely through a thousand miles of Maratha land."

He paused to let us take that in. The new men just had blank uncomprehending looks on their faces but we knew what it meant. A thousand miles would take at least forty days. Even if we were all mounted it would be the best part of a month. We said nothing but each of us would have our own views. In my case it was the thought that there might be some opportunity, during such a long journey to escape. Even as the thought flickered through my mind I saw Sergeant Grundy. If he was a well man then I would go but I felt obligated to watch over him.

Albert Wishart asked, "Oudh, Sir, where is that?"

"It is the northernmost part of India. The Himalayas lie to the north of it and it is a rich kingdom."

For the first time I saw Thompson and his friends take an interest.

"There is more good news, Major Tucker will be with us."

I was not so sure about that. I had been almost thrown to the wolves by Lord Mornington and Major Tucker. I was no longer so desirous of his company as I had once been. What I knew was that there would be danger and, in all likelihood, not all of us would return.

95

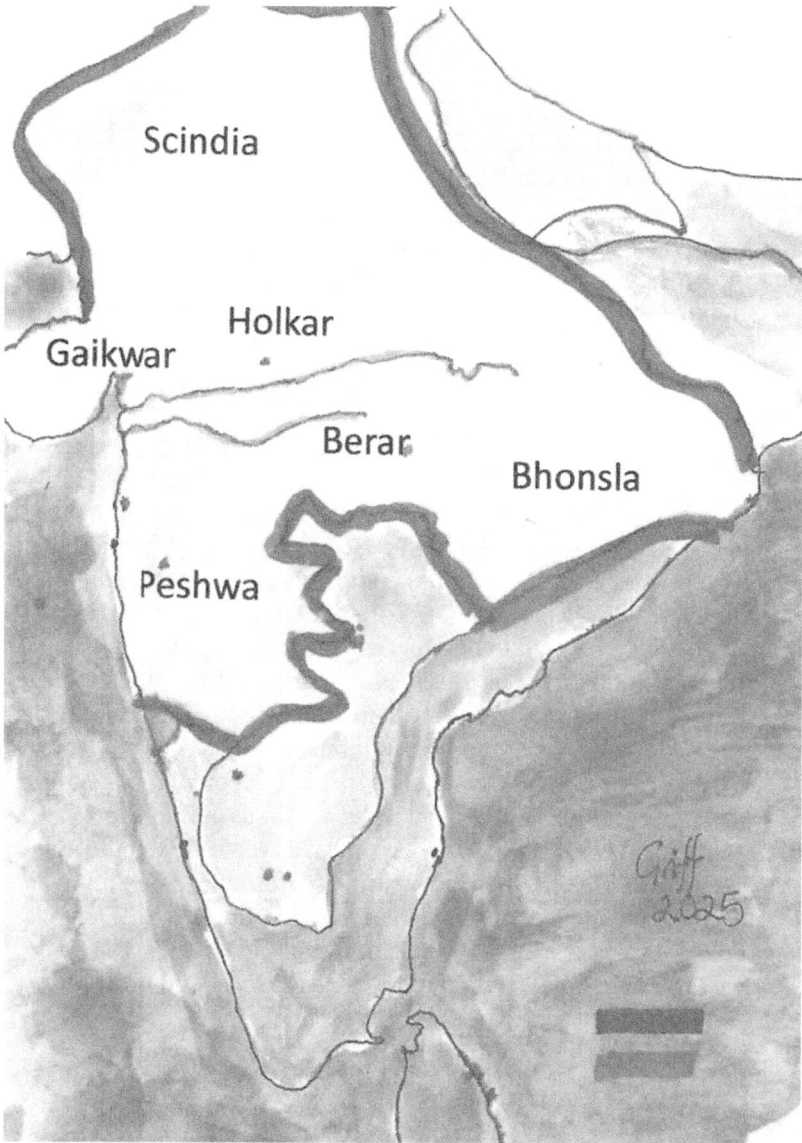

The Maratha Lands

Chapter 8

We discovered that we would be leaving in three days. That gave us three days in Seringapatam to find as much food to take with us as we could. We were scavengers and knew that the road would be a hard one. We had spent long enough in the town to know where to find food either legally or illegally. We were also supplied with another horse for the captain. I guessed that the two men we were escorting would be mounted too. We were given a cart that would be pulled by the mules. That sounded a good idea but the two mules had never been used in that manner and it took Aadyot and I two days to get them used to it. It meant the rest of the platoon had to gather all that would be needed. There was another tent for the two officials and their attendant bedding. We were also forced to carry more food. Although there was no war between either the company or Britain with the Maratha states, we could not guarantee food on the road north. There would be gold to pay for accommodation but that brought attendant problems. Once we began to use the coins then those who would wish to take it for themselves would know we carried silver and gold and we could be ambushed.

Major Tucker and our passengers did not come to our camp. They enjoyed the roof of the palace, soft beds and food served at table. The morning we were due to leave we headed to the main gate to await them. There was curiosity from those on duty when they saw the laden carts and smart new uniforms. It was ten o'clock before the three of them appeared. I knew that Major Tucker would not wish to have a late start and it did not bode well for the rest of the journey.

The captain had met them at dinner when they had first arrived and he had not been impressed. He did not confide in us but Sergeant Grundy. He said that the two men had never travelled in Indian countryside before, having come from Bombay where they had lived in a fine house with servants and plenty of food. While the diplomat was what one might term a gentleman, meaning he could dress and talk well, probably ride and might even know how to shoot, he would have no common sense. The servant was a clerk, so the captain said, '*all inky fingers and pale skin.'* It meant he rarely ventured out of doors. Until we reached our destination then they would need to be cossetted and carried.

The two civilians, when they eventually arrived, were dressed in dark clothes and wore wide brimmed straw hats. The hats bespoke advice from someone who had travelled abroad in the land. The dark clothes were well made but I wondered if they were robust enough for the rigours of such a journey. The one I took to be the servant had two bags which were precariously hanging from the horses. One of them rode well enough but the other looked like a badly loaded bag of grain.

Major Tucker saluted and said, "Sorry about the late start, Richard, but..."

One of the two men, the one who looked more like a gentleman, interrupted, "I do not see why we need to begin so early. I had to rush my breakfast."

The captain nodded as he mounted his horse, "I fear, Mr Beaumont-Smythe, that breakfasts will be, perforce, early and we shall be on short rations for most of the journey. The late start means that we will have a late camp. I intend to make thirty miles today."

The look on the official's face was a picture and made the Devil's Dozen smile.

The captain looked at the two bags and knew that they would end up falling off. "Smith, put those bags on a cart."

"Sir."

I went to the bags and unfastened them. The servant said nervously, "You will look after them won't you, Private? Mr Beaumont-Smythe has his best clothes in them. He must be attired appropriately."

"Don't you worry, Sir. I will guard them with my life." The man nodded. He did not hear the sarcasm.

Sergeant Grundy rolled his eyes at my comment and waving his arm said, "Platoon, march." I would have to start after them when I had secured the bags. I wanted Duchess to have a balanced load to pull.

The official, the major and the man I came to learn was a clerk and servant to the official, rode just behind the captain and the sergeant. As I was at the rear with the mule men then I would be able to catch up. The two mule men would have an easier time thanks to Aadyot and me. We had done this many times and knew how to coax and cajole obstinate animals. Aadyot had his musket slung over his shoulder and he would be the rearguard.

When I caught up with them I could not hear the official but I could see his gestures. He was clearly unhappy and appeared to point and gesticulate in every direction. But for my capture by the Tiger I might have felt some sympathy for Major Tucker but I found myself smiling at his obvious discomfort as he explained to the official the problems of travelling in India.

As noon approached we were tiring but the late start meant a late meal break. To make it easier Sergeant Grundy said, "Seamus, how about a marching song to raise the spirits, eh?"

He was right to make the suggestion. When we sang the pangs of hunger seemed to fade. It was two o'clock when we finally stopped for food. The captain intended to keep to a schedule and four hours of marching were what was needed. The official and the servant would have a harsh lesson in army life. We found shade and water but there was no village. We had passed one four miles back but we had to keep up the miles. It was cold food we ate. We had cheese between pieces of flatbread that was already crisper than it should have been. The eating of the cheese we had brought was necessary. It would not last in the heat. We were used to the cold tea but Robert Beaumont-Smythe was not. His servant, Josiah Brownlee, approached Sergeant Grundy and me nervously and asked, "Is there no wine or small beer? Mr Beaumont-Smythe does not drink cold tea."

"He had better get used to it, Sir, as it is safer than drinking the water." The sergeant spoke politely to the man.

"Oh dear." He half turned and said, "Is this a foretaste of what is to come?"

Sergeant Grundy shook his head and said cheerfully, "Oh no, Sir, it will get much worse, I can assure you." The clerk's face fell.

It was not quite dark when we stopped and this time there was a village. While we erected the tents the captain and major, along with Aadyot, went to buy food from the locals. It would save us from having to cook. Our late arrival at the camp meant that it would be almost nine o'clock when we ate if we cooked. The official might enjoy late dining but soldiers liked regular meals. The original section were happy with what was bought for it was a local dish made with a small amount of goat meat, lentils, greens and was heavily spiced. Thompson and his cronies, not to mention the official, would not even contemplate eating it. They had the same food as at noon. Bread and cheese but this time with hot rather than cold tea. The bread was also stale.

That first week was the hardest as the official moaned and complained the whole time. We took great pleasure in waking him with a noisy camp, well before dawn. The captain wanted early starts to get through land of Hyderabad which was relatively safe. Once we reached Holkar and Indore land then we would need to move a little more cautiously and watch for ambushes and enemies. We also knew that if we started early then we could have a longer break at noon when it was hotter.

One night I was on duty and Major Tucker rose to make water. Aadyot was the other sentry and leaving him to watch the camp I went with the major with a musket that was ready to fire. We did the same for anyone making a nighttime toilet. There were real tigers and panthers in this land and an unwary man dropping his breeches needed a bodyguard. As he fastened up his trousers I asked, "Sir, what is this all about?"

"This, Smith?"

"You know, taking Mr Beaumont-Smythe to Oudh."

He paused and then said, "It isn't really your business, Smith, you are just here to protect us but you are a bright lad and have done me favours in the past so I will tell you. Lord Mornington has a treaty which we want the Nawab to sign. His land is bordered on three sides by Company territory and the Himalayan mountains on the other. His lordship wants to ensure that we have a peaceful frontier to the north."

I nodded, "Because there is more likely to be war in the south."

He laughed, "You are a clever soldier but you do not know everything. If there is war then it is likely to be between the Maratha princes. Nana Farnavis was the politician who guided the other princes and has kept them strong and at peace since the last war with the Company. Since he died they are fighting amongst themselves. They have a prime minister, the Peshwa but he was Nana Farnavis' man. There are other princes who think they can do a better job of keeping the Maratha Confederation independent. It is a matter of time before it becomes open war as they fight to see who will be ruler and when war comes we will be ready."

"To take Maratha land."

He shook his head but said nothing and I knew that I was right.

Once we crossed the Godavery River we were in Berar State and the land of the Marathas. As soon as were on the northern bank we adopted a different formation. Corporal Neville, Seamus and Dai became an advance guard who walked a hundred yards ahead of the captain and sergeant. Corporal Teach joined us at the back. My musket was no longer slung in the back of the cart but hung from my shoulder. If there was danger then we all had to respond quickly. I saw that both the officers who rode at the front had two loaded pistols in their saddle holsters and another two in their waistbands. It was a measure of the danger they thought we were in.

Nagpore was the largest place we had passed through since the city of Hyderabad. Listening to the officers and official, as I stirred the pot the night before we entered the city, I learned that the ruler of the state was Raghoji Bhosale. He was not in the city when we arrived for he was in his summer residence in the hills. The city had been badly burned thirty-five years earlier and there was much rebuilding going on. Despite the maharajah's absence we were allowed to stay in the palace, or the two officials and two officers were. We reached there in the early afternoon and as Mr Beaumont-Smythe wished to speak to the men who ruled this land, we would have an afternoon without marching. We would have a longer break in the city than we had enjoyed hitherto. We camped in the grounds of the palace but at least we were fed by the maharajah's servants and that meant we did not have to use our rations. As the city had a market Aadyot and I were sent to buy provisions. The markets started early and we left our tents well before dawn to be there when the stalls were being set up. We would be able to buy the best produce. The others were given permission to visit the market but I suspect most of them sought an illicit drinking hole.

The Tiger and the Thief

The East India Company took pride in the coins they used. Major Tucker had been given a chest with gold and silver. I had been given silver coins which we used judiciously to barter for what we needed. The coins were freshly minted. No one had tried to nick them and there was, as yet, no teeth marks on them. When I took them from the purse the faces of the men from whom we bought the food lit up like a sunrise over the sea. I had been given more than was needed. The rest would be given back to the captain when I returned from the shopping expedition. We managed to buy two kids which were butchered for us. The fresh fruit and bread would last four or five days and we might be able to buy more further north. Our welcome in Nagpore had been a pleasant surprise.

We left soon after breakfast the next day. Mr Beaumont-Smythe complained even more than normal. He had enjoyed the relative comfort of the town. I think he wanted to stay where it was marginally, in his view, civilised.

The food we had bought was in my cart and I made sure that it was kept cool by placing it beneath the tents. It meant the water skins, filled with tea, hung from the side. That was no bad thing as the heat of the day would keep the tea warm. Aadyot had enjoyed his time in the market. He liked to teach me how to barter and what to buy. I was learning all the time. In addition, each time we were amongst those who did not speak English my skills with languages improved. In Nagpore they were speaking words which Aadyot did not understand and we both learned together. Those times were special for me. I regarded the sepoy as my closest friend. Back in England I had never really had a friend. I had people I spoke to and ate with but they were not friends. I doubted that any of them would have given my disappearance a second thought. My enemies and the constables might have thought about my sudden vanishing but their thoughts would have been malevolent ones. As for family...I had been abandoned and that said it all. True friends were different, they knew secrets and were able to keep them. I felt I had such friends here in the platoon amongst the Devil's Dozen.

We travelled through land which was cultivated land. There were still trees and the occasional patch of tangled jungle but for the first few miles it was open land and less oppressive. There was a generally good mood amongst the men. The ones who had wanted a drink found a couple of places in Nagpore that served alcohol and the diversion put them in a happier frame of mind. We had enjoyed a day without marching and that was always good. We stopped to eat, close to noon, in a village that looked prosperous. They had many goats and the fields looked to be well-tended. There were drainage ditches next to the fields and the lush undergrowth told me that the farms were fertile. The smell of food being cooked as we entered was enticing. The old woman who was cooking, what looked to be a very large pot of food, offered to sell us some. I was surprised that she had so much to spare but we did not look the gift horse in the mouth. It meant we would be able to spend a few coppers, for the officers bargained with her, using Aadyot of course, and have freshly cooked food. It was simple fare, just lentils cooked in a broth but, for us it was that rarity, hot food at noon. The villagers went out of their way to be helpful and we bought more of their food. Captain Crozier was anxious to move on but it was hard to do so. We seemed to be popular. We spent longer at the break than was normal.

As we left the village Aadyot said, "That was strange, Smudger."

I had enjoyed the spicy stew and flatbreads. I was content. "Their kindness, you mean?"

"Everything. There was enough food for us all and yet the old woman looked to live alone. She had cooked a large pot of food."

"Perhaps she had a family and they were working in the fields."

He shook his head, "In this land they take their food to the fields and work all day."

I shrugged, "Then they were just kind people, Aadyot. It does happen."

He shook his head, "Not in this land. I shall load my gun."

Aadyot was not one given to fancy and so I loaded mine. Corporal Teach saw what we were doing and said, "What are you two up to?" I told him that Aadyot was suspicious. He laughed it off, just as I had done but now, as I loaded and mulled over his words, I began to think that perhaps Aadyot was right. I had been lulled by the generosity of the people but if I had been in England I would, like Aadyot be suspicious of such an act. The tilled fields now looked more sinister. The ditches and the fences looked more threatening than they had before. I studied them, carefully.

The men who rose from the drainage ditch to our left did not have muskets but they had swords and axes and they rushed from shelter to charge us. Aadyot and I had muskets in our hands already and as Corporal Teach shouted the alarm, we raised and fired them. The men we hit were less than twenty feet from us and our balls tore through not only them but spent themselves in the men behind. As the rest of our men first raised, then levelled and then fired their weapons some of our men fell. There were new ones who were slow to react. The Devil's Dozen might have been replete after a hot meal but they were veterans. Some of the new men were like lambs ready for the slaughter. They stood and stared with open mouths as a large number of men with bladed weapons raced at them. Even as they reached for their muskets four were hacked down in the slashing of a handful of blades. The two officers emptied both their pistols as I picked my pistols from the cart and discharged them. We had hurt some of them but now, seeing the laden carts, six ran at the five of us guarding the cart and mules. They were after what we carried and, perhaps Aadyot and me. It struck me that they seemed to know we carried coins.

Tom and Jack had fired their weapons but were struggling to react quickly enough. I would not have time to reload and so I drew the hanger from the cart and took my bayonet. As Aadyot and the corporal fired I ran to block the swinging sword of one of the men. He was using it two handed and I could barely hold it with the short sword. I used his momentum to allow the blade to slide to my right. The bayonet in my left hand drove up and into his chest. As the blood spurted and he slipped to the ground I looked, through the swirling smoke, for another attacker. The axe that was swung at my head would have taken my head off had Aadyot not fired his musket. As the man fell I recognised him but I had no time to do anything for there were still enemies there and they had killed some of my comrades. Corporal Teach slew another and as Tom and Jack levelled their muskets the three survivors at the rear of the column turned to run away.

As Sergeant Grundy shouted, "Cease fire!" silence descended. There were only the dead before us.

I was angry. I looked at the bodies of the four men who had been butchered so quickly that they had not even had the chance to unsling their muskets. Their bloodied bodies had been hacked by a number of blows. I ran after the men who were fleeing and brought my hanger down to slice into the back of the tardiest of the three. My blood was up and I think that I might have continued to run after the survivors had not Sergeant Grundy roared, "Smith, stand fast!"

I stopped and turned. I looked at the four dead men. I had not known Will, Edgar, Thomas and Archie. I had spoken to them at meal times and I knew their first names but I knew Tom and Jack better. I had not found out about their backgrounds. I had thought we had a whole journey to Oudh for that. I was wrong. The four had died mercifully quickly. Their blood was puddled around them. Blades do that to a man. Stephen and Harold, two other new men, were slightly wounded. Bob was tending to them. Their wounds did not look life threatening but the fact was that we had lost four of the thirteen new men we had gained and a further two wounded was dispiriting. Edmund Byers had been our only casualty thus far. I looked at Zebediah Thompson and his cronies. If it had been them then…There was no point in thinking that way.

The officers dismounted and came over to me. Captain Crozier said, "You and Aadyot were the first to react. Well done."

I shook my head, "We should have said something, Sir. Aadyot was suspicious about the people in the village."

Major Tucker said, "The village?"

I nodded, "He was right to be. He said that old woman did not need all the food she served us. Somehow she knew we were coming and it was done to allay our suspicions."

"Really, Smith…" I heard the disbelief in the major's voice.

I went over to the man I had stabbed with my bayonet. I turned him over, "This man was in the market yesterday. He served us and sold us the two kids. He commented on the silver coins we used to buy the goats. There were goats in the village and I think he came from that village. They sought to take our money." I nodded to Aadyot, "Aadyot commented on the food the woman was cooking. Major Tucker, why did she have such a large pot of food? The only reason was to make us stop and eat so that the men of the village could be ready to ambush us. Men with full bellies tend to be relaxed and we were. They thought to take us unawares. If they had slaughtered us then who would have known? This is Maratha land."

"Then they are not in the pay of the maharajah?" I heard in the voice and saw in the face of the major that he had already assumed the attack was politically rather than economically motivated.

"If you were to ask me I would say they saw their chance to take us when our guard was down and they were almost right."

The captain and the major exchanged looks. Seamus and Dai were busy searching the bodies. The Irishman looked up, "Poor as church mice, Captain, and not a musket between them. They are more like bandits than warriors."

Major Tucker nodded, "Desperate men then. They risked an ambush, thinking that we would be unwary." He turned to Aadyot, "Thank you, Aadyot."

He bowed, "I am just sorry that I did not speak out sooner, Sir. Those four boys might be alive."

Our journey was delayed by an hour as we buried the four men. I found the interment hard for we barely knew the men. I could count on two hands the number of times I had spoken with them and, for some reason, that made me feel guilty. I decided that, perhaps, I should make more of an effort with Thompson and the others. The two wounded men were able to walk but we let them do so at the rear where they could lean a little on the carts or the animals. I made a point of speaking to them. My days of being a lone wolf were long gone. I knew the value of comrades. I appreciated having men around you on whom you could rely. I made a start with Stephen Hill and Harold Reed as we warily walked north.

We made a late camp for despite the ambush the captain was keen to keep up the same pace. As usual the chest with the money was taken from my cart, when we camped, and put into the care of the two officers. This time, however, I noticed the looks that Thompson and the others gave me as I did so. Did they resent the fact that the chest had caused the deaths of four of their number? They had not seemed close but they had travelled from England and such journeys do bond men. The other thought was a slightly more sinister one. Did they covet the coins?

The next day, as on the previous afternoon, the advance guard walked not with muskets slung but held before their bodies and ready to be used. My musket and pistols were on my cart along with the muskets of the wounded men, Reed and Hill, who were also using the carts for support. The men might be wounded but they could fight. I determined to get to know the two men. I did not want them to die and my only knowledge of them to be the backs of their heads. I chatted to them and found their stories were similar. Both had wanted to join a regular regiment but had failed. They had met a sergeant recruiting for the East India Company and whilst the service would be far from home the pay was an inducement and neither man had strong ties to home. Stephen Hill's parents had died of some wasting disease and he had been left to make a living as a labourer. As he said, sharing lodgings with six other men was little different from a tent with soldiers and at least this way he was fed regularly.

Harold Reed's story was one of a young man who wanted to be educated but his family was too poor and without a skill found labouring the only answer. Harold was a serious thoughtful young man. I am not sure he was cut out for the life of a soldier but he was making the best of it and he was enjoying seeing a new country.

The three of us chatted about how we adapted to the land. Harold was interested in learning the language when he heard my story and he and Aadyot began lessons. Stephen just wanted to be a better soldier. "I want to be as good a soldier as you, Smudger."

I laughed, "I am not a good soldier."

Corporal Teach had been silent, walking behind us, but he said, "You are, Smith. You and Ganguly both. You two reacted quicker than anyone when we were ambushed and you both reloaded so quickly that it was like a blur. You are a young soldier. How did you get so polished so quickly?"

"Practice, Corp, and the necessity of war. For me it started on the ship out here when we were attacked by pirates and at Mallavelli, well, it was either fire faster than the enemy or be buried where I fell."

We walked in silence for a while. I think the corporal was working out the words he would choose. Aadyot and Harold were still speaking, Hill was resting his arm on Duchess and the corporal's words were quietly spoken and intended just for me, "I have changed since I came out here. I thought that the rank of corporal was mine by right. I was wrong. We got off on the wrong foot for we were told that the rest of you were the scum of the earth. The title Devil's Dozen seemed derogatory. Now I can see that it is a badge of honour. With luck we can change men like Zeb Thompson."

I was silent too but encouraged by the familiarity of the corporal's words I went on in a low voice, "I am not sure, Corporal. There are some men who can't be redeemed. The rest of the lads had been in prison but this is their chance to be free from that. They all wanted to change." I did not say that I had changed too but I had. I no longer looked after just Bill Smith. "I get the impression that Thompson is hiding here and this is a step on a journey." Perhaps my insight was because that was my story too. The difference was I was making the best of it.

Corporal Teach nodded, thoughtfully, "You might be right. Thompson was the last one to join us and it was just a day before the ship sailed. He seemed to be anxious to be away from England. Your ideas make sense to me. He might be seeking a new start in a new world."

I made the effort to engage with the new men when we camped. I used the ambush as a starting point. Thompson was surly to the point of aggression and I backed off. It seemed he wanted to keep control of his gaggle of confederates and enjoyed the division between them and the rest of the platoon. The four of them were isolated but having lost four we would need them if it came to another fight. We had been attacked not by enemies but desperate men. There would be more organised bandits not to mention enemies the deeper we went into Maratha land.

One effect of the attack was to make Mr Beaumont-Smythe more nervous. He insisted upon riding between the two officers with his poor servant left behind and alone. The official wanted the protection of two bodies if we were attacked again. Another effect was that we were warier when we entered any village. We had been duped once before and even when people smiled we were suspicious. Another change was that he ceased to complain as much about the early starts. The two wounded men only used the cart for support for one day and, much to my relief and Duchess' they marched next to the cart.

After ten days we had travelled another three hundred miles and Reed and Hill's wounds were getting to the itchy stage and they left the rearguard and became the guards for Josiah Brownlee. The poor man had a stiff neck from constantly looking around him for another ambush. The two soldiers flanking him were reassuring. Harold still continued his lessons with Aadyot but they were around the fire, when we cooked.

Once we neared the land of Oudh and began to pass through safer land which was under East India Company control, we felt a sense of relief that we would be able to wash, hopefully have a roof over our heads and not need to march every day. Aadyot told us that it was only the British who called it Oudh. The people who lived there called it the kingdom of Awadhe. As we neared the capital, Lucknow, he gave Corporal Teach and me lessons in the politics of India.

"This is a rich kingdom. The Nawab and his ministers control the passage of the mountains and their princes and rulers are said to be the richest men in India."

"Then why do they need to be our allies? Surely they could ally with the Marathas."

Aadyot smiled, "This land has been at war for a long time and Awadhe and the Marathas are mutual enemies. They may not like the British but as they are surrounded by British controlled land then it is in their interest to have an ally who can defend them against the Marathas." He shrugged, "Perhaps they hope that they are too far from the residents to be controlled."

Mr Beaumont-Smythe made us stop at a small village ten miles to the south of Lucknow. He wanted to be smartly dressed for his meeting. He scowled at us as his servant tried to clean his jacket and boots. I knew that we all looked ragged and dirty. Major Tucker understood the look and said, "Captain, have the men smarten themselves up. We represent not just the East India Company but Great Britain too."

We spent an hour cleaning boots and taking our black hats from our bags to wear the uniforms that marked us as red coats. I had walked in sandals and worn a straw hat for the journey and most of the others had also worn straw hats. Our collars had been open and our red jackets in our bags. We transformed ourselves and, as we slung our muskets, marched. Those ten miles were hard and we all appreciated the easy-going journey up to then. The woollen tunics made us bake. Had our officers insisted we would have had to march the one thousand miles suffocating in wool.

The transformation did have an effect. As we marched, arms swinging by those not leading animals, people gathered to watch us as we passed the houses close to the city of Lucknow. We were a novelty. We were European soldiers wearing red uniforms. Children giggled as they ran alongside us to march like soldiers. When we reached the palace there was a crowd gathered. The sentries at the palace stood to attention as Sergeant Grundy dismounted and ordered us into a line and to present arms. Even Thompson and the other three managed to do so quite well and the snap of palms on muskets was almost simultaneous. We looked like proper soldiers.

Major Tucker said, "Thank you, Captain Crozier. I will enter with Mr Beaumont-Smythe. I will take Smith with me and he can act as a messenger."

The captain nodded, "Smith, leave your musket here and go with the major. Grey, and Ganguly, take charge of Smith's cart."

My heart sank. I was leaving the comfort of the platoon. I hated the thought of going into another palace. The Tiger's lair had almost proved fatal.

Chapter 9

I hurried to follow the official and his servant who had not
waited for me to join them. When I reached Mr Brownlee's horse
I marched as smartly as I could manage. I wondered why the
major had asked for me. I looked on the positive side. I knew
that the palace would be cooler than where the platoon stood,
baking in the hot sun but I feared that I would be placed in
danger once more.

We were stopped at the entrance to the palace and Mr
Beaumont-Smythe presented his credentials. We were made to
wait and, surprisingly, the representative of the British
Government and the East India Company did not seem to mind.
He had complained about every other delay we had endured. I
stood with Josiah and said, out of the corner of my mouth, "Why
am I here, Josiah?"

It was Major Tucker who answered. He said, quietly,
"Because you are a sharp young man and you are able to keep
your eyes and ears open. You will be ignored so play dumb."

It was what I had asked Aadyot to do once before and I knew
the value of appearing to be one without a mind. We were
escorted through the palace.

I was seeing a different side to Mr Beaumont-Smythe for he
appeared unflappable now. The road was not a natural place for
this diplomat but here he was calm and in control. "Lord
Mornington has judged the matter well, Major. The ruler of
Oudh sees the advantage of an alliance with both the British and
the East India Company. Our approach north alerted him and he,
no doubt, thought it might be prudent to speak to us." He smiled,
"I am confident of a favourable outcome."

The opulence of the palace reflected the riches of the land.
The sentries looked splendid but the soldier in me wondered if
they were just for show. Our platoon did not look pretty but we
knew how to fight. Just as with Tipu Sultan, the ruler of this
northern land had a large throne that was raised on a dais and he
was protected by well-armed warriors. When we had found the
Tiger of Mysore's body he had been with servants. His warriors

and defenders had fled. I was no longer as impressed by such shows of power.

As Mr Beaumont-Smythe introduced himself and the major and explained the purpose of his visit I did as I had been asked to do. I looked around the room. The guards I dismissed. I was looking for people who should not be there. Lurking at the back I saw a European face. Being to the side I had a better view than did the major whose vision was impaired by the throne and guards. I did not recognise the uniform but it was not French. It was green and I could see that it belonged to an officer of some importance for there were markings of rank on the collar. I took them to be those of a colonel but I was not sure. The sword's hilt was magnificent and I knew that such a weapon would be expensive. The man was also trying to be hidden. He could see the major and Mr Beaumont-Smythe and his eyes never left them. Having seen one I sought a second and was rewarded by another soldier, this time of a much lowlier rank, who stood just behind him. I spied him when the officer moved a little to get a better view when Mr Beaumont-Smythe presented the letter from Lord Mornington. He was a proper soldier. He also wore a green uniform and I saw the stripes of a sergeant. My ears had heard nothing of note but my eyes had seen plenty.

When the major and Mr Beaumont-Smythe bowed and began to back out, Josiah and I did the same. The interview was over. We did not turn our backs on the ruler of this northern kingdom until we reached the door. This time we were met by two servants. Clearly chosen because they spoke English, one of them said, "If you would follow us we will take you to your quarters."

Josiah led and I followed behind. I noted the corridor and the route. As I had discovered in Seringapatam such observations could be the difference between life and death. We took a right turn and I saw that this corridor was not quite as well decorated as the one we had just left. We stopped at a room and the door was opened, "This is for you, Mr Beaumont-Smythe, and your servant."

The other went to the room opposite and said, "This is for you and your man, Major Tucker."

The major said, "And our bags?"

The first servant said, "We will escort your servants to fetch them."

I saw that Josiah was waiting and Major Tucker said, "Tell the captain that all is well, Smith." He pointedly tapped the hilt of his sword. I nodded my understanding. He wanted me to bring back some weapons.

Josiah and I did not speak on the way out. The two men who escorted us could speak English and just as I was to pick up what I could, I knew that they would be doing the same. It was a game. My time with Major Tucker had been well spent.

When we reached the tents I took charge and said to the servants who had accompanied us, "If you would wait here, we will fetch our bags."

It was Ben Neville and George Mainsgill who were on duty and Ben said, "Not staying with us, Smudger?"

I shook my head, "I am to fetch the major's bags." I nodded to the two men and said, "These two chaps speak English, Corp. You might want to ask them about Lucknow, find out if there are places to drink."

I was warning the corporal that it would be wise to be close mouthed. I hoped he understood. I headed to the tent that the major and the captain shared. Captain Crozier was waiting, "Well?"

"We are to stay in the palace, Sir. The major sent me for our bags. I saw two Europeans in the court. They were wearing green uniforms." As I fastened the major's bags I saw the captain frowning as he tried to work out the nationality. They would not be French or Dutch. "I had better get my bag. The major wanted me to be armed." I headed out of the tent, carrying the major's bag.

As we entered my tent I was aware of the keen eyes of the Devil's Dozen on me. They would be curious and concerned. When we entered the captain followed and closed the flap. Although the two servants were twenty yards away and the cooking pot was between us he did not want to risk them observing what we were about to do. We took my satchel and I emptied out what was within. I put in two pistols, ball and powder. I took two of the daggers taken from the ambush and slipped them inside. I placed my lockpicks there too and finally added a clean shirt and breeches on the top to give the illusion that it contained nothing but clothes.

"Do you think you are in danger, Smith?"

"No, Sir. Mr Beaumont-Smythe seemed happy enough. I just think that the major is being cautious."

Suddenly he said, "Russians. Those men you saw must be from Russia. We are close to the land they regard as their empire and as I recall they wear green."

"I shall tell the major, Sir."

Josiah had their bags ready too and when I had hefted them on my back we walked towards the waiting servants, "How the other half live, eh, Smudge?"

I grinned, "The life of luxury, Seamus. Enjoy your stew!" I waved cheerily and followed the two men. I knew I would not enjoy whatever was on offer for the memory of the Tiger's trap still lingered. We were far from British controlled territory and a platoon of soldiers and a diplomat might make interesting hostages. Jahan Cholan had been a lesson. Until I was back with my platoon I would not relax.

We followed the two men back into the palace. Our journey was smooth and uninterrupted. I saw nothing of note and when we reached the rooms I saw that the corridor was empty. The two servants left us and I entered. I handed his bag to the major and then took out my weapons. I unfastened my tunic and placed one dagger in my belt. I saw a mattress on a cot. It was clearly intended for me and I slipped the second beneath the mattress and the cot. I handed one pistol to the major and left the other in the bag beneath my clothes.

"Well, what did you see?"

I sat on the chair that was there and began, "I saw two Europeans, Sir. When I described their uniforms, they were green, to the captain, he thought they were Russians. One was a senior officer, he might have been a colonel, and he had a good sword."

He nodded, "Green would be right. I didn't see them, where were they?"

"Keeping out of sight behind the throne but watching you, Sir."

"Anything else?"

"You mean apart from the fact that we have been given rooms in a less well decorated part of the palace? No, Sir." I was a thief and noticed such things.

He looked around the room and saw that it was plainly decorated. The furniture was functional rather than aesthetically pleasing and the mattress on the bed was not a good one. "You are right, Smith, and shows that you have sharp eyes. Now what does that tell us?" I knew it was a rhetorical question and I did not answer. "It could be a message for Mr Beaumont-Smythe that we are not as welcome as Lord Mornington might assume."

"Sir, what happens now?"

"Now?"

"I mean here, in the palace."

"Ah, your role I think you mean?"

"Yes, Sir."

"There is to be a banquet tonight with Mr Beaumont-Smythe and myself in attendance. It will be the preliminaries to the negotiations that begin tomorrow. You and Mr Brownlee will not be dining with us. I am guessing that there will be a second place for your to eat. I need you to listen to what the servants say. If they think you can't speak their language then they might make slips."

"Sir, I can speak a little of Aadyot's language but this one sounds different."

"It is but they all come from the same mother tongue. You are a bright lad and you can join up the words you recognise. We just need to know who is influencing Oudh."

"So I just chat to Josiah and listen."

"Exactly."

The same servants who had taken us to our rooms knocked on our door. The senior one escorted the major and the diplomat back the way we had been led while Mr Brownlee and I were taken in the opposite direction. It was clear to me that we were heading for the parts of the palace used by servants. It reminded me of the palace of Tipu Sultan. It was well lit but the walls were unadorned.

When the doors were opened at the end it was a relatively brightly lit room and there were long tables and benches. It was where servants ate. The man who had taken us said, "This is where you eat. There will not be many here until the banquet is finished. You will be quiet here."

I asked, "Do we serve ourselves?"

He shook his head, "There are servants who will fetch what you wish. I am sorry but they do not speak English. If you do not want what they bring then shake your heads. There will be some of the palace guards eating here and they do speak English." With that he left us.

As there was no one around I said, "Josiah, the major has asked me to pretend I can't understand them."

He smiled, "I wondered why he brought you. I can play the game. Mr Beaumont-Smythe also asked me to keep my eyes and ears open but as I do not understand a word that is said, it will need to be my eyes that do the work."

It was the two soldiers who sat close to us that initiated the conversation. Their English was heavily accented but understandable. They spoke to me rather than the civilian. One said, by way of introduction, "We were on duty when you and the other red coats arrived." I was chewing and so I just nodded. "They are fine muskets you all have. Are they accurate?"

I knew the weapons that were used in the land of the Marathas and I assumed they would be the same here. "If I rest it on something I can hit a target two hundred paces away."

They were both impressed. "Does it take long to load and fire?"

I knew it would not hurt to keep on adding to the skills of my platoon and I shook my head, "We can fire four times in a minute." When I saw their frowns I knew that they did not totally grasp the concept of a minute. "If you count from one to sixty that is a minute."

I saw them counting and one grinned and nodded, "That is fast."

The other said, "Have you fought in many battles?"

I felt as though I was on safer ground for we had never fought any who lived this far north. I said, "Two big battles. Mallavelli and Seringapatam."

Their eyes widened, "You were there when the Tiger was slain."

"I was and he was a brave warrior. He kept fighting when many had left him."

"That is what you need in a leader."

"Your leader is a good warrior?"

For the first time they looked guarded and that look told me all I needed to know, "He is a great man."

He was not a soldier and that meant he would not wish to risk a war with the British or even the company. I had learned enough through just my English. My uncomfortable questions seemed to make a barrier and they began talking to each other in their own language. I listened although I was looking at Josiah. Josiah nodded and then began talking quietly about the food. It allowed me to pretend I was listening to him when, in reality, I was picking up nuggets from the guard.

I learned that they rarely fired their muskets. They did not like their leader and that they feared a war with the Marathas who, it seemed, coveted their riches. It was all valuable intelligence. By the time we had finished our food the two soldiers had gone and the room was half filled with other diners. We left and, as we had no escort, I said to Josiah, "Let us explore." We closed the doors behind us.

"That may be dangerous."

I smiled, "We say we were lost. We play the foolish Englishmen."

We moved down a corridor that led from the right. Our room lay ahead to the left. I adopted a quizzical expression but, in reality I was searching. We moved slowly and quietly and when I heard voices, I stopped and held out my to arm to arrest the progress of Josiah. He was really there to disguise my furtive exploration. A soldier might be suspect but Josiah looked so harmless that I hoped he would act as a disguise. I listened to the voices at the open door. They were speaking a language I did not recognise. That ruled out French and Dutch. I had spoken French when I had scouted with Major Tucker and I had met many Dutchmen back in London. I deduced, from the sound, that it was Russian and when I heard a word that sounded like *Andgridchairman* I thought it sounded like Englishman. There was no point in risking walking past the door and so I turned and led Josiah back to our rooms.

"Those men, we heard, Josiah, did you recognise the language those men were speaking?"

"It sounded like Russian to me."

"Me too and one of the words sounded like Englishman. I might be making that up but it makes sense."

He nodded, "I shall mention it to Mr Beaumont-Smythe." He smiled, "It is most illuminating being in your company... Smudger."

"And yours too." I went into the room I shared with the major and prepared for bed. I took off the tunic and folded it, placing the dagger beneath it. I washed in the bowl provided and then lay down on the mattress. I was tired and the mattress was comfortable. I would not be sleeping on the ground. I forced myself to stay awake until the major returned. Thankfully I did not have to wait long. I heard the voices of the two Englishmen as they came down the corridor although I could not hear their words. The door opened and the smell of cigar and whisky greeted me. I had left the lamp burning so that the major would not trip over.

"Still awake, Smith?"

"Yes, Sir," I rose and went to the door. I opened it and saw two guards walking down the corridor towards us. I closed the door and saw that there was no key. I took my boots and laid them behind the door and balanced my bayonet on the top. If anyone came in the door would open but the bayonet would fall to the floor and as the floor was some sort of stone it would clatter. I had been a thief and knew what would cause a problem to those who preyed on the sleeping. I told the major, as I returned to my bed, what I had discovered.

He nodded as he undressed, "They are Russian but only one was at the dinner and he left early. You did well. Tomorrow the negotiations will start. You will be present so make sure you are smartly dressed. Mr Brownlee will have a seat but you will have to stand."

I did not relish the duty. "Sir, do I have to?"

"You will be there as my servant to find things for me. I will use you as my eyes and ears."

"Sir." As I closed my eyes I thought that I was being used once more. It was strange. When I was away from the others I just wanted to leave the East India Company and flee but when I was with them there always seemed to be reasons to stay. The more I was with Major Tucker the more I wanted to run.

Army habits die hard and I rose early and made water. I moved my trap which had not been disturbed. I peered outside the door and saw two men lounging against the walls. They were either there for our protection or, more likely, to stop us from leaving. I closed the door without them noticing me. My closing of the door woke the major. I acted as his servant and helped him to dress. I polished both his boots and my own. There was a knock on the door and when I opened it I saw the two servants from the night before. The watchers had gone.

"We are here to escort you to breakfast."

It was clear that we were not supposed to wander the palace alone. As the door to the other bedroom opened I reflected that they had slipped up the night before. Mr Brownlee and I retraced our steps behind the servant to the functional dining room. It was busier. I suspected that there would be fewer servants needed to serve at breakfast than at a banquet. We ate and this time the servant who had taken us down also ate and kept his eye on us. When we rose he did too. That was when I knew that the previous night had been an error. We were supposed to be escorted to and from the dining room.

When we entered the room where the negotiations would take place I saw that there was a long table. On one side sat the ruler with his half a dozen advisors as well as the officer in the green uniform. His sergeant was not present. On what I thought of as our side of the table there were just three chairs. Mr Beaumont-Smythe sat in the middle. I stood behind the major. I realised that the Russian was studying the major and then his eyes flicked to me. I took the opportunity to examine him. He had sharp features and what I would term a cruel face. He had angry looking eyes that seemed to dart like a sword's blade. He had a waxed moustache. As the meeting went on I noticed that he often stroked it. It told me he was vain and liked his own appearance.

The negotiations were in English. That the Russian did not need a translator spoke volumes. The Nawab, Saadat Ali Khan, surprisingly, said little and allowed his Prime Minister and another, who was clearly a soldier to put points to the British

diplomat. Mr Beaumont-Smythe was in his element. He had
been briefed well and kept his arguments focussed. Britain
wanted the territory of Rohilkhand and the land between the
River Ganges and the River Jumna. I could see, from his face,
that the Russian did not like that proposal. He leaned over and
spoke in the ear of the soldier next to him and it was the soldier
who voiced his objections. Mr Beaumont-Smythe would not be
moved and refused to budge on those demands.

When there as a break for lunch and the opportunity to make
water I went with the major and the other two to a room set aside
for us. Josiah and I waited until our betters had used the facilities
and then used them ourselves. The major said, when I had
finished, "Smith, watch the door and make sure we are not
disturbed or overheard."

"Sir."

I opened the door a little and peered out. There was a sentry
but he was ten feet away. I turned and nodded.

"Well, Major, you know these people better than I do, what is
your opinion?"

"The Nawab seems weak." The diplomat nodded. "The
Russian clearly had influence." Again there was a nod. "From
what I have seen from the palace, while this land has money it
does not have an army that could stand up to ours. The threat of
force will win."

Mr Beaumont-Smythe nodded, "In the preliminary
negotiations the Nawab offered to abdicate and let his son rule.
Lord Mornington rejected that suggestion. I think if we leave
their treasury intact they will be forced to agree."

The major nodded, "And we would have troops placed here
on the northern border."

"Just so."

I wondered if that would be East India Company soldiers or
British ones. I knew that there were British soldiers in Egypt and
that Napoleon had been defeated there both on land and sea.
Were there enough British soldiers? I suspected that it would be
East India Companies who would police this border.

After lunch the negotiations continued. Mr Beaumont-Smythe
had clearly been chosen for the right reasons and the treaty was
agreed. The Russian was obviously angry about it. His eyes

glared at the two British negotiators then his eyes narrowed and seemed to pierce even more. He was not happy.

Mr Beaumont-Smythe had the last word. "We will return to Bombay and I will hand our copy of the treaty to Lord Mornington. The battalion of soldiers will arrive within the next six months." He smiled, "That should give you the chance to make the necessary arrangements." His eyes fixed on the Russian. We left in silence and headed back to our room. The treaty had to be secured by Mr Beaumont-Smythe and the major and I would ensure that no one saw where it was hidden. We stood outside the door while the two men went inside.

"So we go home tomorrow, Sir?"

"We do."

"Good. I shall be glad to get back to the platoon."

I think I had hurt the major's feelings, "I thought you might have enjoyed this."

"It has been interesting, Sir, but I like the routine of the platoon."

That evening as Josiah and I ate, he asked me some strange questions, "Bill, is your room comfortable?" He waited until no one was seated close by.

I shrugged, "As I am used to sleeping on the ground then any room with a bed is more comfortable than I am used to."

"No, I mean, is it quiet?"

I thought about it. The previous night I had not heard a sound, "Like the grave. Why Josiah?"

"Mr Beaumont-Smythe could hear noises in the night. The window opened to a courtyard and he heard the sentries talking."

"We have an outside wall and it was silent, even with the window open."

I thought no more about it but when the major returned Mr Beaumont-Smythe came into our room. He said, peremptorily, "This will do nicely, Major. If you and your fellow here would vacate it…"

The major nodded, "Of course, Sir. Smith, take our gear to Mr Beaumont-Smythe's room."

It was clear that Mr Beaumont-Smythe had had the same conversation. "Sir." Remembering to take my dagger from beneath the mattress I crossed the corridor. The guards had not

yet come on duty. Mr Beaumont-Smythe's room was similar to
ours and I put the major's bag on his bed and mine next to my
cot. I put the dagger beneath the mattress again. The major
entered. I could hear the noise from outside and said, "This will,
apparently, be a noisier room, Sir."

He smiled and nodded, "I think we can live with it. We are
soldiers and used to worse things than a conversation in the
night."

I went to the door and opened it. The two guards were
heading down the corridor. I closed the door and laid my trap
again. This time sleep was easy as I knew we would be going
back the next day and I would be with my friends and Duchess. I
missed her.

I think it was the silence outside that woke me. I had heard
the chatter as I drifted off to sleep. I woke. I think I needed to
make water but the silence seemed eerie. The two civilians had
found it noisy and yet now it was silent. Perhaps the guards had
slipped off for a smoke or a drink. The major suddenly snored in
his sleep before becoming silent once more. I rose and went to
the pot in the corner. It was white and my eyes had adjusted to
the dark. I made water and headed back to bed. What I had
noticed, since coming to Oudh, was that it was slightly cooler at
night. The window had no glass and the room was a little cooler.
I snuggled beneath my sheets. It was then that I heard the noise.

It was not the noise of voices but scraping and it came from
the window. We were on the ground floor. When I had been a
thief I had not had the opportunity to enter a bedroom on the
ground floor. I had always been forced to climb. Someone was
coming through the window. I put my hand beneath my mattress
and drew the dagger. My eyes were still adjusted to the dark and
I saw the hand on the sill. I slipped from the bed and crouched
on all fours by the side of it where I would be hidden. I crabbed
sideways to our door and grabbed my bayonet from the trap by
the door. A second figure entered and it was then I shouted.

"Major! Awake!"

The two men raised weapons. I saw that one had a cavalry
sabre and the other a wickedly curved blade. The major sat up in
bed, looking wildly around as one does when awoken from a
deep sleep. "What!"

As the sword swung down to split his head I blocked the blow with my bayonet and then slashed with my dagger at the assassin's middle. The dagger was sharp and the man cried out. The second man lunged at me with his sabre and I was only saved when the major threw a boot at him. The man I had wounded was slipping out of the window but the sabre wielding killer turned his attention to me. His sword came down and there was no boot to save me. I heard the major getting out of bed and seeking his sword. He might be able to help me but I would have to defend myself. I made a cross out of my weapons and sparks flew as the sabre struck them. He was a strong man and a soldier. He was European and I knew, as his face neared mine, that it was the Russian sergeant. As I was forced down I did the only thing I could think of. I brought my knee up between his legs as I fell backward. The pressure of the sword eased as he grunted in pain and I pushed with my blades. The weight of his fall and the position of my bayonet meant his cheek was pushed against my blade. Blood flowed on my face and it was not mine; the blade had ripped open his face. I heard the major's sword drawn from the scabbard and my attacker rose, slashed his sword in the major's direction and then dived out of the window.

"Are you alright, Smith?"

"Yes, Sir." I rose. The door opened, pushing my boots aside. We both whirled and I saw Josiah looking terrified, "We heard a noise and…"

I said, "What about the guards?"

"What guards?" I glanced down the corridor and saw that it was empty. The guards had been removed.

I said, when I came back in, "Sir, they intended to kill Mr Beaumont-Smythe."

He nodded, "You are right. We will all share the same room. Bring our bags. Josiah, help him and I will explain to Mr Beaumont-Smythe."

We closed our door and slipped across the corridor. The major had explained and the diplomat seemed relieved to have our company. Josiah slept across the door and I slept beneath the window. It was uncomfortable but necessary. No one could get in without moving one of us. I was grateful when dawn came. I had barely slept.

Mr Beaumont-Smythe was his old self when he had dressed, "We say nothing about this. It would be fruitless to do so anyway. The Nawab and his advisors would deny their involvement and this way we leave them guessing. We smile and pretend that we had a good night's sleep." He turned to me, "I understand that it was you who saved the major. Thank you, Private. It just goes to show that appearances can be deceptive."

I suppose it was a compliment. I didn't care. I had survived and within hours my duty would be over and I would be back with my friends.

Chapter 10

No one said goodbye to us. We ate breakfast and headed out of the palace at Lucknow almost like thieves in the night. That no one wanted the treaty was clear. It was the threat of British might that had won the day. I was too lowly to understand all of it but it seemed to me that if they could avoid the treaty reaching Lord Mornington then they would all be happy. Josiah clutched the satchel holding the treaty as though it was the crown jewels. We saw neither the Nawab nor the Russian. I felt as though every eye was staring at us and I worried about a sudden knife in the back. I know it was irrational but we had come close to death in the palace. I felt a profound sense of relief when we reached the camp.

Major Tucker said, "We can leave immediately, Captain, our work here is done."

"Successfully?"

He glanced at me before replying, "Eventually. Private Smith can keep you entertained with the story as we pack."

As I helped to pack the cart I told the captain all that had occurred. Unlike the major and the diplomat, both of whom appeared to think that this was all over, the captain frowned. "If they attempted to kill the diplomat in the palace then they will try again. If Tucker thinks otherwise then he is a fool."

"Yes, Sir, that is what I thought and it was one of the Russians who came to do the deed. I marked him but he is still alive."

"Then the journey back will be even more fraught with danger. We will keep the same formation." He called over Sergeant Grundy and told him of the attack and the need for vigilance.

I nodded to Josiah Brownlee, "Sir, Mr Brownlee has the treaty. That is what they will want. He will need guarding on the road and when we camp."

"Then Sergeant Grundy and I shall ride next to him and we will have a sentry watching our two civilians at night." He shook his head, "It means more duty for a depleted number of men." We had lost four and the four we had lost had been more reliable than Thompson and his friends.

He left to inform our companions of his plans. The rest of my friends all came, ostensibly to help pack the cart but the reality was they wanted to know what had gone on. The only ones who appeared to have no interest whatsoever were the four men we all viewed as outsiders.

Tom and Jack's eyes widened when I spoke of the attempted murder. Tom said, "You could have died, Smudger."

Sergeant Grundy patted my back as he passed, "Smudger is a survivor. He has the face of an angel but the heart of a killer. Stick close to him you two and you have a good chance of surviving this journey home." We had learned that we were heading for Bombay. It was closer than both Madras and Seringapatam.

"Will there be more trouble?" Jack's voice was filled with fear.

The sergeant nodded, "I am guessing there will be. We have a long and dangerous road ahead of us and we will all have to watch out for each other."

Despite the danger that I knew lay ahead I was happy to be back with my section. Even Tom and Jack had become familiar faces. In many ways I saw myself in them. They were not thieves but they were new and unlike the Thompson crew appeared willing to learn. Duchess was glad to see me, too, but the most effusive welcome came from Aadyot. The others treated him well but I was unique amongst the platoon, I was Aadyot's friend. He asked me about the palace, food and the people that I had met. I had learned, since I had been in India, that they were not one people and like people everywhere had their prejudices. Aadyot only really trusted those who came from Calcutta. The men of Awadhe were to be viewed with suspicion and he was not surprised at the attempt on our lives.

We all travelled prepared for danger, even the diplomat. He now had a pistol hanging from his saddle. I was not sure he would know how to fire it but a man always feels better if he can defend himself. My musket lay on the cart, a ball and cartridge in the barrel and ready to fire but I also had two loaded pistols hung by lanyards from my neck. They were not that heavy and they were a comfort knowing I could lift, cock and fire quickly if I needed to.

The day passed without incident and, that evening, while we were cooking I asked Captain Crozier if he thought I had exaggerated the potential danger.

"No, Smith. I think that there is the real threat of danger to us. You and the major are right to be worried. I believe that the attempt to stop us will be made away from Oudh."

"But why attack us? The treaty is signed."

He smiled, "I am just an officer of infantry, Private Smith, but I am guessing that if the treaty does not reach Lord Mornington then it is not valid. Men would have to try a second time and delay suits both the Russians and the men of Maratha." I frowned and seeing it he added, "There is discord in the lands of the Maratha princes. Lord Mornington needs the treaty so that we have an ally in the north. From what the major tells me he is a reluctant ally but the treaty binds him. When we have men in place in Oudh then the Marathas are surrounded. The Marathas control the heartland of India and Britain just pecks at the borders. That is why the battles at Mallavelli and Seringapatam were so important. They tied Hyderabad and Mysore to the British cause and cut a large slice of land from the Marathas."

The village where we were camped that first night was poor and mean and I waved my hand and said, "And Britain wants this?"

He shrugged, "You and I are soldiers. We face our front and do our duty. We rely on our betters to make important decisions."

"But are they our betters, Sir?"

He laughed, "Well, they have risen to the top, like cream I suppose."

I shook my head, "Not everything that rises to the top is like that, Sir!"

He put his arm on my shoulder, "You are too much of a thinker, Smith. That is not always a good thing in a soldier."

At the back of my mind was the feeling that we had escaped too easily. They had tried to kill the diplomat in Lucknow. I suspected they were not finished with us and I was proved right. The attack came the next day when we had just crossed the border into Holkar territory. I knew, from Aadyot, that Daulat Rao Scindia ruled in Holkar and was ambitious. We should have realised that the Russians might want to pre-empt a war between

Holkar and Britain. Our formation was wisely chosen. Ben, Seamus and Dai managed to see the barrels of the muskets poking out from the trees and they were able to shout a warning. It came before the guns fired. Every one of us, the two civilians included, grabbed a weapon and looked for an enemy. We took cover. The four on horses dismounted. The two civilians were protected by horseflesh and the officers. We all had loaded weapons and no one needed the order to fire. It was a matter of self-preservation. Aadyot was on the other side of the carts with Tom and Jack. Corporal Teach was next to me. We both knelt and I levelled my musket as I sought a target. The white face stood out. As I aimed at the chest below the face I saw that it was the Russian sergeant. I recognised the fresh angry scar across his face. I saw the barrel of his musket swinging in my direction as he saw me and I fired. Smoke rose from the end of my musket and the stock rammed into my shoulder. Even as my ball hit him, his weapon discharged but he was falling backwards and the ball he fired flew in the air.

I reloaded quickly as balls slammed into the cart and whizzed over us. I heard a cry from the far side of the wagon but I had fought enough times to know that until the battle was over you ignored any cries. To do other increased the chances of your own death. A soldier had to fire and keep on firing as quickly as he could. If someone was wounded they would have to fend for themselves. We were a handful of men and surrounded by an unknown number of attackers. I raised the musket as four men burst from the trees. They had fired their weapons and now ran at us with swords. They wore no uniforms but they were clearly soldiers. The swords they carried were those used by soldiers rather than warriors. The Nawab of Oudh's army might not be a good one but they had good weapons and I had seen similar swords in the palace. I did not panic as the men neared the corporal and me. I fired and hit the man, who was eight feet away, in the chest. It blew a hole in him and threw him back. I dropped the musket and simply grabbed and cocked a pistol. When I discharged it I hit the man in the face when he was about to swing his sword. If he had held a musket with a bayonet I might have been struck. Smoke swirled from the muskets and pistols. All along our small column men were still fighting. I could hear the clash of metal on metal as swords were used. There were shouts and screams. Seamus and Dai, in particular, were always vocal when fighting. Their wild cries must have terrified enemies.

I heard a cry from the corporal. He had downed one of those attacking him but the second man had struck down with his sword. Although his musket partially blocked it, the sharp edge of the blade still caught his arm. His tunic slowed down the blow but I saw blood. The corporal's attacker was so close to me that I was able to draw my dagger and ram it under his chin and into his skull. I did not look down at the corporal but levelled my last pistol in my left hand. Another soldier, thinking that all our weapons were discharged, charged with a musket and bayonet. I steadied and aimed the pistol and waited until he was just a few feet from me before I fired. My left hand was not as accurate as my right. I hit his chest but he was a big warrior and he kept coming on. I swept the bayonet away with my pistol and then slashed at him with the dagger. I think he was already dying but the razor-sharp blade across his throat gave him a quicker death than the stomach wound the ball had given him.

I reloaded but risked a glance down at Corporal Teach while I did so, "How are you, Corporal?"

He was holding his neck cloth to the wound. "It is just a cut but it is bleeding heavily. Sorry, I can't reload while I am holding this cloth."

"Don't worry. I think we have stemmed their attack. Aadyot, how are you doing?" I did not turn my head.

Tom Finn shouted, "He caught one in the arm but we have stopped the bleeding."

"Reload and keep firing. Aadyot can see to himself."

Corporal Teach said, "You should be the corporal and not me."

"You have not fought as many times as I have." The smoke began to clear and the sounds of conflict were diminishing. I heard the pop of a pistol and then Captain Crozier shouted, "Cease fire."

I waited until I could see the enemy bodies before I laid down my musket and took a bandage from the cart. I took off the corporal's tunic and unfastened his shirt. The cut looked to be clean but I poured some vinegar on it to make certain. He winced. I then put a dressing on the wound and bandaged his arm. I handed him my loaded musket. "I will see to Aadyot." I went around the cart and saw that Aadyot had taken off his tunic. He had been hit by a ball. A ball was always more dangerous than a cut for often the ball would drive fibres into the wound.

Aadyot gave me a weak smile, "Unlucky, eh, Smudger?"

I nodded but said nothing. I poured vinegar onto the wound and then rubbed it with my neck cloth. It came away dirty. I kept rubbing until I had removed the majority of the fibres. The look on my friend's face showed the pain he endured stoically while I did so. The cleaning of the wound was not good enough. "Aadyot, there may be some threads left in there and it is still bleeding. I don't want you to lose your arm."

He knew what I was going to do and he nodded, "I am ready, Smudger."

"Tom, Jack, come and hold his arms." The two held his arms so that he could not involuntarily thrash. I put some powder in my hand and then spread it in the wound. It seemed to hurt him more than the vinegar. I took my flint and said, "All three of you, look away." When they had done so, I made a spark and the powder ignited with a flash. Aadyot cried in pain but did not pass out. I let it burn for a few seconds to seal the wound and then put the flames out.

Sergeant Grundy came down, his musket at the ready. "How are you, here?"

"Aadyot was hit by a ball and the corporal by a sword."

Albert said, "And Duchess has a wound."

I jumped up and ran to my horse. A ball had scored a line across her back. I took the vinegar and spoke gently, "Poor lass, this will sting but it will heal you." I rubbed the vinegar across her back. I had wisely stood to the side for she kicked out with her hind legs when the acid met the wound. Her hooves struck nothing. I laughed, "Does that make you feel better?" She whinnied.

Sergeant Grundy said, "Mr Brownlee was nicked by a ball. Thompson has a bayonet wound to the leg but Hill and Reed are both dead." He shook his head, "Poor little buggers, some men have no luck. Wounded in the first skirmish and dead in the second." He turned, "Grey and Finn, watch the wounded. The captain wants us to check the rear of the column. Corporal Neville is at the head." The two dead men had the potential to be good soldiers. Now they would be given an unmarked grave far to the north of any Indian land ruled by England.

I took my musket from Corporal Teach and we walked towards the site of the ambush. As we passed the bodies we checked to see that they were dead. When I reached the Russian I saw that he was not wearing a green uniform but civilian clothes. I prodded him with the musket. He did not move and I knew he was dead. "This is the sergeant who tried to kill us. I gave him that scar."

The sergeant and I found eight bodies. There had been horses, we saw their dung but the survivors had fled, taking all the animals with them. We searched the bodies. We hoped for some identification which might be used to prove that they were Russians. I examined the sergeant first. I was rewarded when I found a timepiece in his waistcoat pocket. It was a rare find for they were expensive. I saw writing on it I did not recognise and assumed it was Russian. It was not exactly evidence but it proved that there was Russian involvement. I wondered how the Russian had acquired such an expensive object. I put it in my satchel along with the coins I found. He also had a pistol and a sword. The others we had killed yielded little. I shared the coins we found with the rest of the Devil's Dozen, along with Tom and Jack but kept the sword, pistol and timepiece.

We buried our two dead. The captain said words over them and then, with the wounded bandaged, set off. I looked back at the little mounds of earth that did not even have a marker. When the rains came the soil would be washed away and the vultures would devour the flesh. I found it sad beyond words. Was this my fate?

Thompson complained about his wounded leg and to shut him up the captain had him placed on the wagon pulled by the mules. It meant that we had him at the rear. I did not like the man and assiduously avoided any conversation with him.

I did keep asking Aadyot about his wound but he was a stoically brave man and he insisted that he was fine. It was in direct contrast to Thompson who moaned about every bump in the road. When we stopped we were all ravenous. The attack had come not long before we would have stopped for food and no one had wanted to eat with the smell of powder and death in the air. We found a small mound in a clearing. There was water but it was two hundred yards from us. That was a small price to pay for somewhere that was dry and easier to defend. The four wounded men were waited on. In the case of three of them we did not mind. No one wanted to feed Thompson and so Sergeant Grundy quickly designated Thompson's friends as his minders. I was cooking when the two officers along with Walter and Ben joined me.

Major Tucker said, "Are you sure it was the Russian sergeant, Smith?"

"Yes, Sir, and he had the scar I gave him when he attacked us."

I showed them the watch and the major said, "Yes, that is Russian writing. Did you find anything else of interest?" He handed the watch back to me.

"No, Sir."

"They were being careful. I didn't see the officer but he must have been close by."

Captain Crozier said, "And that means we risk a second attack. We beat off the first one even though they outnumbered us. They may well send for more men and the next time they might succeed. I am not bothered about the treaty but I do not want to lose any more men." The major frowned and then nodded. "Listen, Major Tucker, the only way we can try to avoid a second attack is to move faster. This pace is too slow and will allow our enemies to catch up with us. I intend to march all day from now on with the shortest of stops at lunchtime. You had better tell Mr Beaumont-Smythe what I intend and I don't care if he is unhappy. It is better to be unhappy and alive than cheerfully dead."

"I will tell him, Captain, and I don't think you will get any argument from him. The two attacks have shaken him and the wound to Josiah has brought the danger home to him."

We marched and we marched hard. I worried about Duchess and her wound but she seemed to cope well. The first day was an exhausting one and, at night, we fell into our beds. When I was woken for my duty I felt as though I would not be able to keep my eyes open. I learned, during those hard days, that men are capable of impossible things. We marched for longer, we had less sleep but we kept going and we were vigilant. After three days we had made almost a hundred miles and the captain decided that Thompson could walk. The angry man was not happy about it but when Sergeant Grundy hinted that disobedience of orders might lead to a punishment and the use of a whip, he decided to walk.

Perhaps the death of his sergeant had affected the plans of the Russian officer or it may have been, as Major Tucker suggested, that he had been wounded in the attack, whatever the reason we eventually reached Bombay safely. We had come back a different way to the road north and that might have confused our pursuers. We were exhausted and we were dirty but we made it. We marched up to the residency and Major Tucker escorted the two civilians inside. We guessed that Lord Mornington was within but we did not see him. We sheltered in the shade of the white walls, away from the glare of the sun for two hours before Major Tucker emerged with the news that we were thanked and could now return to Seringapatam. No mention was made of our dead and while Major Tucker's thanks were heartfelt I was most unhappy that Lord Mornington had not bothered to speak to us. The least he could have done was give us a 'well done'.

The captain was also unhappy but for different reasons. We were in no condition to march back to Seringapatam. "Major, we have six hundred miles to travel and we have neither the supplies nor the boots for such a journey."

Concern finally flooded the major's face. I think the euphoria of having succeeded had made him forget the arduous nature of the journey. "Wait here and I will see what I can do." I do not think the major was a bad man but his first promotion must have made him see the possibilities of more.

As we waited this time, we chatted. "A long way to go, Smudger."

I turned to Albert Wishart. He and I got on well, "It is but at least it is through friendly land now. Our enemies are to the north and west."

Sergeant Grundy was seated on the ground and smoking his pipe. He nodded, "And there is no rush to get back to Seringapatam. There is neither war nor urgency." He shook his head, looking wearier than at any time since Mallavelli, "Travelling more than thirty miles a day might have shaken off our enemies but it nearly did for me."

That was the first time I had heard any kind of complaint from the sergeant. We had almost forgotten his ailment in the heat of battle and flight. I caught Seamus' eye. He normally had a quick wit and was able to inject some humour into a situation. The big Irishman said, smiling, "You are right, Sergeant. We have a leisurely stroll ahead of us. Why we could be rich, young gentlemen enjoying the grand tour."

Tom asked, "The grand tour, Seamus?"

"Aye, rich nobles with more money than sense who travel around Europe to see the sights." He laughed, "They probably all come back with a dose of something and are a lot poorer. As we can't become any poorer then our grand tour is already more successful."

The sergeant laughed at the thought. We would speak to the captain and make sure that the six hundred miles to Seringapatam was taken at a much slower pace. We were in no hurry to return to duty.

The major returned with a chit for the East India depot in the port. Being a port of entry for East Indiamen, the depot would have plenty for us. The major said, "You will notice, Captain, that the chit is for all supplies and equipment that you might need." He smiled, "Lord Mornington is grateful to us all."

If he expected fulsome gratitude from the captain then the major was in for disappointment. Captain Crozier merely saluted and said, formally, "Thank you, Major. Until the next time you need a group of expendable men, farewell." The major might not like the use of the word expendable but it was true. The major did not have to bury the dead men that we had.

We turned and headed to the bustling port I had first seen a couple of years ago when I was still fresh from my flight from danger and when I barely knew what it meant to be a soldier.

There was also a barracks at the depot for newly arrived soldiers often needed accommodation. It meant we had beds and were able to use the kitchens to cook our food. It felt like we had reached civilisation. While food was being cooked we were given our new equipment. We had not needed muskets: we had the ones from the dead men and in six cases they were barely used. The new tunics and breeches would be kept safely in our packs and the carts. We did not mind marching in tattered and faded uniforms. We also put the boots away. The judicious use of hobnails would ensure that the ones we wore would last until Seringapatam. The underwear, however, we would wear immediately. The food we had been given included fresh meat that was not goat. We ate well that night. The only shadow was cast by Thompson and his fellows who asked the captain if they could go into town to visit a bar. The captain refused their request. Seamus and Dai would also have liked to enjoy a night spending their pay, which we had also received, but they accepted the decision. Thompson and the others did not and in the barracks, that night, we heard them chuntering and complaining. It took Sergeant Grundy's stentorian tones to silence them. I wondered what might happen as a result of the refusal.

That single incident soured the whole march back to Seringapatam. Thompson was further smarting about being forced to march when he thought he should have been carried on the cart added to the lack of opportunity to visit an ale and whorehouse, made them almost a separate detachment. When we stood duties the captain ensured that the four were split up and that meant we all had to endure the company of someone we did not like. It was a more leisurely march but it was not a pleasant one. However, Sergeant Grundy found it a little easier and that was enough for most of us.

When we reached Seringapatam we headed for our usual camp. I noticed that there were fewer battalions camped around the fortress and only one of them was a cavalry one. The captain headed for the headquarters to speak with General Wellesley. When he returned it was with the news that the general was visiting Bombay and his brother. It was General Harris who was in command and that was bad news for us. He did not like us and as General Baird was now in Ceylon and Sir Arthur in Bombay, we could not expect to be treated kindly.

We were not disappointed. We were given the duty of escorting wagons to and from Mangalore, the port a hundred and twenty miles to the west of us. The city had been briefly ruled by the Tiger and he had renamed it Jalalabad. We learned that and many other things as we wore out our new boots on the road to Mangalore and back.

Chapter 11

We came to know both the villages and the villagers as we spent almost every day either heading west to the port or escorting laden carts east back to Seringapatam. My language skills had improved to the point where Aadyot was not always needed. We both learned the local dialect and customs. The two of us spoke to the headmen of the villages and I knew the right tone to adopt. It meant that we were welcomed both going and returning. In fact we had a better welcome on the road than we ever received in Seringapatam. All our good service was forgotten as officers sided with General Harris and treated us like pariahs. We brought the wagons back with supplies and were then simply ignored. Thompson and his three companions apart, it made the rest of us closer. Finn and Grey were now part of the platoon and fitted in well. The only advantage that Thompson and the other three brought was that we had more men to stand watch and we had to keep a good watch at night, especially when we had a laden caravan. The villagers were kind to us but there were bandits. The wars with Dhondia Wagh had meant there were many deserters and freebooters from the defeated armies. They were armed and desperate men. We kept a good watch to see that they did not take our cargoes.

We were able to do the journey in four days. Usually we had a two or, sometimes, a three day wait in Mangalore and we used the time to buy things we could not get in Seringapatam. They were quite pleasant days as we stayed in the barracks and could use the facilities of the port. I would also study the HCS ships in the hope of seeing old shipmates or even *Campbelltown*. I never did. Perhaps it was no surprise for the distance to England was the journey of months and Mangalore was not as big a port as either Bombay or Calcutta. I still enjoyed speaking to the sailors. Part of me yearned just to slip aboard and hide once more. I knew that while most of the ships would simply turn around and head back to England or Bombay, some, one or two perhaps, would sail to exotic or remote islands further east. I still wanted an escape but now there were fetters, they were the human ones that tied me to the platoon. Others in the platoon took advantage of the leisure time. The captain often allowed us to go into the port to enjoy the markets and places where those who wished could drink.

Our first journey back from the port was a big one. We had the pay for the garrison to escort. The sight of the chests hauled aboard the wagons was tempting for all of us. Bob Cathcart, Eddie Lowe, John Williams and Albert Wishart were all like me, thieves. Whilst I had been the most successful, in that I had never been caught, the others licked their lips at the sight of enough silver to set a man up for a dozen lifetimes. The boxes with freshly minted silver brought from England were loaded into the wagon and then we hauled the heavy and most valuable cargo back to Seringapatam. The captain, especially, was nervous and I am not sure he got above an hour of sleep each night on the four-day ride back to the fortress. Each of the watches had an officer in command but Captain Crozier often rose in the night to see that all was well. We had incurred the wrath of General Harris just by existing. If we lost his payroll then who knew what the punishment might be? When we reached the fortress the relief was palpable. He was so pleased he allowed a double ration of rum to celebrate. As we had two days back at the camp we were able to relax a little.

The two young soldiers, Tom and Jack were now truly part of the platoon. They could take the banter without either blushing or getting upset. They knew how to be soldiers. The lessons in cooking had paid off and we no longer had to endure raw food when they were the cooks. The ones who were never given the task of cooking were Thompson, McKenzie, Talbot and Watts. None of us wanted spittle in our food. Instead they were given more sentry duties than the rest of us. When we had escorted the pay chests we had all had to have more watches. The captain insisted on four men a watch. He did not trust Thompson and his crew so they were split up and Edward Teach and Albert Wishart joined them for one watch and Ben Neville and Eddie Lowe for the other. I was just glad that I was not on watch with them.

On the first day back after the payroll duty Seamus asked the captain if we could go hunting. He craved action of any description. We had seen, from our camp, small deer. The captain was in a good mood and five of us left the camp. Aadyot stayed

to cook but Tom and Jack came with Seamus, Dai and myself. I
had proved to be a good shot and, more importantly, was able to
move silently. Seamus moved like a lumbering bear. He was
there as muscle to carry back whatever we caught and to act as a
rearguard.

We knew where we had seen them and Dai moved us around
so that the breeze was in our faces. It took an hour of seeking the
trail and avoiding the serpents that hung from the trees before we
found the spoor. We primed our weapons and with Dai and
myself in the centre, flanked by the young soldiers we headed off
to try to get venison for the pot. Seamus let us go twenty yards
before he followed. There were animal predators in the forest
and leopards liked to leap from branches onto men who were
hunting. Seamus was there to kill any that did so. I think he
hoped that one would. He had a kind of madness about him. I
was wearing sandals and they helped me to move silently. I
chose the places where I would step and our progress was slow.
None of us were worried for when we had seen the small herd
we had noticed that they moved slowly as they grazed. So long
as we were on their trail and did not frighten them we would get
our chance.

I heard them before I saw them. I held up my hand and
listened. They were hard to hear but you could just make out the
slight sound of grass and leaves being brushed and then the noise
of deer chewing. I raised my musket, even though I could see
nothing. The deer we hunted were little bigger than large dogs
and even the smallest of us would tower over them. I took
another step and peered through the undergrowth. I spied a
movement. It was a pair of grazing deer. Having seen the closest
deer I was able to make out the one I would target. I could have
fired then and hit the deer which was just forty paces from me
but we wanted as many as we could get and that meant Dai
needed a target. I glanced to my right and saw him nod at me and
raise his musket. He too had seen one and as he aimed, so did I. I
saw other animals, drifting into view. I felt, rather than saw the
other two lift their muskets. I aimed for the middle of the animal.
It might make a mess of the skin and create a large hole but we
needed to kill. I squeezed my trigger. The crack sounded like
thunder and was followed a heartbeat later by Dai's and then the

double crack from Tom and Jack. I reloaded for I could see nothing through the smoke. I could hear the herd of deer as they fled. We moved forward and found two deer, one was dead and the other dying. There was blood on the leaves of the nearest bush and that meant at least one was wounded.

"Seamus, two here for you. We will get after the wounded one."

"I will deal with them, Dai."

We hurried after the small herd which had cut a swathe through the undergrowth. The wounded animal managed to run two hundred paces before it expired. There might have been another wounded one but we could not find its trail. Tom used his bayonet to cut a sapling and thrust it through the hind he and Jack would carry back. Seamus had gutted the two deer and when we had found and cut two more saplings we carried our treasure back to the camp. There was a great celebration in the camp for the venison was more than welcome. We would eat well for our two or three days in camp and we could dry the meat with salt and preserve any we did not eat straightaway. The skins could be used, so we pegged them out and we all made water on them to tan them. The bones, when we had boiled them for stock, could be used for carving. I did not do that but many of the others did. Tom surprised me when he asked for the leg bones. He wanted to make a chess set. I had no idea that he liked the game. Albert was good at carving and he set about making a model of an East Indiaman. He had a good eye and a fine hand. I watched the lump of bone change each day as he took small pieces from it. It was painstaking work. Albert had been a thief but I thought it sad that he had not had the opportunity to use his real skill as a craftsman. England was a hard place to live unless you had money or influence. The thieves in the Devil's Dozen had little choice over their careers. It was either theft or starvation.

Those days were almost like a leave for us. When we escorted the empty pay wagons and the civilians returning to England we stepped out in a spritely manner.

That step became jaded over the next two and a half months. We rarely had the luxury of three days at camp. Often we would arrive back at noon one day and leave at dawn the next. As we had wagons to escort we did not need our carts and the mules and Duchess were left at our camp and Aadyot volunteered to look after them and our tents. He seemed happy with this duty. I found, as we marched along the familiar road, that I missed his company. When we returned to the camp he was always glad to see us. We got on well and seemed to enjoy hearing about the other's life before the East India Company. I became closer to Tom and Jack during those days. The three of us and Albert would often sit at night in the barracks talking, carving, playing cards and the like. Others liked to enjoy the port of Mangalore but we enjoyed each other's company. One good thing was that when we were in Mangalore, and it normally involved at least one overnight stay and sometimes two, our barracks was a slightly more pleasant place. The captain didn't notice it but I did. Thompson and his three confederates sloped off as often as they could into the port. The captain gave all of us permission to visit the bars. I rarely availed myself of the opportunity but Thompson and his terrible three went as often as possible. As the captain was often with the resident or dining with other officers they were able to do so. I thought, at first, that they were deserting but they always came back. It surprised me and I wondered if I had misjudged them. I didn't care that they seemed to take advantage of the rest of us for every moment when they were not in the camp was happier than when they were there. Sergeant Grundy turned a blind eye to their excursions as the barracks was a more pleasant place without them.

We were looking forward to the next payroll duty, if only to guarantee three days in our camp. There was a good reason to be leaving the camp for General Wellesley returned to Seringapatam with four more battalions. The place was filling up and whilst we were happier that we had a better general in command of us, the four days on the road would be pleasant. For one thing we had wagons in which to travel and, for another, we were welcomed in the villages through which we passed. I was put in charge of Tom and Jack. I had no stripes but Sergeant Grundy referred to me as Chosen Man. The action on the way back from Oudh had shown, I think, that I was a natural leader. The captain approved and, if I am honest, I quite enjoyed the responsibility. It meant that when we had a night watch I was in command. I know why

Sergeant Grundy gave me the responsibility; it allowed the captain to have four watches. He could supervise watches, when he chose, but he had four men whom he could trust to keep an eye on the wagons at night. The first time I was in charge of the night watch I smiled to myself. The thief had come a long way since he had lived in the east end of London.

When we reached Mangalore we saw **HCS Bridgewater**. She was a large ship and well-armed. She had twenty guns, all nine pounders. She was on her way to Madras and had only called in at Mangalore to drop off the payroll. I think the captain was glad to be rid of it for it was three times the size of the first payroll we had taken. The battalions brought by General Wellesley needed to be paid. There were just two wagons for us to escort but they would be well laden. We were quite happy, when we set off from Mangalore as there would be no rush to get back to the port. We would have at least three days in Seringapatam. The two carters asked us if they could share our camp by the river. I knew why, they would save the money they would otherwise have to spend on accommodation and food. We had travelled with them before and the captain agreed. We sang and joked on the way back in anticipation of three or four days at what we now considered our home.

Panchavalli was a small village that marked the start of the Deccan Plateau. It was a day or so from Seringapatam and was a place where we could relax a little. We had left the lush jungle and begun the climb towards Seringapatam which lay just forty miles away. It was always a good place to stop for the small village made us welcome and the bullocks enjoyed the rest after that first slog of a climb. It prepared them for the next two days. For us the plateau was less oppressive than the road close to the coast. My section had done two watches on the previous nights and we were happy to have a night off. The two night watches would be taken by the two corporals. We always took pleasure when that happened because Thompson and his friends seemed to think that they were being picked on. They were not but we enjoyed watching their sulky faces when the rest of us retired for the night.

We slept under one of the wagons. This coast had sudden and heavy rain showers that would soak you. The wagon beds gave good protection and it saved us from having to erect the tents. We still erected one for the sergeant and the captain but the rest of us used the wagons for a roof. I always slept well beneath the wagon bed but that night I was disturbed. I thought it might be an animal of the night. They did not worry me but if it was the slithering of a snake…I chose to rise and check to see if it was an animal. The ones who had the next duty used the other wagon.

The first thing I noticed was the silence. That was rare. The horses made noises as well as the men on watch. There was nothing. I checked first to see if there was an animal lurking near the food. Foxes often came to try to steal from us. There was nothing. I turned to look for Corporal Neville and Eddie Lowe. They were the ones on watch. I saw that there was a figure lying on the ground. I was shocked. It was not like Ben Neville to let one of his men sleep. I walked over to shake the man awake and when I pulled at his shoulder I saw that it was Eddie but he was bleeding. The blood was matted around his nose. I looked around and saw that there were no sentries and, more alarmingly, the horses were gone.

"Stand to!" I grabbed my musket. They were all stacked together. My first thought was robbery. Someone had taken the pay chests.

I then knelt and felt Eddie's neck. I could feel the heartbeat. He was alive. Captain Crozier was the first to join me. He stood, half naked, wearing just his breeches. "What is it, Smith?"

"Lowe has been hurt and I can't see Corporal Neville or the other two."

He turned and shouted, "Corporal Teach!" There was no answer. "Sergeant Grundy, search the camp. Hogan and Evans, go with Smith and search the trees and village. Finn and Grey see to Private Lowe."

The two sleepy Celts, half naked like the captain, had their muskets ready and followed me as I headed along the road to the west. I found Corporal Neville as he moaned. He was just ten yards from the camp. We ran to him, "Are you alright, Corp?"

He looked up at me and said, "What happened?"

"The horses are gone and Lowe is out cold." Seamus and Dai helped him to his feet.

He started to talk as we helped him up. "I was on duty when I heard a noise from these trees. I wandered over the next thing I knew was that someone smacked me from behind." He held his hand to his head and it came away bloody.

I said, "Seamus, take him back. Dai, let's continue searching." It was the glint of silver in the moonlight that told us that the thieves had headed along the road. I picked up the fresh silver coin. It was part of the payroll. "They went in this direction." I listened and could hear nothing.

Dai shook his head, "Whoever they are they are long gone. We had better report back to the captain."

There were lights in the camp as we approached. Muskets swivelled in our direction as we neared them. The two carters were stood in shock and were staring at a blanket covered mound. I shook my head as I flipped the coin to Captain Crozier, "We found this on the road west, Sir, but we heard nothing. Whoever took the horses took some of the payroll and headed west."

Sergeant Grundy walked over he said, "One of the chests is half empty."

I looked around at the faces and saw that six were missing. I said, "I can't believe that Corporal Teach and Albert Wishart would join Thompson and his band to rob the payroll."

Behind me I heard Edward Teach's voice as he said, "I didn't and neither did poor Albert Wishart. Someone hit me while I slept."

Bob Cathcart said, as he nodded towards the blanket covered mound, "Albert was stabbed. We have lost another comrade."

Those words upset me more than I could say. We had lost Edmund Byers but that had been in battle. Albert and I had been close. We were of a similar age and backgrounds. While Aadyot was my best friend I often found myself talking to Albert as he carved his bones.

Captain Crozier shook his head, "From what I have been told this is what happened. Corporal Neville was lured from the camp by one of those on watch with him and then he was sapped. Someone then sneaked up on Eddie and did the same to him."

Eddie Lowe had his head bandaged and he said, "They used a sap, a leather bag filled with sand. I heard something and half turned. I saw it just before he hit me. I saw Thompson with one the other day after we had been to the market in Mangalore. I should have asked him why but…"

Captain Crozier shook his head, "It is not your fault. I think that Thompson and Talbot along with the other two who were ready to come on watch took Corporal Teach and Wishart as they slept. Perhaps Wishart heard something and woke…"

George said, "He would have shouted out."

The captain had clearly thought of this already, "Not if they held a hand over his mouth."

I became angrier. They had murdered him. I could imagine the hand over his mouth and the blade sliding in to end his young life. In my head I swore vengeance. It would be unlikely that I would have it but I promised myself that if I had the chance then the four would die.

John Williams said, "They can't be moving that fast, Sir. They only have two horses and…"

"And we have none. We have two wagons to escort and a payroll to deliver."

Sergeant Grundy said, "The general won't be very happy."

"You are right, Sergeant, and that is another reason why we will get back as soon as we can. We have to report to the general so that men can be sent to hunt them down." He looked at the body of our friend. "We will bury Wishart now and then leave. I don't think any of us will sleep."

When we put Albert in the ground I found that I was weeping. I had seen men die but Albert was my friend. I thought back to the last night when we had joked about the food that Jack and Tom had cooked. The last memory I had of Albert was his laugh. Now he was dead and would laugh no more.

We were well on the way to Seringapatam by the time dawn broke. The three injured men and the sergeant rode in the wagons. I was at the rear with Finn and Grey. There was a sombre mood without any banter or chat of any kind. I was running through what we could have done and, perhaps, should have done. Tipu Sultan had been called a tiger but, in reality he was not. Zebediah Thompson was the real tiger. We had been stalked since he had joined us. Everything became clear to me. The first payroll wagon and the subsequent trips had allowed him to establish how we worked. Our visits to Mangalore meant he used the time there to get what he needed for his robbery. The only thing out of his hands was the timing of the watches. He had chosen Panchavalli to rob the wagon because that was when he and his band of thieves were on duty. I even knew where he had gone. He would be hiding close to Mangalore. He had not taken all the silver but he had more than enough to use it to hide and then to do as I had wanted to do and to escape to the east and the islands. There were ships other than East Indiamen who used Mangalore.

When we arrived in Seringapatam and delivered the payroll the captain went to headquarters to report. He was away some time. As time dragged on we knew it did not bode well for us. None of us were surprised when a platoon of armed soldiers from the 33rd, led by Sergeant Charlton, came to escort us inside.

Sergeant Grundy said, "Heads up, lads, we did nowt wrong. We are still soldiers."

Sergeant Charlton roared, "Silence in the ranks."

I knew that would anger Sergeant Grundy but he said nothing. The house General Harris was using had an inner courtyard and garden. We were marched inside. Captain Crozier was stood before the general and some other senior officers. I saw neither Colonel Stephenson nor General Wellesley. They would have offered us some support.

Sergeant Charlton roared, "Attention."

We all snapped to attention, mindful of Sergeant Grundy's words. The general walked along our line and glared at each of us. When he reached me he stopped and gave me a look as though he had stepped into something unpleasant and he chose that moment to speak, "I should not be surprised that this band of thieves and vagabonds cooperated in the theft of the payroll. I warned others of the perfidy of such men. I was ignored and now we have lost a substantial part of the payroll that was to be used to pay good soldiers. This platoon is not only to be disbanded and its officers stripped of rank but there will be a court martial and, if I have my way, a term in gaol. Sergeant Charlton…"

He got no further for I heard from behind me a voice I recognised, "Sergeant Charlton, I do not think we need your platoon here. Take them back to the camp. I will take charge now." It was General Wellesley.

"Yes, Sir. Platoon, slope arms. About face. Quick march." I did not turn but heard the platoon march through the gate we had used to enter this courtyard.

General Wellesley and Major Tucker walked into my eye line. They did not look at us but strode to the senior officers. I had sharp ears and although they spoke quietly I heard most of what they were saying. General Wellesley dismissed the senior officers and then told General Harris that he had acted hastily. I heard him say, "General, think about it, if the rest of the platoon was implicated then they would have stolen the whole payroll and disappeared completely. From what Major Tucker tells me and from what I have seen this platoon is resourceful enough to do that. They did not. They returned here to face the consequences." The general objected but I could tell that General Wellesley must have enjoyed another promotion for he gave orders. The orders were clear enough for us all to hear. "General Harris, have light cavalry search for these..." he turned to Captain Crozier. "How many men was it?"

"Four men and two horses, Sir."

"Four men and two horses. I will deal with this platoon."

"Sir." The general was red faced as he saluted and left us. He would not forget his humiliation and would blame, unfairly, us.

When he had left us General Wellesley said in, for him, a gentle tone, "Captain Crozier, I am sorry that you had to endure that. The major and I had just arrived at headquarters moments after you left. The officer of the day gave us his report. Your three wounded men should be in the infirmary and not standing in the sun." The captain said nothing. I think that, like the rest of us, he was just stunned at the reprieve. He had been within minutes of losing his rank and facing not only a court martial but, with a court chosen by General Harris, probably a gaol sentence. "I am afraid I need you to return to Mangalore tomorrow. The wagons need an escort and I need to inform the authorities there of the theft." I saw a rare smile, "And I think that you and your men need to be away from Seringapatam for a while. I do, in any case, have a task which is eminently well suited to your depleted platoon." He nodded to Major Tucker, "The major will explain." He stood to attention and saluted.

Sergeant Grundy roared, "Platoon, attention." We snapped to attention.

Major Tucker said, with a smile, "Come along, Captain, let us retire to your camp. There is much to say."

Aadyot was pleased to see us but the looks on our faces clearly confused him. Major Tucker said, "Private Ganguly, we need a pot of tea, I think."

"Sir."

"Gentlemen, sit. I think that you all deserve to hear what I am about to tell you."

We sat and there was a subdued and angry silence. We had returned and were being blamed for the action of four men we never wanted in our midst.

The major spoke calmly, "The robbery aside, I will come to that in the fulness of time, I was coming today to give you another task. There is a war to the north of us. The Peshwa of the Marathas is being threatened by an alliance led by Daulat Rao Scindia, the Maharajah of Gwalior and Jaswant Rao Holkar, the Maharajah of Indore. It is in Britain's and the Company's interest that we profit from this war. The Peshwa is a relatively weak man and Lord Mornington believes that with British guidance he can become stronger. We are going to Poona to offer the Peshwa British support."

Captain Crozier said, "Then why not send an army, Sir?"

"Ah, there's the rub. If we send an army then it looks like imperialism and other disaffected leaders might join the two maharajas and this little war might escalate. You were in Oudh and know that if the Nawab of Oudh threw in with the Marathas we would have a hard war to win on our hands. No, Richard, this way the Peshwa will, hopefully, invite Britain to be his allies. That is the other reason you are returning to Mangalore so quickly. Your time in Seringapatam was up before this unfortunate incident."

Albert Wishart was dead. It was more than unfortunate. I could not contain my anger and I burst out, "But, Major, what about Thompson and his killers."

He turned to me, "He will be caught and punished. You heard the general, horsemen will be sent to find him."

I knew that they would fail. I saw a lot of me in Zebediah Thompson. I had planned my escape many times and I had thought out ways to avoid being found. He was just as clever as I was and he was also ruthless. I was not a murderer. I knew who had used a bayonet to end Albert Wishart's life.

Captain Crozier caught my eye and gave me the slightest of shakes of his head.

Aadyot came over with the pot and Major Tucker beamed, "Ah, a pot of tea. Just the ticket, eh lads?"

As I sipped the tea Captain Crozier came over and said, quietly, "You know something about Thompson, Smith?"

I nodded, "I suppose I should have mentioned it at the time, Sir, but when we were in Mangalore Thompson and the others often sneaked into the port. They went when they weren't given permission by you. We did not say anything, Sir, as, well, to be honest it was more pleasant without them in the barracks." He nodded his understanding. "I think he was making connections, Sir. The general's horsemen will not find them. The two horses will either be dead or have been sold. They will not wear uniforms and they will know where to hide."

He sipped his tea and nodded, "Just like you would."

I met his gaze and nodded, "Yes, Sir, you need to set a thief to catch a thief. Eddie, Bob, John and I are all thieves. The difference is that I was more successful. If the major gives us the time, Sir, then I reckon I can find them."

"Say and do nothing, Smith. I will speak to the major. Despite what many other officers think I believe that this platoon is a good one. I want our honour to be returned. We have a stain on our name and while I doubt that we will ever change General Harris' view of us, I want other soldiers to know that we did our duty."

Chapter 12

Surprisingly it felt sad to leave our camp. We were not unhappy to be leaving Seringapatam and the wrath of General Harris but we had enjoyed our camp by the Little Cauvery. It was the longest time we had spent in one place since we had arrived in India. Aadyot was the saddest of all. When we had been the escorts it had been his home. Sergeant Grundy rode Duchess and we put one cart in the empty wagon. We still had the mules to pull the second cart and Major Tucker managed to acquire another horse for the captain. Our cargo was, apart from our three wounded, the family of an East India official who had died of some illness. His wife and four children were returning to England. I don't think that Mrs Grant was sorry to be leaving India. When I spoke to her around the campfire I had the impression that her husband had been ambitious and saw himself as a powerful man in the lands controlled by the East India Company. She saw England and her family as more important. I do not think she would grieve overlong for her husband. The company was generous to such families and she would be a rich widow.

As we journeyed west I saw Captain Crozier and Major Tucker in deep discussion many times. I knew what it was about. He was attempting to persuade the major to let us hunt for Albert's killers. The payroll they had stolen meant nothing but they had killed a good man. They had taken just what they could carry. Four men riding the two horses would be a heavy burden. I knew how much silver weighed. When I had been a thief I always preferred houses with the odd piece of gold. It meant I had less to carry. We also spoke of the men we intended to hunt with or without permission. I spoke to the others about what we might do to find the four men. The others, it transpired, had been as suspicious as I had. That we had never spoken together before the attack was sad and had resulted in Albert's death.

"Four white men hiding in a place like Mangalore will stand out. Even if we just walk around the port we should be able to spot one of them."

"A good idea, Smudger, and I think you are right. They will stay in Mangalore. It is clear to me that they had been planning this for a while and will have set up something before they took the silver. We know that the bastards will hide and they will hire local men to protect them." Seamus was every bit as angry as the rest of us and I saw his hands clenching and unclenching. If he got hold of Thompson this time then he would beat him to a pulp.

I nodded, "You are right, Seamus, but we have a secret weapon, Aadyot. I have spoken to him already and he is more than happy to pretend to be a newly discharged hand from a ship and sniff them out. You know they will be wary of white faces and not someone like Aadyot."

Dai added, darkly, "And I want no interference from the officers. We will find them and we will punish them."

Tom asked, innocently, "Punish them?"

"Kill them, son, that is what he means." Bob and Albert had been friends and tentmates. Such bonds were deep ones. Bob Cathcart had a dark side to him too.

I had never killed in cold blood and I was not sure I would be able to. I had killed but in battle or situations where it was kill or be killed. Dai and the others seemed quite happy to hunt knowing that, as with the deer, there would be death at the end of it. We did not mention any of this to the five officers. Major Tucker was not one of us and the others might baulk at such drastic measures. Sergeant Grundy and the two corporals wanted vengeance but they were non-commissioned officers and breaking the rules was not in their nature. When we hunted it would be Albert's tentmates who would do the hunting.

When we reached the port the major and the captain went to report and to deliver the messages at the East India Company offices. We would be housed in the barracks and we made ourselves comfortable before, while the officers were away, Aadyot and I slipped into civilian clothes and headed out into the port. We did not stay together for we knew that might endanger Aadyot. I had picked an easy part to play. I was a sailor who had jumped ship, fed up with the punishments. I would seek a place to hide. To disguise myself I wore a patch and a sailor's cap. It hid my hair and disguised my face. None of the officers appeared to have noticed that I had not shaved since Seringapatam. I looked as unlike a soldier as was possible. I wore a sailor's dirk in my belt and I had a dagger secreted beneath my top. I wore sandals and, as I had worn them before, my feet were not the pale white ones of a soldier who never took off his boots. While we were away the rest would cover for us. The sergeant and the corporal would, hopefully, not notice our absence or if they did might assume we were at the market. One thing we were all good at was telling lies. Tom and Jack were the worst liars and Seamus and Dai intended to keep them busy so that they would not have to lie.

The two of us separated from the others as soon as we left the back door of the barracks and did not look back. In my case it helped that I looked furtive. I made my way to the port. There was a frigate, **Comet**, in port and a small ten-gun East Indiaman, **Alexander**. I hung around with the others who were either seeking to steal from the cargoes or to gather information. I stood there for half an hour, chatting to the other idlers and gathering information, and discovered the names of the ships and their sailing times, not to mention the names of their captains. As I had learned in my former life as a thief, the more detail you had for a story, the more believable it was. I also made sure that I kept myself hidden either by others or by objects. I did not think one of the evil four would be there but I would not take a chance. If they were in Mangalore itself then we would quickly find them and deal with them. I thought they would have a lair that was hidden and secret. Until the furore of the theft died down they would want to be hidden from view. What Aadyot and I were doing was what I had done with the others when we hunted deer. We looked for their sign. We would listen for conversations about strangers in the town. All men need food and paying for food with freshly minted silver would give us a clue that the men were in the area.

When I left the quayside I did so as though I was trying to keep hidden. I moved in the shadows. I kept as close to crowds as I could. In that way I moved from the harbour side to the commercial buildings. I found a tavern close to the port. It would be run by a European but the ones who worked there would be local. It would be rough and it would be noisy. I entered and found myself in a fog of pipe and cigar smoke. The air was redolent with the stink of ale and poor bathing. It was noisy and the faces were threatening. It was the perfect place to find out information. I headed for the bar rather than trying to find a table with a spare place. Such a move would have sparked violence at some point. I waited until there was a space and then inveigled myself between two men. In that time I had been listening to the drinks men asked for and the prices they paid. I ordered myself a gill of the cheapest locally made alcohol I could. I had no intention of drinking much of it. It would serve as a tool and mark me as someone who was down on his luck.

I then found a wall against which to lean. I did not approach anyone. That would be a mistake. Instead I stood, apparently sipping the fiery liquor. I knew that at some point I would be spotted and approached. If no one else came then my nursing of the drink would mean they would ask me to leave. The greasy looking man who did so had a small moustache that was oiled. He had lank hair that was visibly thinning and his hands were grained with powder. The man had been a soldier. He was the same height as me but his stomach showed that he liked his food. He had a pint pot and a pipe was jammed in the corner of his mouth. He chose the moment to approach me when the wall next to me was vacated by someone going to make water. I glanced at him and then sipped my drink again.

"Haven't seen you in here before, young un." I said nothing and my face remained without expression. "My name is Dutch Bill." He chuckled, "Don't take that the wrong way, I am an Englishman but my father was a Dutchman and the name stuck. What is your name?"

There is an unwritten convention that if a stranger gives his name then you give one in return. I said, "Bert." I used Albert's name. In my mind I was playing the part of a young sailor and Albert's name seemed right.

He nodded and said, "Just Bert?"

"No," I paused, "Bert."

He laughed, "I can see you have wit but now, Bert, tell me what brings you here? You look like a sailor but as far as I know no one was discharged from the two ships in port lately."

I shrugged, "I have just arrived in Mangalore and," for the first time I let the hint of a smile pass over my face, "I am exploring the possibilities it presents. The life of a sailor was not what I expected when I left England." I was not saying it but hinting that I had jumped ship.

Dutch Bill nodded and emptied half of his pot. He gestured with it, "Can I buy you a drink? Some food perhaps? You look as though a good meal would not go amiss."

I shook my head, "I am unused to such kindness and I do not want to be beholden to someone I barely know. Besides, I have a little food at...the place I sleep."

He was not put out by my refusal, "No harm intended. You are English as am I and this country is full of foreigners who will slit your throat for the price of a bowl of rice."

I frowned as though I was thinking through his words. "I will not be bound to you?"

"You have my word."

Licking my lips I said, "Then I accept."

He was clearly a man who was known and he shouted, "Two bowls of food." We strode over to a table and he growled, "Move." The two men obliged.

We sat and I felt the man studying me. He said nothing until the food came and we ate. I played the part of a man who was starving, aware, all the time of the man's furtive scrutiny. I wolfed it down while he leisurely picked at his. When we had finished he asked, "What did you do before you were a sailor?" I said nothing. "Come, I am interested."

"Aye, but why? I am unused to this sort of kindness and it makes me suspicious."

He sighed and lowered his voice, "I may have work for you but it depends on your answers. Come, you have enjoyed a meal, now share a little of your story."

I sighed and took a breath as though I was revealing something important. I knew he would expect something in exchange for the food. "I was a thief."

He nodded, "You have the furtive look of one. Here in India?"

I shook my head, "Back in England."

I saw him drawing his own conclusions from that. He seemed satisfied with my story and he lit his pipe. "You say you have somewhere to sleep. That is good. Come back here in," I saw his face as he calculated, "two days' time. I may well have an offer of work and, if not, will treat you to another meal."

I nodded, "And if I am not here then you know that I have found another offer of…" I paused and smiled, "employment."

"Just so but know that the men with whom I work have great plans and we are talking about making ourselves as rich as a maharajah." He smiled, "I thought I was the top man here until they came and in a short time they have shown me that my thinking was too small. They think big. They are tough men and not to be crossed. I will offer them your services and we shall see. They need thieves but prefer English ones."

I stood and nodded, "Thank you for the food, Dutch Bill. I will think about your offer." I did not offer to shake his hand but turned and slipped out of the tavern. Once outside I moved around the side and darted down an alley that ran behind the warehouse and tavern. It was empty and when I had run forty yards and seen a pile of rubbish I ducked behind it and peered back. I was rewarded by the sight of two half naked men who searched for me down the alley. I was hidden behind a broken chair. I peered between the shattered spindles. I waited for five minutes after they had left before I moved. I used the back alleys to make my way back to a main throughfare and then chose my moment to disappear into the throng. I was confident I was not followed.

I found a quiet place to discard my eye patch and sailor's hat. I waited until I saw Seamus, Dai and Bob returning from a visit to an alehouse that lay close by to the company barracks. I slipped out and was between them so fast that I heard the intake of breath from Bob. Seamus might have enjoyed a drink but it still did not dull his wits. He said, quietly, "Hiding?"

"Let us say that I would rather not be seen entering the barracks."

He and Bob put their arms around me as though I was drunk. It effectively hid my face from view. The legs could have belonged to anyone.

The sentry on the gate merely nodded. One did not argue with Seamus. Once inside the barracks, having made sure that the corporals were not there and the officers still absent, I told them what I had found out. Tom and Jack were both innocents and could not make the connections that the others did.

Tom shook his head, "It sounds to me, Smudger, that you have found a gang to join but that does not bring us any closer to getting the four who killed Albert. It may well be that the man who has taken over, the one Dutch Bill said, *'thought big'* might well be Thompson but a two day wait suggests that they are not close."

Eddie smiled, "I disagree. The men who took over Dutch Bill's gang came recently. They were described as tough men. We all know what Zebediah was like. It makes sense to me. The money they took on the two horses and carrying four men could not have been a huge amount. It would be enough for them to set themselves up. It might be that they plan piracy. A laden East Indiaman is a good prize and Smudger was dressed as a sailor."

Dai added, "And the two-day delay might be because they are seeking others. He was always a cunning man. Thompson was a careful bugger. He must have planned every step of this."

Jack nodded, "Now I come to think of it, each time we came to Mangalore the four of them would disappear. Tom and I happened to be going in the same direction as them once, towards the quay and we were warned that we would have a beating from them if we continued to follow them."

Dai said, "It makes sense but we do not know, yet, where they are holed up."

"I know but tomorrow I will adopt another disguise and follow Dutch Bill."

John Williams shook his head, "Too risky. I will follow this man. He does not know me and while I may not have been the thief that you were, Smudger, I know how to hide in a crowd. I could pick a pocket as deftly as any."

"But you do not know the man."

"You come with me and identify him. I will follow him and you can follow me."

Seamus said, "A grand plan but do not forget the officers. They will be suspicious."

156

"We have to find a way to stay here for another two days." Dai smiled, and waved a hand at Seamus and Bob, "The three of us had some bad food. We play act being sick."

"Will it work?"

"Smudger, we can try. We will be in the latrine. When they return and ask where we are the rest of you need to convince them that we have spent a long time emptying our bowels."

I nodded. It was a believable story. The food in some inns and taverns was often poorly made and induced vomiting and diarrhoea. "And we have yet to hear from Aadyot."

The corporals and Sergeant Grundy returned first. They had enjoyed grog and food and were in a good mood. The three men who purported to be sick had no sympathy from them but there appeared to be no suspicion. Aadyot returned before the major and the captain. We were all eager to hear his news but the presence of the non-commissioned officers made conversation impossible.

We ate, or rather most of us ate, and we secreted some bread for the three who were feigning illness. The two officers returned from headquarters. The rosy glow from their cheeks and the smell of spirits on their breath and tunics spoke of a fine meal. Captain Crozier announced an impromptu officers' call and the five of them left us alone. I had feared that they might include me for I was seen as a Chosen Man but they did not.

Bob stood watch at the door. He could hear what we said and watch for the return of our officers at the same time. While Seamus and the other two devoured the bread and food we had brought Aadyot gave us his news. "I found the places where those of the lowest castes congregate. The four we seek are not in Mangalore but have taken over a house a mile or so outside, to the north. I could not discover the exact location, Smudger, for it would have looked suspicious." I nodded my understanding. "The four do not want any with a dark skin to work for them. They only want white men and preferably Englishmen."

"That ties in with what Dutch Bill said."

"They have been in Mangalore for just over a week but already they had taken over a gang of thieves. I was told that the Englishman who ran the gangs was found floating in the harbour. This was when you were here before. His throat had been cut, his eyes removed and he had been castrated. He had been a smuggler and a pirate." He had clearly met his match in Thompson.

Seamus nodded, "A warning then. You were right, Jack, they have been reconnoitring on our previous visits. They must have seen their chance when we escorted the pay chest. It is seed money. From what Smudger was told there are more riches to come. The question is, what is it?"

John Williams said, "If the chap who was murdered was a smuggler then perhaps smuggling or piracy."

I said, "You don't make a fortune quickly by smuggling." I had known smugglers in London. They had a steady income but that was all it was, regular.

Dai shook his head, "It doesn't matter. We have the chance to get them now, while they are still gathering a gang. Aadyot, where is this house?"

He shrugged, "North of Mangalore and close to the sea, that was all I was told."

"You have risked enough, Aadyot. Tomorrow, if we are able, then John and I will follow Dutch Bill. Failing that we search the land to the north of the port. They must be close enough for Dutch Bill to report to his new masters. I saw neither horse nor mule and he must be walking."

John Williams said, "But will we be allowed to do this?"

Bob said, "Heads up."

The three sick men immediately went to their beds and disappeared beneath the sheets. They moaned, but gently. It would not do to over egg the pudding.

Captain Crozier and the three non-commissioned officers entered. He looked at the three heaving bunks and said, "How are those three?"

Eddie said, "You know what it is like when you have the squits, Sir. They have been up and down like a fiddler's elbow and now they are exhausted."

It seemed a plausible explanation and none of the four appeared suspicious. "Well, they have three days to recover. Major Tucker has decided that we need horses. It will take time to get us a dozen or more horses. There will also be new uniforms. You have two days' leave in Mangalore but," he pointed at the three sheet covered men, "No silliness. Drink and eat, aye, but in moderation. We shall need our wits about us when we head north."

We had no further opportunities to either plan or talk for the non-commissioned officers were with us. However, we had planned enough to allow John and I, suitably disguised in civilian clothes to slip away early. Tom, Jack, Eddie and George came with us to help with our disguise. We headed for the ships. The *Alexander* had gone but there was a small schooner docked in her place, the *Mandalay*. While John and I lounged with the other idlers on the dockside the other four headed first to the tavern and then into town. As we had walked to the water we had come up with this extension to our plan. Their presence would draw the eyes of Dutch Bill's spies, and having been in the tavern, I knew that he used others there for just such an enterprise. We watched the tavern from the crates that had been unloaded from the schooner. We saw our companions leave and the two half naked men who followed them were the same ones as those who had followed me. It seemed that while the gang leader only employed white men, Dutch Bill was more democratic. The two men would follow our companions and when they had established where they were housed would return. I hoped that Eddie and George would lead them on a merry dance.

We waited until I saw Dutch Bill emerge. It was past noon and we had been moved on at least once. We now lounged next to boxes that were waiting to be hauled from the warehouse next door to the tavern. As they were being loaded onto wagons, they were a perfect hiding place. Dutch Bill was filling his pipe and I saw that the two men with him were the ones he had evicted from the table. He spoke to them and then set them off.

I said, "That is Dutch Bill."

John said nothing but was studying him. I had no patch but, instead, had a neckerchief tied around my head. John wore a battered tricorn hat he had found discarded in the barracks. Dutch Bill looked around him as though he was just filling his pipe and enjoying the day. I knew that he was looking for another like me or for anything suspicious. It took some time to get the pipe going, he had to go to a brazier burning discarded packaging to get a light and that afforded him the chance to scan more of the busy quay. Seemingly satisfied, he set off and headed north along the road. John had been a thief but not one who broke into houses. He had been a cutpurse. He knew how to use crowds. Dutch Bill was alone but there were others who were leaving Mangalore either having finished their business or bought what they needed from the market and were returning home. My friend joined a group of those. He was invisible. I just kept him in sight. I often lost sight of Dutch Bill but John, in his tricorn hat, was always visible. We walked for two miles and the numbers on the road thinned out as people took side paths to their homes. When Dutch Bill paused at the side of the road to fill his pipe again I ducked into the shelter of a stand of huge trees that grew by the side of the road. John carried on walking with his new companions. He had struck up a conversation with them. They passed Dutch Bill who waited until they had disappeared from sight and the road was, apparently, empty. It was only then that he headed down the track that led through more trees towards the sea. I waited. An hour after he had gone John, minus the hat, appeared next to me having made his way, not along the road but the side.

"I thought you would be here. Where did he go?"

I pointed, "Down that track." I had been studying the ground and I said, "If we go down the trees to the left of the track we should be able to see where they went."

We headed through the trees towards the sea. I pointed to the figure lurking behind the wall that marked the boundary of the property that we saw.

John spotted him, "If this is their lair then they will have more watchers than just that one."

"I know. All we need is a glimpse of one of the deserters and then we know if we are right."

My head told me we were right. Unless there was a completely different group of men who had recently arrived, taken over the gang who ruled Mangalore then it had to be Zebediah Thompson and his men.

I took out my dagger. It was not a great weapon but it was better than nothing. John followed me. We moved back a little closer to Mangalore and, hidden by a bend in the road, crossed it.

I sought a route through the undergrowth that looked safe from obstacles that might trip and reptiles that would bite. We moved slowly. There was little need to rush. By my reckoning it was mid-afternoon and we had hours until darkness. I smelled the woodsmoke and knew that there was a house ahead long before I saw it. The house when we saw it, proved to be just a half a mile from the road and was on a piece of ground just forty yards above the beach. I saw that it was a small cove. Even I recognised that it was a perfect place for smuggling and I spied a boat drawn up on the beach. The boat had a reefed lateen sail and was about forty feet long. It could smuggle and, packed with pirates, would be able to cut out a ship like the schooner I had seen in the port.

Being this close we moved even more slowly and were both careful not to make too much of a disturbance to the undergrowth. A sudden flight of wings could prove disastrous. We stopped two hundred yards from the front of the house which overlooked the beach. There was a veranda that looked over the water. I heard voices and we ducked down. Men came out onto the veranda. They were preceded by a cloud of smoke from their pipes. I recognised Dutch Bill and he stood with his back to the sea and faced the other men. There were six of them and their backs were, annoyingly, to us. Four of them had the build of the four deserters but they could just have been the smugglers who used the house.

There was a sudden burst of laughter and one of them, choking with mirth, turned to spit at the ground. It was Talbot. We had spied one and that was enough for me. I was about to leave when another of them turned to re-enter the house. It was McKenzie. It was confirmation. I backed away and John did the same. We never took our eyes from them until we were far enough away to stand. I pointed to the sea and we made our way through the trees to the water. We were on the next beach beyond the cove. I said nothing but pointed towards Mangalore, hidden behind more trees.

I waited until we were half a mile along the beach before I spoke. "I saw Talbot and McKenzie."

"And I am sure I saw Watts. We have them, Smudger."

"Then we now need a plan to get here with the others and take them."

"And that will be easier said than done. They are clearly being careful. There are only nine of us."

"Eleven if you count Tom and Jack."

He scoffed, "They are bairns and still wet behind the ears."

"And they are part of our section. We need them, John."

"Then I hope that they are good enough for the ones we are hunting are as deadly as cobras."

Chapter 13

While it took longer to reach the barracks by the route I had chosen I felt that it was worth it. We would now have a way to reach it without being seen by the watchers in the tavern. Having done part of the journey at twilight I knew we could make an approach that would be hidden from the men in the house. The sentry at the gate recognised us but gave us a strange look. We headed for the barracks. We had missed mess but we had learned enough to regard the pangs of hunger as worthwhile. We opened the barracks door and were greeted, not only by our friends, but the five officers.

Captain Crozier stood and said, "Well, Smith, did you and Williams have a profitable day?"

The old thief in me came to the fore and I lied, "Sir? What do you mean, profitable?"

Walter Grundy shook his head and said, "The others have come clean, Smith. We know you were looking for Thompson and the deserters. Did you find them?"

I wondered if it was a trick and I looked to Seamus who nodded, "Just tell them, Smudger. We will take whatever punishment they say, eh?"

I sighed, "Yes, Sir. We found Talbot, McKenzie and Watts in a house two miles up the road on a beach that looks as though it is used for smuggling. We didn't see Thompson, Sir, but Williams and I are convinced he is there."

Major Tucker smiled and stubbed out his cheroot, "Very enterprising, Smith."

"And what were you going to do with this information? Tell the authorities? Me?" The captain's eyes bored into me.

Dai came to my defence and said, "No, Sir, we were going to go and kill the bastards and return the payroll to shove it up General bloody Harris'…" If we were in trouble then the truth would out.

I saw the smirk appear on the major's face.

"You realise, Evans, that such an unofficial action would result in a court martial."

Seamus grinned, "If anyone found out, Sir. After all we are the Devil's Dozen and we would have simply let the sharks eat the bodies and tell the company that we found the payroll."

"A little thin, Hogan."

Seamus' face became serious, "Captain Crozier, we owe it to Wishart not to mention Eddie and the corporals, to pay them back. Besides, our name was besmirched." He smiled, "It will be like spitting in General Harris' eye and even a whipping would be worth that."

The captain nodded, "You will all be confined to barracks until further notice. Sergeant Grundy, they are your responsibility."

"Sir."

The two officers left. I looked at Seamus, "How did he find out?"

Aadyot looked distraught, "It was me, Sir. The captain began to question me and I could not lie to an officer."

Seamus said, "To be fair, Sir, the captain had an idea of what was going on and picked on the one he knew wouldn't lie."

I looked at Sergeant Grundy who shrugged, "The major saw you yesterday with the eye patch and sailor's hat. He saw through your disguise and watched you. He knew you had to be up to something and as Aadyot is your mate, well..."

I sat on my bed and shook my head, "We were so close, Sarge. We even had a good plan. We could go to the house using the beach. John and I found a way. There were about a dozen men that we saw and we worked out we could easily eliminate the sentries and that would lower the odds. They would not have weapons at the ready. We could have had them and then redeemed our name."

Sergeant Grundy shook his head, "If you think that returning the silver to the general will do anything then you are wrong. He hates us and wants us disbanded. The deserters will have spent some of the money and the twisted mind of General Harris would lay the blame on us." He took out his pipe. "It is a good plan though, Smudger. You have a clever mind. You can put all this behind you when we leave for Poona in a day or two." He stood, "Right lads, me and the corporals will be on duty, between us, all night. Thank you for depriving us of a night in our beds."

164

There was no rancour in his voice and a smile played upon his lips. "I daresay they have food for you two. You have been busy boys today."

He closed the door and Aadyot, Tom and Jack produced two plates laden with food. Seamus poured two mugs of what looked like grog. He said, "You did well, lads, but the game is over. Those four are going to get away with it."

Tom said, "They will be judged in heaven."

Seamus snorted. He sounded like a wild bull, "Bugger that! They will be in hell but I wanted them to suffer in this life. I was going to finish what I started when they first came. I intended to beat him to a pulp."

John and I ate but it was mechanical. We were filling a hole. There was a larger one already that was the void of our failure to have vengeance. Despite the fact that we were not going to be able to do what we intended, the others, even Tom and Jack, were keen to have a picture of the house. Afterwards they speculated about the series of events that led to the deserters gaining such power so quickly.

"They must have met this Dutch Bill and the smuggler they killed at that inn. Once they knew who ran the criminal side it must have been easy for Thompson. He is a clever man." Eddie had run with a gang in England. Whilst very low in the pecking order, he understood how such organisations worked.

"What do you think the big job is that Smudger mentioned?" Bob had a curious mind.

"If they have a ship then it is likely they could pirate an Indiaman."

I shook my head, "No, Tom, I sailed an Indiaman and they are not easy to take. They might take a little Indiaman but that would not be carrying enough to make them a fortune. If they see a sail then they are wary." Even as I said the word, 'fortune' I knew what they would seek. "I think it is more likely they will take the whole of the next payroll." Every eye swivelled to me as though I had a fortune teller's mystical ball. "Think about it, the only reason they didn't take the whole thing the first time was that there were only four of them and they had just two horses. They have a gang now and as they are recruiting that gang will only grow. They could strike closer to Mangalore and this time take everything: the payroll, wagon and horses. They would also have the weapons and powder from the guards. If they chose the right place and killed everyone then it might be a week or more before Seringapatam knew anything about it. They have enjoyed just over two months to recruit and plan. They already know where the escorts stop and they know the routines of loading and unloading. It is a lot safer than taking an Indiaman."

George laughed, "I am glad that you are a reformed character, Smudger. You have a devious and cunning mind."

Dai shook his head, "And we might have stopped it but now they will get away with it and we will be off with the major risking our lives again."

He was right and that made me angry. I did not sleep well that night. It was a mixture of the thought that the deserters had got away with it and my black heart reminding me what I was really like.

We woke at reveille. There was a bugle and other soldiers and so we were in a more military routine than at Seringapatam. We went to the mess and ate along with our non-commissioned officers. The three did not seem annoyed or angry at their lack of sleep. I think that they sympathised with us. Three of them had been laid out by the deserters and could easily have suffered the same fate as Albert.

As we ate Seamus asked, "And are we still confined to the barracks, Sergeant Grundy?"

He shrugged, "I am not sure. We shall see but I don't think any of you will be allowed to wander free."

"Looks like cards or dominoes then lads."

Without the deserters there was now more good humour in the platoon. We would amuse ourselves but the reality was that we really wanted to carry out our act of vengeance.

After breakfast some of the men sat around the tables in the barracks and either played with the tattered cards or else they played with the dominoes made from ivory. They had come with the barracks and looked ancient. Tom was carving his chess pieces. I took the East Indiaman that poor Albert had been carving. I was not sure if I would be any good at it but I felt I owed it to Albert to at least have a go. Somehow it seemed to keep his memory alive. I also had the advantage that I had served, albeit briefly, as a sailor on an Indiaman. It would help. I began to carve tiny slivers of bone and the slow and steady work seemed to calm me.

The NCOs came in and they too began to amuse themselves. At about ten o'clock the two officers returned. Even as we all began to rise the captain said, "As you were."

Major Tucker lounged laconically by the closed door and smoked a cheroot. Sergeant Grundy looked at the captain and said, "Orders, Sir? Do we know when we are leaving?"

"The horses will be delivered the day after tomorrow and that means we can leave the next morning."

We all nodded. Being back on the road might help to put the whole incident behind us. Even as the thought flicked through my mind I knew that it was not true. Until the four were dead they would haunt us. To betray your own tentmates was the most heinous of crimes.

Major Tucker blew out a plume of smoke and looked at me, "You were supposed to meet this, what was his name, Dutch Bill, today?"

My spirits rose a little, "Yes, Sir."

I caught the glimmer of a smile on Major Tucker's face and Seamus and Dai nudged each other.

"And what was the purpose of this visit?"

I calmed myself, "For my part I hoped to find out where the deserters were and for Dutch Bill's side of it I think he was going to decide whether or not to involve me."

Captain Crozier said, "And if you do not turn up?"

I shrugged, "It might be that he will assume I have found another occupation, or…"

The captain nodded, "Or he might become suspicious and return to the gang." He had his hands on the table and seemed to be smoothing out invisible creases on a tablecloth that was not there. "Major Tucker and I have been talking. We debated telling the resident about these deserters but as only you two have seen them then an assault by the garrison might harm innocent people." I did not think it would but I said nothing. I was afraid that if I spoke it might break the spell. "And if it is true then I am not sure that the garrison would emerge unscathed. These are desperate men. Although it is not a situation of our making we

believe that we are the only ones who can bring it to a
satisfactory conclusion. If you are willing, Smith, I would like
you to meet this Dutch Bill. Make up a story that while you
might wish to join him, you need to fetch your belongings. I rely
on your honesty to give a fair appraisal of the situation. If Dutch
Bill is just a minor criminal then live and let live but if he is a
confederate of Thompson and the deserters then they should be
brought to justice." He saw the grins on the faces of the rest of
the platoon. He shook his head, "Firstly, we are going to do
things legally and secondly, I only want volunteers." Every hand
went up. He laughed and shook his head, "You are all as mad as
Smith here."

I went to get changed into my outfit before he could change
his mind. John Williams would follow me this time. We would
reverse our roles. The rest of the men prepared for an illegal
sortie by our platoon. Captain Crozier insisted that we did not
wear our red coats or hats. We would leave, if my mission went
well, after dark so that we might not be noticed by the ordinary
folk of Mangalore.

I made the same approach to the tavern as I had the first time.
John Williams, minus the tricorn hat, lounged with the idlers and
smoked a pipe. I wandered into the tavern and walked straight up
to the bar. When I saw the two men seated at the same table as
the other day then I knew that Dutch Bill would be inside and if
all went well would seek me out. I bought the same drink and
stood in the same place. Sure enough he wandered over. I had
not seen where he had been and that meant he was good at hiding
in plain sight.

"Well, Bert, you returned. I am glad. We need young men like
you for our enterprise."

"I have been thinking about that. What sort of enterprise?"

He laughed and tapped his nose, "Not yet, my young friend. I
need to take you to speak to the leader of our little band. When
you have finished your drink I will take you to him."

"If I am accepted will I be staying with you?"

"Of course."

"Then I need to go back to my lodgings and collect my
belongings. I don't have much but there are some things that are
precious to me."

He frowned, "If you are not back by sunset then all bets are off."

"I will try to get back as soon as I can. You said riches beyond my wildest dreams?"

"I said as rich as a maharajah, but yes, more silver than you have ever seen in one place."

"Then I will be back!"

I downed my drink, the raw alcohol almost burning me, and headed outside. I did not try to lose my followers, not straight away, for I knew that John Williams would be watching. I had plans to lose them but this time in the market. I set off at a smart pace and did not look behind me. When I reached the market it was so busy that it was hard to find a path through it. When I was surrounded I dropped to my knee, as though I had tripped and in one move removed the patch and sailor's hat and jammed on John Williams' battered tricorn which I had secreted beneath my dirty shirt. As I rose, I turned and pulled the front of the hat down to cover a little of my face. I stooped a little and set off. I saw the two men sent to follow me. They were scanning the crowd for a sailor with an eye patch. I walked straight past them and they did not see me. When I spied John Williams I turned and headed for the barracks.

When we neared the gate I took off the hat and John walked next to me. "That was a clever trick. If it was not for the fact that I recognised the hat I would not have known you."

I waited until we were in the barracks before giving my news, "They are after the next payroll. Dutch Bill told me that it would be more silver than I had ever seen in my life. That means the payroll."

Captain Crozier nodded, "Then we leave here after sunset." We cheered. He held up his hand, "When we are at the house then no one fires until I give the command. I will not shoot down men with no warning. I will ask them to surrender."

We said nothing and, to all intents and purposes, we would attempt to heed the commands but this had been our idea and I knew, without the words being spoken, that we would ensure that the four deserters all died.

I chose to wear my sandals and the old brown breeches I had worn when sneaking into Seringapatam. I took my sailor's dirk,

169

bayonet and dagger. I would take a pistol in my belt. The trickiest part would be passing the ships and the tavern for there would be many people around. To minimise our presence we divided into two. I would lead one party and John Williams the other. To disguise our muskets we improvised what looked like crates to be loaded onto a ship. They were in fact empty boxes and the muskets were disguised as handles. Captain Crozier came with us and walked next to me. He adopted the manner and pose of an overseer. We moved as though we were carrying a heavy load and passed the first two ships. We headed for the schooner which was the last ship in the line. We were lucky, the tide would turn in an hour or so and she was loading the last of her supplies. To a watcher it would look as though we were also loading the ship while those on the schooner would be too busy to notice the lost labourers.

Once we had passed the schooner we dropped down to the sand of the beach. We moved along until we were hidden from the port and then took our muskets and loaded them. John Williams led Major Tucker and the others to join us.

Captain Crozier nodded to me, "Your show, Smith. What are your orders?"

"Major, if you go with Williams. John, head to the trail that leads to the house, the place we first watched. There is a sentry there. When you have dealt with him make your way to surround the house on the landward side. We will head to the beach side and deal with any sentries there. On the beach side we will spread out and when we are close enough the captain can call on them to surrender."

I could not see the faces in the dark and neither could the captain. He said, "I want it understood that you will all wait until I have given them the chance to surrender."

George said, "They gave poor Albert no chance, Sir."

"And that is why they will hang but if we are to do this then we do it my way."

We murmured, "Sir."

"Off you go, Major."

We all set off along the beach but when we neared the other cove Williams led his half through the trees. We had one more man than they did for I believed that they would run to the boat and we were covering the beach. The night was quiet and there was no moon. The sea lapping to our left was one sound while in the trees to our right came the noise of the night. Owls and bats flew through the trees and foxes and wild dogs hunted in the undergrowth. The smell of woodsmoke alerted us to the house and then we heard the noise of merriment. Thompson and his new gang would be enjoying themselves. They thought they were hidden. I had no idea where the horsemen were who were searching for them but they were nowhere near Mangalore.

We had to cross rocks and wade through water to reach the other cove. I did not want to risk alerting a sentry. Once around the headland we sheltered near the rocks and I pointed to the house. There was the brightness of lights spilling out but there appeared to be no one on the veranda. That had been a fear. Shadows passed before the lights. They were inside. The sound of the sea hid our voices and I said, "Once we have seen the sentry we can move up the beach." The captain nodded in the dark. "I would like to close their back door too, Sir."

"Back door?"

"Their ship. We don't want any to escape, do we, Sir?" He shook his head. "When we have the sentry I will eliminate their escape route."

Seamus pointed, "There he is, sat on that rock just below the veranda." The sentry was off to the side. He was smoking a pipe and we could see the glow.

Ben Neville handed his musket to Seamus and took out a leather sap. He patted it into his palm. "Time to pay one of them back for the lump on my head." I could guarantee that the man Ben hit would stay down. We watched the shadow that was the corporal move along the rocks and scrubby grass to our right. The sentry, whose face we could see, appeared to be watching the sea. Ben worked his way around so that he approached the man from behind. We watched with bated breath. It seemed to take an age but we had all the time in the world. When he was behind the man we saw his right hand come up and we heard the dull thud as he smacked him on the back of the head. His left hand stopped the sentry's fall and Ben laid the man to lean against the rock. He would look as though he was still watching. Ben waved to us.

I handed my musket to Aadyot and then ran across the beach. This was the most dangerous moment. If someone came from the house they might see the figure flying across the sand. The ship was tethered to the sand by a large metal spike. The tide was still coming in and the ship was moving towards me. I laid my pistol on the sand and then waded through the water. When I reached the stern I grabbed the rope and climbed aboard. I had feared that someone might be aboard but it was silent. The ship had a simple tiller attached by ropes and fixed in place. I cut the rope and then lifted the tiller. I slipped it over the side and it fell to the seabed. If they did make the ship they would not be able to sail it. I waded ashore and recovered my pistol. I waved to the captain and then made my way up the beach. I saw the rest of the section emerge from the rocks like disturbed ants. I would be in position first. I stopped just below the veranda. Aadyot joined me and handed me my musket.

The others were spread out in a line. We were kneeling and would be able to rest our forearms on our knees We would be smaller targets and be able to aim better. I was at one end and Ben Neville the other. The captain was in the middle. He hissed, "Present." We all lifted our muskets. They were primed and ready. We aimed at the veranda. The captain, satisfied we were in position, called out, "Zebediah Thompson, this is Captain Crozier. Come out with your hands up and I shall see that you have a fair trial."

A voice, I recognised it as Talbot's, snarled, "Go to hell!" and there was crack from a pistol. I saw the flash from the veranda but it was a wild, unaimed shot. It hurt no one and marked where at least one man was.

I heard Thompson's voice, it was angry, "Fire on my command, damn you."

Captain Crozier said, "Platoon, you may fire when ready!"

This was a battle of wits and I wondered if Captain Crozier, through his honourable gesture, had just handed the gang an advantage. The men inside poked their weapons through the windows. We were ready and I aimed at the barrel. I fired first and the flash from my musket lit up the porch. I heard a cry and then the night erupted in the cracks and pops of pistols and muskets. We had the slightest of advantages in that we knew they had to use the windows and the door. The building was a wooden one and if we hit the wood then, as I knew from the Indiaman, splinters could be as deadly as a direct hit. We were able to move and I did so. As soon as I fired and while I was reloading I moved five feet to my left. In the dark all one saw was the flash of a weapon. You had no idea if it was aimed at you or not. A ball flew over my head and zipped through the leaves of the tree that lay behind. I fired at a flash from a window. I could not tell if I hit anyone or not for there were cries and shots from within and without. I just did as Sergeant Grundy had taught me. I loaded and fired. I was fighting my own war.

Suddenly there was the sound of a volley from the landward side of the house. Major Tucker and the other half of the platoon had got into position and the major had ordered a volley. It was clever for it suggested more men than we actually had. The result was instantaneous. I heard Dutch Bill shout, "We are surrounded. Make for the ship."

My estimate of numbers inside the house had been a rough one and when a large number of men charged out I knew I had underestimated or they had gained more recruits in the day since I had scouted. There were fewer of us but we had one advantage, a charging man cannot aim as well as a kneeling one and that first volley from the eight of us took out six straight away. Not all would be dead but a wounded man cannot move as quickly as one who is whole. I discarded my musket and drew my pistol.

Dutch Bill was less than eight feet from me and he shouted, "You!" He raised his pistol as I raised mine and we fired, seemingly simultaneously. My shot must have been fired a heartbeat before his as he dropped his pistol as his ball flew alarmingly close to my head and he ran to the water clutching his arm. I might have run him down had not another man charged at me. It was Watts and he had his musket with a bayonet attached. I threw my pistol at him and then dived to the sand before him. The pistol hit his shoulder and distracted him enough to make him fall over my body. I whipped out my dagger and as he fell stabbed at his leg. The blade was sharp and ripped through his breeches and flesh. He screamed and tried to club me with the stock of his musket. I moved my head to the side and slashed with the dagger. I was lucky and the edge sliced though the back of his hand. He threw the musket at me and took off, limping, to follow Dutch Bill.

He was going to escape and then I heard the crack of a musket and Watts fell. Aadyot nodded, "That is one deserter dead, Smudger."

After sticking my bloody dagger in my belt I picked up and reloaded my musket. Some of the platoon were racing down the beach to catch Dutch Bill and those trying to reach the ship while Captain Crozier had taken the rest into the house. I could hear the pops of weapons and see the flash from musket and pistol. The night was punctuated with cries and shouts. Aadyot ran into the house as I reloaded my pistol too. It was as I did so that I saw a figure slip away to the trees on my left. I jammed the pistol in my belt and followed the figure. It was foolish I know for I was alone but the man, whoever he was, thought he had escaped and if I shouted for assistance then he would know he was being pursued. He was hard to see for he was a shadow in the dark and I did not want to risk missing. I followed the movements of the shadow. The man was clearly heading somewhere, but where? I moved silently as I closed with the figure. All that I knew was that it was a man and he had a musket. He could have been one of the original smugglers in which case he would know this part of the world well.

I caught a glimpse, through the trees, of the sea. It was another cove. Soon I would see him and have the chance of a shot. I moved steadily for he kept turning. When the figure reached the beach he turned. All I saw was the flash of a white face and when I saw it I froze. It was Zebediah Thompson. I raised my musket and aimed at his back. He was one hundred yards away but I was confident that I could hit him. I was about to squeeze the trigger when he did something unexpected. He laid down his musket and began to pace. I took a breath and my finger from the trigger. The man was unarmed. I was about to shout for him to surrender when I stopped myself. What was he doing here? It was at that moment I saw the dory drawn up on the beach. He had another means of escape. He had deserted the platoon and now he was abandoning those who thought they were his friends. He began to dig. I was a thief and I had done just as he had. I had buried my treasure. He was digging up the payroll.

I was about to shout out when, from behind me, I heard Jack shout, "Smudger, are you here, we have them all."

Thompson had quick reactions. In one move he had pulled and fired a pistol at Jack. Even as I raised my musket and fired I heard the cry that told me that Jack had been hit. Thompson spun around and dropped to one knee. I had hit him. I let go of my musket and drew my pistol. As much as I wanted to go to the aid of the young soldier I could not let this last rat have the chance to escape.

"It's over, Zebediah!"

"Not yet it is not!" He grabbed a bag of silver and ran to the dory.

He had a start of one hundred yards. If he could launch the small boat then he had a chance to escape. I ran. The sand sucked at my feet. It was as though I was running in slow motion. I took heart from the fact that Thompson had the same problem and he was wounded, carrying silver. He reached the dory when I was still twenty paces from him. He threw the bag in the dory and was pulling the dory into the water. He was a cunning and clever man. He was using the dory to protect him. I stood stock still and levelled the pistol. I used my left hand to support it and I aimed at his middle. There was a loud crack and I was temporarily blinded by the flash. When I looked up I could not see him. I drew my bayonet and walked to the small boat. I saw the coins inside and I moved along the side to the front. Thompson was still holding the painter, his body moving with the tide. He had blood pouring from his chest. He spat, "I should have slit your throat back at the camp instead of Wishart. You…" He got no further.

I grabbed the collar of his coat and dragged him up the beach beyond the high-water mark. He was going nowhere. I went back for the bag of silver and then ran to my musket. I picked it up and shouted, "Jack!"

I was relieved when I heard his shout of, "Here, Smudger."

I found him sat on a tree branch and tying a bandage around his leg. "He just nicked me. Did you get him?"

I nodded and held up the bag, "And the payroll too. Come on, I will help you back to the others."

By the time we made our way back to the house, dawn was breaking in the east. Anxious faces were looking for us in the darkness to the west as Jack and I emerged from the trees.

There was a cheer and Seamus said, "I told you Smudger would be alright. He is a lucky bugger."

I saw Captain Crozier having his arm bandaged and said, "Did we lose any men, Sir?"

He shook his head, "No, but four, five counting Grey here are wounded and Thompson escaped along with the payroll."

I held up the bag, "No Sir, here is the payroll and Zebediah Thompson is on the next beach. He is dead."

Major Tucker laughed, "Smith, you are either the luckiest soldier in the East India Company or the best."

Sergeant Grundy said, "I think he is both, Major. I am damned glad that he is one of us."

I felt myself grow at the fulsome praise. Once more the thoughts of flight and escape receded. How could I leave this band of brothers?

Just then I heard a neigh and knew that it was Froggy. I hurried along to an outbuilding and found the two horses there. The recovery of Froggy and Duchess was as important to me as the payroll.

Chapter 14

Not all the gang had died. The four deserters had, thankfully, all perished along with another six of Zeb Thompson's command. The others, there were ten of them, were either wounded, as in the case of Dutch Bill, or simply surrendered. We marched them to the residency and we watched them while the two officers went inside with the payroll and the details of what we had found. Our wounded, four of them, were taken to the barracks' infirmary. We did not let the prisoners out of our sight. None of their injuries were life threatening.

Dutch Bill glared at me, "You have no honour, you rat."

I laughed, "A smuggler and a killer of men calls me dishonourable." Shaking my head I said, "I outwitted you and I am proud of that, Dutch Bill."

He could not help talking, "When you did not return, Zebediah was suspicious and when I described you he said he thought he knew who it was." He grinned, "He planned on having you gutted like a pig and fed to the fishes. How I would have liked to see that."

"But he did not and if you want to speak of honour, you fled your men and your leader sought to save his own life and make off with the payroll. I will sleep easier at night. You will have haunted dreams until you are hanged."

"I will not be hanged for I have not committed a capital offence." He was a clever man who had survived many years on his wits. I wondered at that. Was he a picture of what I might have become had I not fled Ralph Every? I wondered if the weasel would escape. That was out of my hands. We had done what we had set out to do. We had even recovered the muskets and uniforms from the deserters. No one would want to wear the uniforms again but neither did we want them disgraced by criminals.

The two officers were inside for two hours and when they came out they were with a captain from the Bombay European Regiment who would take charge of the prisoners. As they were shackled and led away I voiced my fears to the captain, "Dutch

Bill might escape punishment. He says there is no crime we can
pin on him."

Major Tucker answered, "Ah, that is where you are wrong,
you see, he made the mistake of registering his ownership both
of the house and the ship when Thompson slew the previous
owner, the leader of the smugglers and pirates. There is enough
evidence to link both the ship and the house with smuggling and
piracy. The owner of the tavern will, no doubt, talk when he is
questioned. Those kind of rats rarely go down with a sinking
ship. They will all hang. Many were known to the resident. They
had been using the house as a hideout. He is pleased and he will
send the rest of the payroll and this time it will be with a strong
escort. General Wellesley will know the truth."

Captain Crozier placed a hand on my shoulder, "And, Smith,
I mentioned your idea that they planned to take the payroll. The
resident is going to increase the escort from a platoon to a full
company. I do not think the regiments that will have to endure
the duty will thank you but the East India Company is grateful.
And now, we have a day of rest before the horses arrive
tomorrow and we can plan our next journey."

Sergeant Grundy said, "What about the wounded, Sir?"

"That is out of our hands, Sergeant. If the doctor deems them
fit enough to travel then they can come, otherwise they will have
to await our return."

In the event all four wounded were in the barracks by the time
we returned. Dai, John Williams and George were old hands and
knew that if they were not passed fit then they would be forced
to stay in Mangalore. They play acted well enough to be passed
fit and Jack's wound was just a scratch. I was glad. It meant we
would all be together and that gave me comfort.

When the horses came we discovered that they were all in a
poor condition. Froggy was a thoroughbred in comparison. I
knew why we had been given them. We needed to move faster
than men on foot. I asked the captain if I could ride Froggy and
my star was high enough for him to accede. Sergeant Grundy
appeared not to mind. Any horse would suit him. I then made the
suggestion that Aadyot should ride Duchess. He knew her and
she was as gentle a horse as there could be. The mules would be
used to carry our tents. The poorest two horses that had been sent

would also be used as pack horses. I was given the task of fitting the panniers and working out how best to load them while Captain Crozier and Major Tucker gave riding lessons to the others. As I was adjusting the panniers that had been sent with the horses I had to hide a smile for none of the horses were large and Seamus' feet almost touched the ground. I heard him joke, "Sure and it might be easier if I carried this wee beastie under my arm."

The lessons took all day and even by the end they all looked as though the horses were being ridden by sacks of grain. The saddles were also not the best and we had to improvise some means of fastening the muskets to them. In the end it proved so difficult that Captain Crozier decided that we would be better off with the muskets slung over our backs.

The day after the lesson the two officers went to the residency to receive their final orders. We went to the quartermaster to pick up our supplies. Aadyot and I went with him. While the two of them made their request, I did what I do best, I stole. I found where they kept the oats and the root vegetables. Horses like carrots and I had learned that they helped to bribe an uncooperative animal. The oats were needed to fatten up the horses. I managed to slip into the warehouse, unseen and take the two sacks, one larger than the other. I then went outside to the cart and mules we had brought to carry the supplies. I placed them on the bottom and had them covered before anyone could see. I then stood stroking the mules' ears while I waited for the other two. There were more oats but they were for us, as well as wheat flour and some barley. We also had salt beef, salt mutton and salt pork as well as tea. The meat would last a month or more but we knew we would have to augment our rations on the road. I hoped that the two officers had been given money to spend on the road otherwise we would have to forage and hunt. We also had onions and garlic. They would last for the whole journey and add flavour to otherwise tasteless food. We had sacks of salt too. What the quartermaster did not supply were the spices that we had become accustomed to. Aadyot would visit the market and buy some from there.

When the officers returned they held a meeting with the other officers and we packed the food so that if something happened to one animal we would not starve. Each mule and horse had a mixture of meat, grain, pots, spare powder, balls and tents. Our blankets would be carried on our horses along with our powder. We would be laden when we rode but at least we would be saving our boots and make the journey quicker. We enjoyed our penultimate meal in the mess. From now on we would be cooking for ourselves. There was beer in the mess and we made the most of that. We all took in a spare canteen. When we had taken the deserters the four canteens we had recovered would be reused as would the ones from the other men who had died. We wasted nothing. We surreptitiously filled the canteens with beer. It was not for the alcohol but it was better than any water we might find. When that ran out we could use cold tea.

Back in our barracks we prepared for our last night under a roof. Sergeant Grundy and the two corporals came in. "Right lads, we now know what we have to do. Three of the maharajas have fought a battle, north of here, at Poona. The Peshwa, the Prime Minister, was on the losing side and our job is to find him and Major Tucker is going to offer him an alliance with the company and Great Britain. That is not for us to worry about. We have to extract him from the clutches of Yashwant Rao Holkar. He was the maharajah who won the battle."

Seamus said, "So he might be a prisoner already?"

"He might be but Major Tucker does not think so."

Dai asked, "What will the weather be like?" It was a good question. If it was the rainy season then we would never be dry and risk all sorts of diseases.

"The rainy season in the area we are going is from June to September but it will be hot as Hades." It meant we had missed the rain but the roads would still be muddy. We would never be clean.

"What do we do when we have him? Fight all his enemies?"

"Lord Mornington has sent an East India Company ship, *Herculean*; she will be sailing along the coast and then up the Ulhas River where she will moor as far upstream as she can. She will wait for us. When we have him we head north for the river. We make contact with the ship and she will take him and us to safety."

To me that sounded more than a little vague. The ship might sail up and down the river searching for us but I had been a sailor long enough to know that the winds might mean she could be well out to sea when we needed her. She might reach the rendezvous and be forced to leave for a whole raft of reasons. It would be a challenge but we would be working on our own again and our platoon had shown that we had skills.

We left Mangalore in better spirits than we had arrived. We would never forget Albert but we had avenged his death. It had also made us stronger. Tom and Jack had now fought alongside us. They had the scars of battle that were badges of honour.

We had to pass the house on our way north. The resident had commandeered it and there was an armed guard at the end of the trail that led to it. I was intrigued. Was the resident using it for the company or was there another motive? I had long ago ceased worrying about the actions of those who were my superiors. The resident's plans would have nothing to do with me for I was leaving Mangalore and it was unlikely that I would return. When we passed a piece of high ground that afforded a view of the cove I saw that there was no longer a boat in the cove. That too had been taken by the resident.

This mission felt different to all the other ones we had undertaken. It was not just that we had lost comrades, it was the very nature of it. We were rescuing an important man. We were travelling through a land where the people were divided about the outcome. Whilst most supported the Peshwa there were others who wanted a stronger leader. The land of the Marathas was a vast one and the people who lived on its borders were as different as a Scotsman from a Londoner. It meant that, as we progressed north, we found out more and more. I was still the one, Aadyot apart, who had the skills to speak to the people and, I would like to think, the right manner and attitude. I always apologised for the limitations in my words and that seemed to make the conversations easier.

While the Peshwa and his allies had lost the battle of Poona, the losses on both sides had not been huge. It meant that the war still continued. It explained why the Peshwa had not yet been taken. When I reported to the two officers I was privy to their deliberations and thoughts on the matter. We were close to the

Portuguese enclave of Goa when we heard that the whereabouts of the Peshwa was in doubt. The best guess was that he was to be found at Wadgaon. That town lay far to the north of us. Major Tucker thought that might be where he would take refuge. "The place is famous for its Jain and Potoba Maharaj temples and Mhadaji shinde garden. It is also where, in the First Maratha War, the East India Company was defeated. Baji Rao was a boy then but such things linger in the memory."

Captain Crozier said, "How far away is it?"

"Three hundred miles."

The captain snorted, "Then it is closer to Bombay. Why don't they send men from there?"

The major sighed, "Captain, we have been sent by two men, Lord Mornington and Major General Wellesley. Both are ambitious men and they do not want the resident of Bombay to take the credit for this. Besides which, both men know the skills of this platoon."

"We are, in effect, their private army."

The major laughed, "I suppose so. You and your men have shown that despite your rough edges, you get the job done." The captain did not look convinced and the major added quietly, "Be honest, Dick, you enjoy being away from the shackles of men like General Harris, do you not?"

The captain nodded, "I suppose so. What if the Peshwa moves? Perhaps he is not even there."

The major put his arm around my shoulder, "Then the redoubtable Smith will, no doubt, find him for us. This soldier has the nose of a bloodhound."

We set off and soon entered Maratha land. General Wellesley was still eliminating the supporters of Dhondia Wagh but it did mean that there was an army close to us and we could use that as a refuge if we managed to take the Prime Minister.

The enemy were looking for him too as well as doing what all victors of battles enjoy, they were raiding and riding at will. We were close to Chik Kodi when we encountered some of the Holkar horsemen. Corporal Neville and Eddie Lowe were the scouts. The first week had seen most of the platoon master the riding of horses. We were riding along a tree lined carthen road when they suddenly galloped back towards us.

"Horsemen! There are thirty or more of them."

We had fought the Warlord Dhondia Wagh and knew that the idea of freebooting warlords was not a new one in this part of the world. In war there is chaos and warlords can exploit such disorder. Captain Crozier took no chances. We were infantry and not cavalry. The captain wanted us to fight as foot soldiers. "Dismount. Finn, Grey and Ganguly, you will be horse holders. The rest load and prime your muskets. Single rank. Fix bayonets too." The loading and the priming were easy enough but once we fitted the long bayonet then the muskets became heavier. The horsemen would have to be very close for us to stand any chance of hitting them.

We heard the thundering of the hooves but we were well practised at what we did and by the time they turned the bend and saw us we had ten muskets and two pistols at the ready. They were not yet aimed at the approaching horsemen but it would take the merest of moments to raise them.

The horsemen reined in. They had lances but I saw that some had scabbards and what looked like carbines. Ben had been right, there were thirty-two of them, a troop. They were irregulars for they wore their own clothes. Some were vain for they wore expensive looking turbans and tunics while others wore more functional clothes. Their leader had no lance but he had a curved sabre hanging from his saddle and I saw a brace of pistols. They stopped just thirty yards from us. They were close enough for us to smell them and to hear the snorting of their horses which stamped their hooves.

"Smith."

"Sir."

"Tell him who we are. Say we are heading for Bombay and wish no trouble."

I handed my musket to Seamus and walked forward. I bowed and put my hands together. I did not know what particular dialect or language the leader spoke but I had learned that there were enough similar words in all the languages to enable communication. I had learned to use the simplest of phrases.

"We are men of the East India Company and we are heading for Bombay. We wish you no harm."

The man's lips curled in the slightest of smiles and he nodded. He spoke in English, "It is good that you show us respect and try to speak our language but know that we do not need foreigners here. Maharajah Yashwant Rao Holkar has taken control of this land. The Peshwa will be offered his protection and once that is done then we will drive you Englishmen from our land. Turn and leave. We will let you live."

As he had spoken English my skills were no longer needed and I stepped back into line and took my musket. Major Tucker walked forward, "We cannot do that. We are bound for Bombay and wish you no harm."

I had been a soldier long enough to learn how to read signs. I caught the slightest of gestures from this chief. I saw the lances being slowly lowered. No matter what the words spoken, this chief intended violence. If we turned our backs and obeyed then we would be ridden down like deer.

The chief smiled and spread his arms, "Then do as I ask. We outnumber you and if I drop this hand then you will all die. My men would like that for your muskets are prized but I am in a kind and generous mood. I give you your lives. Turn and live. Stand and die."

Captain Crozier hissed, "Stand by." He was far more experienced than I was and if I had seen the signs then I knew that he had too.

Just as the horsemen were preparing their lances and, no doubt, readying to spur their horses so we began to raise, albeit slowly, our muskets.

The major smiled and gave an elaborate bow. I knew what he was doing. He was readying his pistol, "I am afraid I cannot do that."

The hand came down and the horsemen charged. They were confident that their lances would soon destroy us but they had not counted on two things. One was that the trees narrowed the frontage that they could use. The second was that we were not afraid. We had twelve weapons that could fire as one. The two officers had a second pistol each and we could reload quickly. We would not bother with a ramrod, just drop a ball and bang the musket on the ground. It was not the regulatory method of reloading but it would work.

The Tiger and the Thief

"Fire!"

We raised and fired our weapons almost as one. The air before us filled with smoke as twelve balls scythed through men and horses. I had my weapon reloaded quickly. I heard the screams of the horses and men as they were struck. I raised my musket as the lance came, seemingly at my head. I fired and then flicked my musket and bayonet to the side. It deflected the lance and the flash terrified the horse which reared and then veered to my right. I had no time to load a second time as another lance and horse came at me. The swirling smoke must have made us harder to see for the lance was too high. I lunged at the horse with my bayonet. I struck its chest and it, too, veered to my right but its body and the leg of the warrior hit me and knocked me to the ground. If another horseman saw me then I was a dead man. Smoke swirled and there seemed to be a mass of horses still before us.

"Cease fire!"

Seamus, grinning, reached down and offered me a mighty mitt to pull me up, "Sure and aren't you a lucky little bugger."

"Reload!" Sergeant Grundy was an old hand and we all obeyed him.

As the smoke cleared I saw that the horse I had bayoneted was on the ground and writhing. The other horses had wandered off. The warrior was trapped beneath the horse I had stabbed. Dai went over and put a ball in the head of the stricken animal. He shouted, "I think this poor sod has a broken back."

Sergeant Grundy shouted, "Put him out of his misery."

Dai's bayonet ended the warrior's pain. The survivors had fled. The chief and what looked like his two subordinate officers both lay dead. There were four horses walking disconsolately around and ten of the warriors, including the one slain by Dai and the three officers, lay dead.

The major said, "I don't think they will bother us again."

Captain Crozier was reloading his pistols and asked, "Anyone hurt?"

Sergeant Grundy came over to me, "You get hurt in that fall, Smith?"

"No, Sarge."

"No one hurt, Sir."

185

"Right, Grey and Finn collect the loose horses. Clear the bodies into the ditch and then we move as soon as that is done."

We were the masters of scavenging and as we cleared the bodies we took everything of value. Seamus had the best reward for he stripped the body of the chief. There were rings and medallions not to mention a purse. No one objected for we all knew that he would share the bounty. The carbines were poor weapons and fired a smaller ball than we used. We left them but made sure that they would be unusable. We took the swords.

Aadyot hacked some joints from the dead horse. Meat was meat and it would augment our salted rations. It took an hour to clear the field and then we headed north once more. This time we were even warier than we had been.

We enjoyed four days without firing our muskets or encountering more problems like the warlord chief. We sought information at every village but all we heard was that while the Peshwa was still free he was being hunted and that the hunters were also looting the land as they passed through. Holkar lay many hundreds of miles to the north and the warriors and soldiers seeking the Peshwa neither knew nor cared about the people ruled by the Peshwa.

We heard the sound of screams coming from the village ahead and stopped. Major Tucker said, "Smith, come with me."

"Sir."

I dug my heels into Froggy and we set off down the road. I had a loaded pistol slung around my neck. If danger came then I would simply grab and fire it quickly. The noise grew louder and a small boy ran into view. He looked to be about seven or eight, I found it hard to judge for they all looked to be smaller than English children. The horseman who galloped behind him had a sword and he leaned from the saddle to swing it at the back of the boy's head. I just reacted. I grabbed and cocked the pistol and prayed that it was primed. I fired. The flash and then the bang made the warrior's horse veer and the boy dived to the ground. The ball struck the warrior in the shoulder and must have driven deep into his flesh for he fell from the saddle.

The major reined in. We had not heard the sound of either muskets or pistols and my shot, whilst it had saved the boy's life, had warned whoever was raiding Sangli, that there were soldiers close by. He smiled, "Nobly done, Smudger, but I fear that we will now be involved whether we wish to or not. Back to the platoon."

"Sorry, Sir."

I looked down but the boy had disappeared. He had been inches away from death but thanks were the last thing on his mind, he just wanted to survive.

The shot had been heard and the platoon were dismounted behind a wall of horses. The muskets rested on their backs.

The major said, simply, "Raiders, attacking the village ahead. Smith shot one but I think we will have company and I suspect they will not bother to talk."

We both dismounted and I unslung my musket. I stood on Froggy's reins and hoped that my horse would not pull. A half dozen horsemen burst around the corner and seeing the muskets and horses turned and fled. Captain Crozier was a soldier while Major Tucker was a mixture between spy and diplomat. The captain took charge. "Into the trees. Tie the horses up and take cover."

None of us questioned the order nor asked what was in the captain's mind. We trusted him. We hurried into the trees. Aadyot, Tom and Jack had the captured horses with them as well as the mules. They would be the slowest to join us. I tied Froggy up and hurried back to the trees lining the road. I laid my musket by the tree and reloaded my pistol. I had another but I knew I might need more than one loaded weapon. When I had loaded all my firearms I fitted my bayonet.

Aadyot and the other two took their places next to me. Tom and Jack looked nervous. I smiled, "Whoever comes down this road are not as good as us. They are attacking civilians. The man I shot was going to split open the head of a little boy."

They nodded. I knew that, like me, their mouths would be dry and they would want to either make water or empty their bowels. It always happened that way. As soon as the action was over the need would disappear.

We heard the noise of the men as they approached. They were on foot and came as a mob. There were too many to estimate but they filled the road. I had time to observe them as I raised my musket. Many had bloodstained clothes. They had a variety of bladed weapons including axes, curved scimitars and even large sledgehammers. I suspect the captain was going to let them pass but one of them spied us and shouted something. It might have been a war cry but I did not recognise the word. As one they turned and ran towards us.

Sergeant Grundy was calmness personified as he shouted, "Present! Fire!"

This time we had every musket and pistol firing and the wall of lead scythed into the leading ranks. The balls we fired were at relatively close range and some went through bodies to hit those behind. I had seen such wounds at Mallavelli and knew that when the ball hit one body it flattened slightly so that when it struck the second man it did not penetrate far but would make a hole the size of a child's fist. One ball could hurt two men. I held my musket in my left hand and aimed my pistol into the fog of smoke. It was on a lanyard and when it was discharged, I dropped it and fired my second. A face appeared before me and I grabbed my musket and parried away the sword that was swung at my head. Sparks flew as the metal blades screeched and scratched against one another. The advantage I held was that my musket was longer than his sword and as I had swept his blade to my right then by back slashing at him as he raced to get at me, I was able to rake his face and shoulder with my bayonet. He screamed, dropped the sword and put his hands to his face to stem the tide of blood. I pulled back and rammed the bayonet at the man. The others had reloaded and I quickly did so and then raised the musket. The warrior was dead. The next man whose face loomed up out of the gun smoke was so close that he almost ran into my bayonet. I fired and the ball hit his face and exploded the back of his skull to shower the men behind.

Seamus and Dai were screaming Irish and Welsh curses while our Scotsman, Bob Cathcart was screaming his clan's war cry. This was war at its most ancient and basic. We were two sets of warriors fighting not for land but survival. I reloaded and was aware that suddenly there was no one before me.

"Reload!" Sergeant Grundy's voice was reassuringly calm.

Captain Crozier said, "Ganguly, Finn and Grey, guard the horses. The rest of you, mount."

As we left the trees I saw the bodies littering the road. One or two moved but from the puddling blood they would be dead by the time we returned. Captain Crozier and Major Tucker led with pistols in their hands. I saw two more men who must have been wounded in the fight. They had made it forty yards down the road before succumbing to their wounds. The two officers slowed as we neared the village.

Captain Crozier shouted, "Smith, investigate, we will cover you."

"Sir!" I had a pistol drawn and I walked Froggy towards the villagers who were tending to their own wounded. I reined in next to a white-haired man whose head had been laid open. He had a long reed streak of blood but he was tending to a young girl whose leg was bleeding.

"We are East India Company soldiers. We are here to help."

He looked up and smiled, "You are the ones with the guns?" I nodded. "Then we are in your debt. We would all have died but for your arrival. They have fled for they are like jackals."

"Who were they?"

He spat, "Men from Holkar. We had no warriors here, they are with the Peshwa. They came for plunder and for our women. Thanks to you they failed. You and your soldiers are welcome here." He stood as a woman finished the bandaging, "We would like you to stay, at least until morning. By then we will have buried our dead and be ready to repel them if they return."

I nodded, "Captain Crozier." The two officers rode over and I told them what had been said.

He nodded, "Of course. Sergeant Grundy, have the horses brought up and set up a line of sentries at the two ends of the village."

"Sir."

"Major, if you and Smith would scout out and make sure that they have gone I would appreciate it."

"Of course. Come along, Smith. Duty calls."

I was more than a little nervous as we left the village and headed north. I knew that it was necessary. We had to travel north and the last thing we needed was to run into the remnants of this band. There was a river to the west of the road and the undergrowth had been cleared to make fields. It allowed us to rein in a mile north of the village and spy ahead. We saw the survivors. There looked to be forty or so men. In my view that was more than enough to take us.

The major took out his telescope and viewed them. He nodded, seemingly satisfied, "They will not bother us again."

"Sir, they still outnumber us."

He turned his horse and shook his head, "They have left a good number behind and I saw wounded amongst them. Men like that seek easy victories. An undefended village promises plunder but a platoon of East India soldiers means they are likely to lose. Come, we can return and enjoy the hospitality of the village and, perhaps, garner news."

Chapter 15

We shared our food with the villagers and they shared what they knew. Their information was marginally more reliable as their men were away fighting for the Peshwa. The Peshwa was still north of us but he had taken refuge at the hill fort of Sinhagad. The good news was that it was closer to us than the place we had heard he was hiding. We only had another one hundred and thirty miles to travel. We were within three days of the man we had been sent to rescue. We learned of the other leaders there with him. Chimnaji, Baloji, and Balaji Kunjar were all generals but Chimnaji and Balaji Kunjar did not like the English. When he learned this the major made a note in his notebook. Our job was to get the major to the Peshwa. His job was to persuade him to ally his land to Great Britain and the East India Company and he needed as much information as possible to do so. We learned a great deal from the wounded headman not least that Maharaja Yashwant Rao Holkar was a very able general who had defeated a larger combined army already. There was respect from the headman who, we learned, had been a warrior in his youth and had fought the British. He knew about able generals.

It was while we were there that the major told us a little more about the man we were sent to rescue. He was not a popular leader. His family had become the rulers of Gwalior through, according to the headman, the murder of the previous incumbent. Although Baji Rao was not thought to have had a hand in it he was tainted by the deed. Daulat Rao Scindia was the real ruler of the land and he had brought the larger part of the army that had been defeated. That Baji Rao had been abandoned told us much about the man and I wondered if this rescue was necessary. He did not seem to be popular.

I asked the major about that and he smiled, "Lord Mornington wishes to have the legitimate ruler of the land of the Marathas as his guest and if we can save his life and preserve his authority then we have the chance to control even larger parts of India. That keeps the East India Company in profit and British interests safer. As you know General Bonaparte and the French

Republicans have their eyes on the riches that are to be found in India. Politics, Private Smith, are complicated in this part of the world. If we can exploit the divisions then our people will be safer."

By safer he meant more profits for the company and more land to be ruled by Britain. All I knew was that to keep those people safe then soldiers like Emund Byers would have to be sacrificed and I wondered if it was worth it.

We moved north as fast as we could but ever mindful of the two fights we had endured. We had been lucky to avoid casualties but nothing could be taken for granted. The horses we had taken were better than the ones we had been given and it meant we moved slightly faster than we might have done. Being as close as we were to our destination we spent longer in the saddle to make the most of daylight and reach the hillfort that would mark the end of this part of our journey.

I worked out that it was the start of November when we passed though the last village before the hillfort which rose ahead of us. I could see, even with my novice's eye, that it was a good place to defend and explained why the Peshwa had not wanted to move from it. With the two thousand soldiers who, allegedly, remained to him he would be able to defend it easily. We camped so that we could look, once again, like soldiers. We put away the straw hats and donned our regulation headgear. We brushed as much as we could from our tunics and our boots were polished.

We left the next morning and as we neared the road that wound up to the top, the sun obliged by reflecting from our shiny boots and newly polished buttons. The defenders would know we were English by our red coats. Would they regard us as friends or foes? The major was confident it would be the former.

The road that wound up the slope of the hill fort told me that if an enemy wished to take this then they would have to be prepared to bleed and lose many men to do so. If the walls were manned then huge numbers would be slain before they even reached the gates. Both our officers were certain that we would be welcomed but I saw few smiling faces manning the walls above us.

When we were admitted, I breathed a sigh of relief. However, when the gates slammed behind us I knew that this could be a prison as well as a refuge. The official who greeted us was able to speak English and we were allowed to put our horses in an open area where they could graze. I saw a large herd of horses already there. There were many buildings and a smaller palace but there was also an area of grass. It could be used for grazing but, if needed, then a large army could camp there. It looked to be an ancient refuge for many people. The headman had told us that two thousand men were still with the Peshwa. I saw evidence of, perhaps, two hundred horsemen. I had counted another hundred or so on the walls. If you trebled the men who manned the walls, the foot soldiers, then you would still only have five or six hundred men still with the Peshwa. Where were the rest?

We were allocated an open area for our tents. Even the officers would have to use the tents. As we erected them I reflected that our welcome was not as fulsome as we might have hoped. The welcome of the village had been warm and we had shared food with the villagers. Here we were allowed to use the well and that was all. I saw that, on the walls, there were more men watching our camp than were on the other walls. We were not, it appeared, trusted. As I had with Jahan Chalan's hill fort, my natural reaction was to look for ways out. There was a gate within a hundred yards of us. When I saw it my fears eased slightly mainly because we had a quick way out if things turned ugly but also because it explained the reason for so many watchers being this close to us.

I was helping Aadyot to cook the food when Sergeant Grundy came over. He took the ladle from me, "Smarten yourself up, Smith, the captain wants you to go with him and the major when they are taken indoors."

"Me, Sarge?"

He smiled, "Eyes and ears, boy; you have sharp ones. Use 'em."

I brushed my tunic and adjusted my belts. The only weapons I would have would be my dirk hidden beneath my tunic and my bayonet, hanging from its frog. I gave my boots a quick rub but it was hardly a polish. The dust climbing to the fort had taken the

shine from them. I presented myself to the two officers. They
had their swords hanging from their belts and both had donned
their good jackets. It was the first time since we had packed them
at Mangalore that they had done so. It was the major who spoke,
"Now, Smith, you know the drill. The eyes of those within will
be on the two of us, the officers. You will be ignored. Feign
ignorance of any words you hear and adopt a dumb expression."

"Sir." I had done this many times as a thief and now almost as
many times in the service of the king and the company. I knew
how to keep an expressionless face that would make people
misjudge me.

"You are there to do as you did at Oudh. Look for the things
we might miss."

"Sir."

I walked two steps behind them as they headed for the main
building. I suppose it might have been a palace once but it was
nothing compared with the one we had seen in Lucknow. This
was a refuge. The rulers of this land wanted to be comfortable.
The men who guarded this lesser palace were both well dressed
and well-armed. Baji Rao was, in effect, King of India and the
men in the palace were his bodyguards. When they saw us
approach, I watched their eyes as they assessed both our
weaponry and our demeanour. I saw the looks of derision when
they viewed me. I was skinny and slight in comparison with
them. I did not look like a threat. Had the officers brought
Seamus then they would have seen a warrior who looked
dangerous. He looked like a fierce tiger and I looked like a
mouse. I helped with the illusion by moving closer to the officers
as though I feared for my safety.

We were led along cool corridors to the main hall. The fort
itself was cooler, because of its height, than the low ground
through which we had passed. I could see why the rulers of this
land had chosen it as a residence. It was bearable. The doors to
the hall were guarded and we were made to wait while a warrior
went within. He was inside for some moments before we were
admitted.

I had been in enough palaces to recognise certain features.
Seringapatam and Oudh both had a raised dais with a throne and
the ruler sat upon it. There were always bodyguards flanking the

ruler and usually the important advisor stood close by. Baji Rao was no exception. Another figure, as richly dressed as the Peshwa, stood next to him. Both men had rings hanging from their ears and were adorned with jewelled and golden medallions and rings. The rulers of this land liked to display their wealth. I also saw something else that drew my eye and piqued my interest. There were two Europeans. They were standing in the shadows and I could not make out their features but they were most definitely not from this land. It was too dark to make out their uniforms as clearly as I would have liked but bearing in mind the attempt on our lives in Oudh it was, I thought, an important discovery.

I watched the faces around as the major spoke, "I am Major Tucker and Lord Mornington has sent me here in response to your request for sanctuary. We can, if you still wish it, take you to safety where your enemies will not be able to reach you."

I expected the man to smile and accept the offer. After all, according to the major he had requested the rescue.

He frowned, "But what price would the British ask, Major. My advisor," he gestured to the well-dressed man next to him, "Balaji Kunjar, tells me that the price to be paid for my safety might be the land of Gwalior." I now knew the name of the man who stood at his side. "When your General Wellesley defeated the Warlord, Dhondia Wagh, he offered to give me sanctuary but we declined the offer. This hill fort is impregnable and I am not certain that I should leave it."

Balaji Kunjar nodded and spoke for the first time. His English was not as good as the Peshwa, "It is what I told you, Peshwa, the British wish to rule this land and if you are their guest then you would be, in effect, their prisoner."

There was silence and I wondered what the major would do next. We had travelled a long way, it seemed, to be turned away. What would we do? The **Herculean** was waiting off the coast or on the river and I supposed that we would board and be returned to Mangalore or Bombay.

"May I speak frankly to you, Peshwa?"

The ruler of the Maratha Confederation nodded, "Although that would be a first, to hear something that might actually be the truth from the British."

Ignoring the barb the major went on, "We have travelled many miles through the land you rule, Peshwa, and we have had to fight off warlords and bands of soldiers who are raiding and ravaging with impunity. The platoon who escorted me had to drive off one such warband who had attacked the village of Sangli." I saw two of the soldiers at the side glance at each other. They were from that village. "You do not control the land that lies within a hundred miles of this hillfort and I have not seen evidence of an army that could face Maharajah Yeshwant Rao Holkar."

Balaji Kunjar became angry, "We do not need the British to offer us assistance. There are others who will happily supply guns and soldiers."

In contrast to the anger of the advisor Major Tucker was calmness personified, "The French perhaps? And what would they demand, Peshwa? Lord Mornington just wishes to offer you sanctuary and safety away from your enemies. If you do not wish an alliance then Lord Mornington will honour that decision. I have no treaty for you to sign. I just offer you the chance to come with us and escape your enemies." He paused, "Or you could wait here until Maharajah Yeshwant Rao Holkar brings his army and takes this hillfort and makes you his prisoner. You might still be Peshwa but of a land ruled by Holkar."

I saw the frown crease the face of the Peshwa. His advisor shook his head, "Once they have you in the lands of the East India Company, Peshwa, you will be their hostage."

The Peshwa looked at his advisor and I saw doubt written all over it. "I need time to think. Return in the morning when I have had the time to digest both this news and my food. I will seek advice from all my advisors and I will make a decision then." I saw the two Europeans move. They left the room.

"And whatever decision you make, Peshwa, will be agreeable to us. We have been sent to take you to safety. That is our only intention. If you decline our offer then we will leave and head to Bombay."

He bowed. The captain and I emulated him and turned smartly to leave. We were escorted back to our camp. No one said a word until we reached it. Captain Crozier said, "Sergeant, have the sentries ensure that we cannot be overheard."

"Sir."

I saw that there were horse guards near to the other horses. While I doubted that they would understand what we said, it was a wise precaution.

The two officers sat on the camp stools we used. I stood and waited. I would be consulted but only once they had spoken. As the major lit a cheroot the captain said, "Not the welcome I expected, Geoffrey."

"I know. I think that Balaji Kunjar has his own plans. He clearly mistrusts us. The other advisors were pro-British."

"And they were clearly not there."

"Quite. We will have to wait and see. I confess that I do not know which way he will jump. I should so hate to return to his lordship with the news that we had failed."

I knew that Major Tucker was looking for more advancement. We were the tool he was using.

"Smith, what did you see?"

"Well, there are soldiers in the hillfort from Sangli. I saw their faces when you mentioned the attack on the village and I saw two European officers hiding in the shadows."

Captain Crozier's head whipped around, "Russians again?"

I shrugged, "I could not see the colour of their uniform, Sir, just their faces. They were European."

"We need to know who else is sniffing around." The major looked at me, "Smith, is there any chance you could do what you do so well and find out their nationality?"

I sighed, "If they catch me, Sir, they will not be happy."

"I know but this is your sort of thing. You still have the clothes from Seringapatam, don't you?"

"Yes, Sir."

"Then go inside the palace and listen. You have good ears and all you need to find out is the nationality of the two men. They could be Russian, Portuguese or French."

"Does it make a difference, Sir?"

"The Portuguese are our allies and their presence would not worry me. The Russians do not normally bother about the lands of western India and if it was them then I would be worried, especially after Oudh, but the French…ah, they have advisors in the army of Maharajah Yeshwant Rao Holkar and if they have

them here then that is a major concern for us and Lord
Mornington. General Abercromby defeated the French at
Alexandria in Egypt but if there were French here then it would
show that they had merely changed their focus further east. The
East India Company won its control of this land from the French.
They may well wish it back." He smiled, "Don't take risks,
Smith, just have a sniff around, eh?"

I sighed, "Sir."

As I turned to fetch the clothes I would need Captain Crozier
grabbed my arm, and said, quietly, "Just listen and keep hidden.
This information is not worth your life." He gave the major a
stern look, "The world will not change if you come back empty
handed."

"Sir."

Aadyot had been stirring the pot and listening. He handed the
ladle to Tom Finn and came with me, "You will need the staining
juice I think."

"I think so."

What I had noticed, when we had walked to the meeting, was
the number of men I had seen of mixed blood. They had some
European in them. I decided to play the part of one of those. I
would not wear a shirt but go half naked. The brown stain would
be an effective disguise, I hoped. We went into a tent so that we
would not be observed from the walls. I took off my shirt and
handed my money belt to Aadyot. He alone knew of its
existence, "Keep this for me, Aadyot."

"Of course." He put the money belt beneath his blanket.

As he began to spread the stain over my back, chest and arms
I mussed up my hair to make it wilder. I then took some of the
juice and smeared it on my face. That done we removed my
breeches and I donned the filthy ones I had worn in
Seringapatam. Since then I had used them, often, to clean mud
from Froggy and now they looked even filthier. I fastened the
tatty belt around them and jammed the dagger in. Most men we
had met had been armed and had such a weapon in their belts. I
would not look out of place.

I said, "Well, what do you think?"

He shrugged, "I would know you, even in the dark, Smudger,
but this should get you past the sentries, if you keep your head

down. Wait here." He left the tent and when he returned he had a pot. It was about as long as my arm and I had seen them used to hold wine, water, beer and milk. "I have filled it with water. Carry it on your shoulder and keep you head down. It will get you in through the servant entrance." He took off his own shirt and donned a turban. I will come with you to the servant entrance. Two of us together will not look as suspicious."

"You do not have to do this."

"I know but you are my friend and it is wrong that you alone take all the risks. I will not come inside."

It was now dark outside. We slipped out of the tent. The rest of the platoon, having been spoken to by the captain, assiduously avoided looking at us. They were loudly joking and talking. It would attract the attention of any who were watching. I was in Aadyot's hands. He had clearly been identifying the points of entry when I had been in the fort. He led me towards the wall and then turned right to head to the small door we could see. I lifted the pot. He began to talk to me. It was to add to the disguise. When we neared the door I saw the sentry. Aadyot said, as we neared him, "I have forgotten something, Sutil. Take the pot inside as ordered and I will join you." He grinned at the sentry, "I would forget my head if it were not screwed on."

The sentry nodded, "I know what you mean." By such a simple ruse I was inside the palace.

I walked through the door as though I had every right to be there. I walked down a corridor and from the noise and the smell I realised that it was the kitchen area. I saw an alcove and I placed the pot there. I might need it later on. I walked down the corridor trying to do so with a confidence I didn't feel inside. I examined everything in case I had to make a hurried exit. I glanced around the door and saw a chaotic mass of men who were busy lifting platters clearly intended for the meal. I was about to turn and depart when a voice shouted, "You, where do you think you are going? Get your lazy self back here or I shall have the skin from your back."

I put my hands together and bowed my head, "Sorry, Sir."

"That's better. Pick up the platter of fowl and take it with the others."

"Yes, Sir."

I picked up the large platter with the twenty small, cooked fowl upon it. The smell made me realise how hungry I was. I followed the man who was carrying a platter of fish and I was ahead of the two men carrying the pot with the aromatic stew within. Others followed us. We went through a labyrinth of passages until we reached large double doors. The two sentries said, "About time. The sooner these are fed the sooner we get off duty."

The man with the fish said, "We have come as fast as we could." The doors opened and I saw that there were forty odd people seated along two tables. Liveried servants waited at another table. The fishman went to the table and deposited his platter. I did so, too, but made sure I did it slowly so that I could listen to the babble of conversation from the tables of diners. As I turned I saw not two but three uniforms and three Europeans. They were blue uniforms. As luck would have it the fishman headed past behind the three as he headed for the door and I followed. Passing them I heard them speak. They were French. I recognised the language and it confirmed what their uniforms had told me. I had the information I needed but now I needed to get back to the camp without arousing suspicion.

I planned to simply carry on and pass the kitchen entrance to pick up my urn and then head back outside. The imperious kitchen overseer thwarted my attempts. He stood barring our way outside. He pointed to the next platters, "Take those and when they are gone then you may have a drink break."

This time I looked at the head of the table when I entered. I saw a fourth blue uniform and he was seated next to the Peshwa. On the other side was Balaji Kunjar and they were clearly engaged in a heated debate. The epaulettes and gorget added to the collar insignia told me that he was a colonel. The first time I had been behind the lines with the major he had taught me such things. It was as I was passing the bottom of the table that I saw some pieces of cutlery had been dropped. They looked to be silver to me. I knelt down and picked them up but, as I placed them on the table I managed to palm one knife. The old thief in me did not miss a trick. The man who had knocked it to the floor said nothing to me. I was the lowest of the low. Aadyot had taught me about the caste system and this was a lesson in its reality.

When we reached the kitchen the overseer was not there. As I headed down the corridor one of the stew men said, "Where are you off to?"

"I need a shit."

He laughed, "You have been eating the food they give to us and not that which we steal. You will learn." He had not recognised me and thought I was new.

I laughed, "A lesson learned."

I picked up the urn when I passed it and simply headed out of the door. The sentry did not see my face and assumed that I had every right to leave the building. I headed for the horse guards to make them think I was taking them a drink. They were close enough to our camp for me to be able to do so without arousing too much suspicion.

I managed to get past Jack and Eddie who were on duty without them seeing me. It was a little thing but it made me feel good about myself. I still had the skills to vanish. I stepped out from behind the tent and Sergeant Grundy laughed, "By, lad, but you are like a bloody ghost."

Corporal Neville shouted, "You pair, keep your eyes open. Smith just walked right past you."

While the others laughed the major and the captain were all business, "Well?"

"There are four French officers. One is a colonel and he and Balaji Kunjar were bending the ear of the Peshwa."

Captain Crozier said, "Well done, Smith. Get yourself some food."

The major tossed the end of his cheroot into the fire and said, "Well that complicates things."

As Aadyot ladled food into a bowl I heard the captain say, "How so? We already knew it had to be one of three nationalities."

"Yes but the French are also advising the Holkar army. From what I learned the French officers in command of the guns were the reason they trounced the men of Scindia." He turned to me, "Smith, what did you notice about the uniforms?"

"Sir?"

"You said that they were blue but were there facings, trims, of another colour?"

I closed my eyes to help me to remember. "The colonel had red trim and I think one of the other three did too but the last two had white trim."

"Good lad, the colonel is a colonel of artillery. The French, it seems, are backing two horses in this particular race. I wonder if the Peshwa knows that. When we speak to him on the morrow, Captain, I shall make a point of telling him," he smiled, "subtly, of course." He turned to me. "We cannot afford them to recognise you, Smith. You had better stay here tomorrow."

Seamus murmured, "You have done more than enough for no reward already, Smudger."

The major said, "What was that Hogan?"

"I just said would he like a little more as a reward, Sir, food, you know."

"Ah."

Seamus winked at me.

I was rewarded. I had no duty that night nor in the morning. The rest of the platoon thought I should have had either more praise or a reward from the major. I had not expected anything and I had a fine silver cutlery knife that I could sell.

We had nothing to do but to watch the guards on the walls and to make sure that no one stole from us. The captain and the major were away for most of the day. We ate a midday meal and then enjoyed that rarest of things, a day of leisure.

When they came back the major looked to be in good spirits. "You were right about the French, Smith, well done. As soon as I mentioned that they were the reason the Army of Holkar defeated them he changed his mind. He will be coming with us."

I was not sure if that was a good thing or a bad one.

Captain Crozier said, looking largely at the major, "And before you all think that this is done and dusted, the men who want the Peshwa are at Poona. We have to pass Poona and avoid their army before we reach the Ulhas River."

Sergeant Grundy asked, "Would it not be easier just to head due west and up the coast to Bombay, Sir?"

"That it would, Sergeant, but unfortunately for us there is a second army and they have Bombay cut off. We have to thread a needle and do so for one hundred and twenty-five miles."

It was impossible and I felt it was a venture doomed to failure.

We

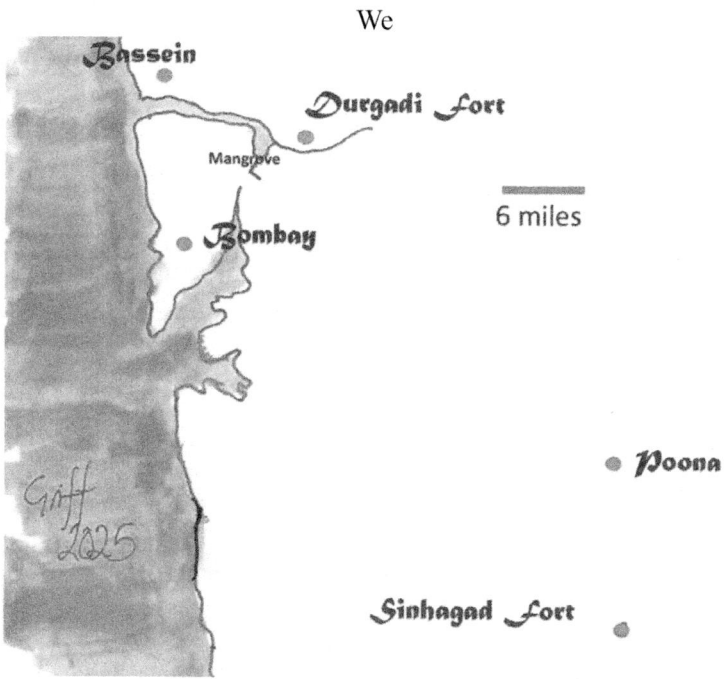

Bassein

Durgadi Fort

Mangrove

6 miles

Bombay

Poona

Graff 2025

Sinhagad Fort

Western India

Chapter 16

The odds became stacked against us when we discovered that the Peshwa insisted on bringing three troops of cavalry with him and a large company of infantry, as well as his wives and servants. While that gave us another one hundred horsemen, we would be slowed down to the speed of wagons. Such a large number of people would be easy to spot. Perhaps this would be the chance for not only me to run but the rest of the platoon. I had no desire to die for this political gesture. I would choose my moment. When we were on the road I would speak with the others. I was no longer thinking about just myself.

We would be leaving in two days' time and that thought depressed me for it gave more time for the enemies of the Peshwa to realise he was leaving and give them the chance to lay an ambush. The officers and Sergeant Grundy were summoned, the next day, to a meeting to plan our route. That was also alarming. I would have preferred Major Tucker to keep his route in his head and only let people know the day we were due to leave. I took the opportunity, while the two corporals were busy checking the saddle furniture of the horses, to broach the idea of running to the others.

"This is doomed to failure, you know."

Eddie Lowe nodded, "It looks that way. I mean how can we be expected to escort wagons and civilians one hundred and twenty-five miles through hostile lands, it can't be done. Smudger is right and the best that we can hope for is to be taken prisoner."

Aadyot shook his head, "You do not want to be a prisoner of the Holkar. They are a cruel people. Better a death in battle."

I measured my words, "Or perhaps we do not die."

Seamus grinned, "I know you have the luck of the devil, Smudger, but how can we escape either death or capture?"

"Simple, we choose our moment and escape."

Dai shook his head angrily, "Desert? Never. I am surprised at you, Smudger."

I had no intention of deserting. Such an act would result in a manhunt and end any chance I had of starting a new life. "I am not talking about deserting, I am talking about escaping with our lives. If we are ambushed it will not be by a warlord or by rapacious bandits. It will be by an army. Now I don't know how good these soldiers who are guarding the Peshwa are but they lost the Battle of Poona and I am not sure they would win in a battle with the same men who beat them in October. Have they suddenly grown into better soldiers in a month?"

Seamus' smile had gone, "Well, what are you suggesting then, if not desertion?"

"I am just saying that when we lose the battle and all is lost, we don't wait to get killed. We try to escape with our lives."

No one argued with me.

Dai just said, "If the officers are still alive and order us to stay, then we stay."

I nodded, "Of course, but I can't see that happening. They will be with the Peshwa and it is he that the enemy will seek to take." I did not like the words I was saying but I was a survivor and this looked hopeless.

The banter and humour went from the camp. I had planted a seed, it was the seed of realism but once planted then the doubts grew in their minds. I was sure I had done the right thing by speaking aloud my doubts. That no one had disagreed with me was evidence that they had been thinking the same thing.

Aadyot spoke to me while we were preparing vegetables, "Smudger, you are my friend."

I nodded, "Of course."

"Then I will speak to you as a friend. You should not have said what you did. You were made Chosen Man and that was for a good reason. You can lead. You need to use that leadership for good. I know it seems hopeless but when you were taken by Jahan Chalan it was hopeless too and yet you survived. You were taken by the Tiger and yet you escaped his lair. This seems hopeless but I believe we will survive."

"But how?"

He smiled, "I do not know but I believe that someone, the major, the captain, the sergeant or, more likely, you, will find a way."

His optimism made me feel even guiltier about opening my mouth and I wished I had said nothing. I know why I had. We had lost too many men already and each death brought my own that little bit closer.

The officers held a meeting with us all when they returned. The meeting was held close to the fire and we were gathered in a tight circle. There was no one nearby but neither of the two officers was taking the chance on us being overheard.

The captain spoke and that was reassuring. I trusted him more than the major. "Now I know this looks hopeless but believe me the major and I have come up with a plan that should mean we do not end up in a Holkar gaol nor having our bones cleaned by vultures. We have told the Peshwa that we are heading for Bombay. That is not our route. We intend to head north and at the crossroads close to Pirangut, we do not turn west but head, instead, to carry on northwards."

He paused so that we could all take that in. Corporal Neville said, "But, Sir, won't the Peshwa's men have something to say about that?"

Major Tucker said, laconically, "They may well do, Corporal, but any protests will only come from those in the pay of Holkar. This group is the only one that knows about the ***Herculean***. Perhaps this is why Lord Mornington arranged for the ship to be there two months since. It was a guarantee that the Peshwa could escape. Once we have passed the crossroads and on the road north we push on as quickly as we can."

He nodded to the captain who continued, "We use the Peshwa's cavalry to range ahead and trigger any ambushes and we use the infantry to guard the baggage. This platoon and his personal bodyguards will guard the Peshwa."

Edward Teach asked, "Sir, does he have to bring his family? Without them we could make better time."

"There is just a wife, Saraswati Bai. They have no children and we have persuaded them to take just four servants. Believe me that is far less than the number they wanted originally. If we need to then they can ride horses and we can abandon the wagons."

Suddenly it looked more hopeful. Perhaps we did have a chance. That evening as we sat around the fire Seamus said, "So, Smudger, are we all going to die now?"

I shrugged, "We have a better chance but we have more enemies than friends in this part of the world."

"Aye, but the quality of friends is greater than those that we shall meet. I will take my chances with the captain and the major. Who knows, at the end of this there may be something in it for us. This Peshwa chap is supposed to be rich. He may well decide to reward us."

I realised that the big Irishman was right although in my experience rich men often forgot any favours that they were owed.

I had not seen the French officers again and neither had our officers. They were of the opinion that, having failed to sway the Peshwa to a French alliance, they had left. I feared that they might run to the enemy. The other absentee was Balaji Kunjar. He was remaining at the hill fort. I could not work out the reason for that. However, as we were leaving it seemed immaterial to me.

The colourful horsemen of the Peshwa's bodyguard led the way down the slope to the plain. The wagon with the wife of the Peshawa and his servants brought up the rear but we rode just behind the Peshwa and his six bodyguards.

That first day was painfully slow and we only covered twelve miles. I wondered if that was planned by the major for it coincided with our arrival at the crossroads. We camped and fires were lit to cook food. We had a ring of enemy camps around us for we were close to Poona and while the whole of the enemy army was not there enough of them, so we were told, were in such numbers as to present a risk of attack. We had half of the army standing a watch. To my mind, this was the most dangerous part of the whole scheme. We were close to Poona and an enemy army lay between us and Bombay. If they chose to attack quickly then we would be caught in a pair of enormous nutcrackers.

The major and the captain went, just before lights out, to tell the Peshwa of the change of plans. The major was a skilled liar and could tell a story as well as I could. Sergeant Grundy went with them and he gleefully recounted how the Peshwa was duped. "The major said that he had news that the French planned to ambush us." He nodded at me, "He used your information about the French officers and the fact that they had fled leant credence to the story. He had planted the seed already about the French being present at the Battle of Poona and the Peshwa was more than happy to approach Bombay from the east and not the south."

"He still thinks we are going to Bombay?"

The sergeant nodded, "He does, Private Williams. Major Tucker does not intend to reveal the presence of the ship until the last minute so keep your mouths shut. We are not sure if there are spies amongst these men."

Jack asked, "Why not tell just the Peshwa about the ship? I mean it is in his interests to escape isn't it?"

The sergeant rolled his eyes, "You came out on an Indiaman did you not?"

"Aye, and a long and tedious voyage it was too."

"And how many passengers were there?"

Jack looked up at the sky as he calculated. "Thirty soldiers and another forty passengers."

The sergeant waved his hand around the fires of the encampment, "Not five hundred though."

I saw realisation dawn, not only on Jack but the rest of the platoon. Many of the bodyguards would be left behind. I had worked out for myself, quite a while ago, that if the ship was to use the river then it had to be a smaller one than the ocean going ship I had used to travel from England. We would be lucky to have a berth ourselves and we would most certainly have to abandon our horses. I told no one this information. We had far to travel and who knew what the future would hold?

Sometimes we give our enemies more credit than they deserve. I had expected swift action from those who wished the Peshwa in their hands. The next day we hurried up the road that would take us to the river where we could contact the ship. This was wilder country than we were used to and that surprised me for Bombay was a large place. It had been the first place I had seen when I had first arrived in India. I had assumed that the East Indian Company would have tamed the jungle. They had not. The road snaked along rivers and we had to ford streams and cross the most rickety of bridges. It also meant that our view of the world was restricted to just forty or so yards ahead and the same behind. As we were in the middle of the column then we were blind. While we would not be the first to feel the wrath of our enemies we would have to rely on soldiers in whom we had no confidence. If the enemy had been better prepared we could easily have been ambushed.

Seamus and Dai were the most optimistic of soldiers and it was they started singing the songs that brightened and lifted our spirits. The noise of hooves and the rumbling of the wheels meant that we were hardly silent. The songs would not alert anyone to our presence but their singing seemed to bond us together. I found myself smiling as we sang and that had to be a good thing.

It was late on the afternoon of the second day after we had deviated from our announced route that we were attacked. The attack came at the rear and the first that we heard was the sound of muskets. I had expected such an attack the day before but the enemy must have searched the road to Bombay first. They would have searched along our planned route and then chased up the unlikely road to the north. The wife of the Prime Minister had the most men guarding her but Captain Crozier was taking no chances. "Finn, Grey and Ganguly, stay with the major and guard the Peshwa. The rest, leave your horses here and come with me."

We did as we were ordered and we unslung our muskets and fitted our bayonets. I hung my straw hat from Froggy's saddle. My face was still dark from the stain and I wanted to be as anonymous as possible in the gloom of the forest road. Horsemen would be coming from the head of the column to help us but the nature of the road meant we would be at the battle first. We heard the clash of steel and the sound of musketry. It was not the regular volleys of British soldiers but was the irregular crack of men fighting for their lives. The dead bullock in the traces of the wagon was a disaster. The wagon could go no further. We saw the servants and the wife of the Peshwa sheltering beneath the stranded wagon. The driver and guards lay dead. The foot soldiers at the rear had been caught and I saw that there were no officers. They were either dead or fled.

Captain Crozier was decisive, "Single line and present muskets."

Already the enemy had carved a path through the defenders and were perilously close to the rear of the wagon. We had come to the rear to support but we were now the rescue. We raised our muskets. We had fired using the bayonet often enough now to know how to compensate for the weight. As the last defenders were hacked the captain shouted, "Fire!" The captain was using a musket too and ten muskets blasted a solid line of balls at the enemy.

Sergeant Grundy roared, "Reload!" It was a race but we were confident in our actions.

Even as the smoke cleared a little and we saw more men rushing over the bodies of the dead to get to us the captain shouted, "Fire!"

The two volleys seemed to put heart into the men around us. When we fired a third time it was not the sound and fury of ten muskets that rent the air but forty as men obeyed the orders of Sergeant Grundy. The fourth was the weight of shot of eighty muskets and by the time we fired a fifth there were almost a hundred muskets firing and there were no more enemies before us. British resolve had put steel into the disheartened defenders of the wife of the Peshwa.

"Smith, tell the wife of the Peshwa that she and the servants must come with us. They will now need to be mounted."

"Sir." I slung my musket and went to the cowering lady and her servants. I bowed and said, "If it would please you my officer asks that you come with us to the Peshwa. Your wagon cannot move. Bring only what you need."

The woman looked terrified but after glancing at the dead bullock and the human slaughter she nodded. She stood and said to the servants. "Fetch the bags with my clothes and those of the Peshwa. Hurry!"

I turned, "They are coming, Captain Crozier."

"We can't afford a delay. Our little action has slowed down the pursuit, that is all."

As we stood, facing down the road where wounded men moaned, I smiled as I saw Seamus hacking a large joint from the rump of the bullock with his bayonet. We would eat meat that night. Our platoon wasted nothing. The servants, fearful for their lives, had quickly recovered the four bags and they joined us.

"Ready, Sir."

"Move." Captain Crozier commanded.

211

"Follow me." I led the lady and the four servants. We left the stranded wagon and the single bullock still in the traces with the dead men. Horsemen galloped from the head of the column. There was a troop of thirty men. Their leader, a havildar, saluted the captain and, drawing his sword led his men to gallop towards the rear. We had time for the horsemen would make those attacking the rear form solid lines to repel them. The horsemen were buying us the time we needed.

Major Tucker and the Peshwa were peering anxiously through the fog of gun smoke that lingered on the road. I saw the relief on their faces as we appeared. The captain shouted, "Get the spare horses. The wagon cannot be used."

The spare horses were brought and the wife of the Peshwa was helped, by her husband's bodyguards, to mount the horse. We had not brought a side saddle and I hoped she knew how to ride. I saw one of the bodyguards take her reins. She would have protection and the Peshwa took his place on the other side of the horse. The servants looked most uncomfortable as they mounted. It all took time and it was almost dark when we rode north. We kept going, riding in the dark, for an hour before the major decided that we had to camp. The seventy men who remained from the advanced guard acted as sentries as we made a rough camp and lit fires to cook food. In the distance we could hear the sound of skirmishing. The rearguard and the troop of horsemen were still duelling with our pursuers.

The meat that we cooked was rarer than we normally ate but it was fresh and it was filling. We put oats and barley in the broth. That would be our breakfast. Captain Crozier came along, "Sergeant Grundy. Divide the men into two. Four hours on and four hours off. The major and I will do a duty too."

We no longer had the same number of men with which we had left the fort. Until the troop of cavalry rejoined us and the remnants of the rearguard we had barely a hundred. I was on the second watch and I huddled beneath my blanket. I did not need the blanket for warmth but to keep away the insects that bit. I would be too hot but at least I would sleep.

John Williams roused me after what seemed like moments only, "Come on, Smudger, rise and shine." I stood and picked up my blanket. He pointed to some men asleep in the forest. They had not been there when we had gone to bed. "Fifty or so arrived about an hour ago. There are more men coming up the road."

I nodded and, as he took my bed I went to make water. I joined Ben Neville and the major when I had finished. Four men approached, three were helping a wounded man. The major said, quietly, "Keep them covered. They could be friends but, equally, they could be enemies pretending to be friends."

For the first two hours of the watch we scrutinised and questioned the stragglers as they made their way into camp. By the time we heard the sound of horses more than a hundred had arrived. This time we levelled our muskets. Out of the darkness loomed the havildar and four men. He reined in and dismounted as did his men. His arm was bloody. "We are the last. The rest of my men kept their oath and we held the enemy. Any who come up this road now are enemies."

He had spoken in English and the major nodded and then saluted with his sword, "Well done, Havildar. Rest while you can. Have that wound seen to."

He looked at his arm as though he had not seen the wound and he nodded. The horses looked weary as they were led to join the other horsemen.

The major said, "So now we have less than two hundred men and the enemy know where we are."

He was not inviting comment and we just peered into the darkness.

The major was making water when we heard the men coming along the road. Ben said, "Ready your muskets."

Although the havildar had said that they were the last I knew that men could have survived and remained hidden. There was a chance that these were such survivors. Ben called out, "Halt, who goes there?"

The voice that answered in English was accented, "Thank God we have found you."

I said, "That is a French accent, Corporal."

"Present." I heard the sound of muskets and weapons ahead being prepared. Ben did too and he shouted, "Fire!" Our eight muskets lit the night and I saw the men in their light. A European led twenty men. The other men on duty with us also discharged their weapons. We reloaded and fired as balls zipped through the darkness towards us.

The major raced from the trees and fired his pistol as Captain Crozier led the rest of the platoon. It was he who shouted, "Cease fire."

We reloaded and waited for the smoke to clear. Ben said, "Smith, come with me."

Captain Crozier said, "We will cover you."

We walked warily toward the men we had killed. Some must have fled for, as we approached I counted just fifteen bodies, but the European who led them had not escaped. Ben and I used our bayonets to turn over his body. He wore a French uniform. It had white trim and that meant he was an officer of infantry. He was also young. Ben undid the dead man's tunic to search the body. There were no papers on the body but he had a good sword and a pistol. Ben took them. "Search the other bodies, Smudger."

The rest had French Charleville muskets. They were not as good as ours but better than those normally used by our enemies. I slung my own musket and whistled, "Give us a hand, lads." There were too many muskets for me to carry. Some of the men who had limped in during the night had lost their weapons. Fourteen could be rearmed.

We left at dawn and we were already exhausted before we began. We had covered a good part of the journey but we had lost more than half of the men with which we had started. The breakfast helped a little but as most of the supplies had been left in the wagon we would be on short rations. The two mules now carried just food. We had discarded the tents.

The next attack did not come from the rear but was an ambush. Perhaps the first attack had been to slow us down, I do not know but not long after our noon break there was a burst of musketry from ahead. A troop of cavalry was our rearguard and the rest were the vanguard. As the havildar had demonstrated, the horsemen were both loyal and brave but their weapons were no match, fired from the back of a horse, for a volley from a company of infantry armed with a musket, even a Charleville one.

"Dismount and form a skirmish line." Captain Crozier rapped out the orders. He turned to me, "Smith, order the Peshwa's men to do the same."

I shouted, "Dismount, form a skirmish line."

Half of the men obeyed immediately and the rest looked to the Peshwa. He shouted, "Do as the red coats command."

It meant we had fifty muskets presented as the survivors from the ambush made their way back. There were just four horsemen and ten loose horses. The four horsemen were all wounded. The infantry that marched down the road were in what I would call a typical French formation. I saw no white faces but guessed that they had been trained by Frenchmen. They were in a solid column eight men wide. That was the width of the road. We were spread out in a loose three-line formation with our platoon in the centre. We had twenty muskets that could bear and fire.

As the enemy halted to present muskets, just fifty yards from us, Captain Crozier said, "Present!" Our muskets came up. The Peshwa's man did not need a translation for that command. "Fire!" Our balls scythed into the enemy and although six or so muskets fired in response they only struck two men. We all reloaded but the platoon's muskets fired before any other.

I heard an order from the enemy and they charged us. We fired two more volleys before they struck us. The superior fire power of our platoon meant that we had fewer enemies. The Peshwa, his wife and servants, protected by his bodyguards were behind us. They knew the value of the red coats and their muskets.

I parried away the bayonet that came at my face. The man wielding it had clearly never used the bayonet in earnest. I back slashed across his face and chest ripping open flesh. He screamed and put his hands to his face. I drove my blade into his middle and he died. The rest of the platoon, even Finn and Grey were enjoying success but the Peshwa's men were not. Had the cavalry at the rear not charged I fear we would have lost more than we did. The handful of men attacked the flank of the men fighting to our left. It began the trickle that became a rout as the survivors retreated up the road. They were out for vengeance and unlike the men who had died at the head of the column, they were fighting men who had discharged their muskets. They hacked, slashed and stabbed at the column of men who had already been badly handled by us. It was no wonder that they fled.

Darkness was falling when the ten surviving horsemen returned. With the four survivors of the ambush we now had just fourteen horsemen. We had lost another thirty infantry and we were surrounded. The river might just be twenty miles away but it might as well have been on the other side of the world.

We did not light a fire but made a camp as far away from the dead as we could manage. The major ordered the bodyguards to stand a watch. They, out of all of us, had yet to fight. While they did so he met with Captain Crozier, Sergeant Grundy and the Peshwa along with the last two officers from the soldiers we had brought from the fort.

We ate the salted meat we all had in our packs and slaked our thirst with the last of the cold tea from the morning.

Seamus chuckled, "Well, Smudger, you are quite the prophet. You were right. We are well and truly up the creek and not a bloody paddle in sight. The trouble is, I can't see anywhere for us to run."

I nodded, "Aye, Seamus, but if we are doomed to die then there is nowhere better to do it than with you lads."

Dai clapped a hand around my shoulders, "Don't be so pessimistic, Smudger. You are our lucky charm and while things look black there is always light at the end of the tunnel."

I smiled but inside I believed that we had finally run out of luck. The money belt around my waist would be found by another, picking over the bodies at the end of the next attack. I did not begrudge the finder the treasure. It was how I had accumulated my fortune, but a fortune was of no use if you were dead.

Chapter 17

"Right, lads, here is the plan." Sergeant Grundy used a stick to draw a map in the mud. "Here is the river. Now here," he made a cross, "is the Durgadi Fort. We had hoped to cross the river there but we think it might be defended and we have too few men to take it. Instead, we are going to head to the river and leave the road. The good news is that it will save us about twenty miles. The bad news is that we will have to find a path through the trees and undergrowth."

John Williams shook his head, "The road is bad enough, Sarge, but this is jungle here."

"I know but one of the bodyguards comes from around here and he seems to think he can find a path through it. He used to hunt here as a boy."

Seamus nodded to the dwindling number of men around us, "And how many of this lot will still be with us when we reach the river, Sergeant Grundy? We are bleeding men every step of the way."

He stood and said, "Enough to die protecting the Peshwa. That is why they are still with him and it is our job to get him to the ship and we will."

I said, quietly, "And if we do get him to the ship, what then?"

The sergeant looked perplexed, "What?"

"You have already said, Sergeant, that the Herculean will be a small ship. It has to be to negotiate a river. The major, the Peshwa, his wife and their servants, they will be able to board, probably the bodyguards too, but us, and our horses? Will we get aboard?"

I saw that he had not even considered that, "The captain will think of something." His voice did not sound convincing. I saw the faces of the others. Even if we succeeded it did not guarantee our survival.

I hoped that Captain Crozier would use his experience to find a way to extricate us from this seemingly impossible position.

By the time we left the road to head into the jungle we had barely sixty of the original men of the Peshwa's army who were still with us. Many had deserted in the night. Fourteen horsemen remained. Not a single officer had survived and they were led by a trooper who had a bandage around his head. As the havildar had said, they had kept their oath. He lay somewhere along the road. He had been a brave man and his reward had been a death unseen by anybody.

The bodyguard found a trail quite quickly but it was barely wide enough for a single horse and that meant our line became longer and we snaked along it. Four of the horsemen acted as a rearguard and the other ten protected our guide. We were in his hands now. He alone knew the way and if he died we would struggle to find the river. It lay to the north of us but that was all we knew. The trees before us were a higgledy-piggledy mess of branches, lianas surrounded by spiky bushes, and thick undergrowth that masked a myriad of dangers. There seemed no way through but he picked his way, it seemed, unerringly towards the river.

It took all day to twist and turn through undergrowth that was deep in parts and in others had been cleared, God alone knows why, to give a few joyful moments of air that was not oppressing. The air, for the most part, was heavy and while it was not the rainy season it felt as though rain was just around the corner. Stinking vegetation hid all kinds of dangers and two men were killed by venomous snakes when they stepped, briefly, from what passed for a path. They were barefoot and we were on horses but as some serpents hung from the trees it was a journey fraught with fear for everyone. When we reached the river I almost wept with joy. The air was slightly fresher and we could see four hundred yards across the brown and murky water to the northern bank. That there was no Indiaman there was not a surprise but the river had to head to the sea and therein lay hope. The map was a guide only but Captain Crozier, when he came to check on the condition of our horses, informed us that we were about twenty miles from the sea. As the ship was supposed to sail up the river that meant we should have largely finished our march. There was, however, bad news too. The bodyguard guide told us that just two miles up the river lay a huge mangrove swamp. Had we been able to cross the river at Durgadi Fort it would not have been a problem for there was a road to the north where there was no swamp but we were south of the river. The guide had found us a place with a beach where the river was wide. It was a good place to camp and a place we could defend. After the horrendous journey through the jungle we needed to recover.

The soldiers with the Peshwa made it into an armed camp as we did not know how long we might have to stay here. Trees were hewn to make barriers and those who knew how to do it were sent into the trees to forage and to hunt.

Captain Crozier said, "Tomorrow I want Corporal Neville, Private Ganguly and Private Smith to go with our guide and find this mangrove swamp. It is not that I don't believe our guide but I would rather have confirmation from my men about the impossibility of travel." He smiled. "If it is impenetrable then I want one man to return, if you are unable to continue west, with the guide here, and the other two can stay and wait for the ship. You can leave your horses here. It is only a couple of miles to travel and will be easier on foot."

"Sir." We all nodded.

"Corporal, take food with you in case the two who are to watch for the ship have to stay there for more than a day."

Ben nodded and said, "Sir, what if an enemy comes? We have not seen them for a day or so but…"

Captain Crozier was an honest man and he nodded, "I think we can expect to meet enemies and if we do then we shall defend ourselves. If we hear musketry then I will send men to assist you." He waved a hand, "This will be Hope Fort for all our hopes on survival depend upon us being able to defend it."

I looked at the dwindling numbers in the camp. If we were attacked again then it would be unlikely that any of us would survive. We had powder and ball for we had taken both from the dead of both sides but what we lacked were numbers of men.

The three of us packed as much as we could in our knapsacks. We made sure we had a pot so that we could brew tea or cook food and we each packed a couple of flints. We hefted the packs on our backs along with our muskets and then followed the guide. He seemed quite at home in this foetid place. I didn't like it for it stank. As we headed west the stink grew. When I asked him what the smell was the guide explained that it was the mangrove swamp that made it smell so. We marched for what seemed like dozens of miles but it was probably just a couple. When he finally stopped I saw what he meant. We had reached the actual edge of the swamp. Trees grew from what appeared to be a lake. That suggested it was shallow enough to walk but that feat would be impossible with the Peshwa and his wife. The water looked brackish and threatening. Who knew what creatures lay below the surface? Birds were in the branches and we saw them swoop to the water to take fish. The smell from the swamp was even worse than it had been as we approached. Vegetation was rotting and the water did not move. While the river appeared to move this water just lurked malevolently as though it was waiting to spring a deadly surprise. Our guide stood in ankle deep water that was so filthy that nothing could be seen. The bodyguard had turned to spread his hands and give us more information when he suddenly screamed and he arched his back. Aadyot pointed at the water snake that slithered away. The man fell into the water. We quickly pulled him from it but he was dead.

The corporal shook his head, "Poor bugger. Well, if nothing else that confirms what he said. We can go no further." He looked east, "Now, which one of you is to go back with the news?"

I shook my head and said, "Corporal, leave Aadyot and me here. The captain is more likely to need a corporal than us two and we are quite happy, aren't we, Aadyot?" I did not relish the walk back and the riverbank looked more inviting than the swamp side. If nothing else it would not stink as bad because the river was moving.

Aadyot grinned, "We are friends, Corporal. I am happy to stay here."

Corporal Neville nodded, "We will bury this chap first. He deserves it."

Aadyot looked sadly at the dead body, "We can bury him but the creatures that lie around here will not leave his body undisturbed. He will be devoured within days."

Ben said, "If it was me I should like someone to say a few words over me."

He was right and we obeyed. We dug a grave and found as many stones as we could to place over the body and then the corporal said words. They were words more suited to a Christian burial but, as he said, so long as some words were said then God would understand. He left immediately.

We sought somewhere close to the river from where we could watch for the ship. The mangrove swamp was at a bend in the river. We had not seen any sign of the **Herculean** upstream and I knew, from my time on a ship, that wind and tides would determine her arrival. We could wish it to be sooner as much as we liked but nature did not obey man. Man obeyed nature. The place we chose to wait was more open and less oppressive. The breeze took away the stink of the mangrove swamp and once we lit a fire then the insects would leave us alone.

We found as much dry wood as we could and got the fire going. As well as stopping flies from bothering us it might discourage spiders and snakes. I had always found a fire to be reassuring and while it might draw enemies to us, the nature of the mangrove swamp was that they would find that as much of a barrier as we had. We put water on to boil. Aadyot threw a couple of fishing lines he had brought into the water. I dreaded him catching a snake but he was sure that the only thing he would catch would be edible. We made tea and drank half. The other half we used to top up our canteens. We then put more water in the pot to boil. If nothing else we would be able to drink the water when it cooled. Surprisingly he did find and catch creatures that we could eat. He caught three crayfish and we popped them into a pot of boiling water. He found some wild greens that he assured me were edible and we waited for the meal to change colour. The crayfish were delicious and that meal was the best I enjoyed, including the rare beef, on the whole journey. We sat with our backs to two large trees and peered into the darkness.

"Well, Aadyot, we can get some sleep now."

"What about the ship, Smudger? Should we not watch for it?" I was the sailor and Aadyot was not.

"It will not come at night. They will anchor, probably closer to the mouth of the river and try again tomorrow."

"I do not understand. The river is wide here."

He was right. It had looked, in daylight, to be about four hundred yards wide but I knew that a captain would not risk ripping his hull out on a river he did not know. "It is but the captain has to think about the tide. He will sail up the river in daylight at high tide, when the wind is right. He will have men with lines to test the bottom. We will see him when he edges his way upstream. He will just have the topsails, the sails at the top of his mast, to make him move. We will see those first."

I had worked out that it was high tide now but there was little wind and it was night. We had until daylight.

"Do we watch, Smudger?"

I shook my head, "We are safe enough here and besides, we are both exhausted. We sleep." I suddenly realised that I was giving commands. How I had changed since I had fled England.

I slept but fitfully. Every noise in the night made me wake. The death of the guide had shaken me. He had been one who knew this land and yet he had been taken. When I woke it was not dawn but I could see that the river was lower. It was between tides. I made water and then rekindled the fire. Aadyot was disturbed and he rose. By the time the sun flared in the east I could see that the river was getting higher. The tide was beginning its turn. Aadyot fished and this time caught two small fish that we gutted and cooked. They were delicious. I decided that I could get used to this sort of diet.

I heard the ship before I saw it. The creaking of the yards and the crack of the sails, not to mention the shouts from the lookouts told me it was coming before I saw the topsails of the one-hundred-and-twenty-foot long ship. I stood and began to wave. I knew there would be a lookout and he would spy my red tunic. I saw the topsails reefed as it turned to come as close to the bank as the captain could manage. I saw just seven gunports. They were all open. The captain was prepared to fight.

The captain cupped his hands, "Are you the fellows we are looking for?"

I cupped my own hands and spoke slowly, "The ones you want are another mile or so upstream. They are close to a beach." I pointed upstream.

"Do you want me to send a boat for you?"

I shook my head and shouted, "No, we will make our own way back." He waved and the topsails were lowered. It moved slowly.

We packed up our gear and began to walk back to the camp. We both glanced at the grave as we passed. This time we did not have a guide and that meant we had to pick our way carefully towards the others. We would find it hard to see them until we were almost on top of them, but we knew that all we had to do was to keep the river to our left and we would, eventually, find them. We had plenty of time for it would not be a quick process to load the small ship. We picked our way looking for the easiest route. It was that care that enabled us to see the blue uniform leading the men with muskets towards the camp. I could just see, above the trees, the mast tops of *Herculean*. We were close to the camp and the blue uniform suggested that this was our enemy. That they were up to no good was clear. They had found our trail, smelled the woodsmoke and were about to end the flight of the Peshwa.

I said, quietly, "Load your weapon, we have to warn the camp."

"Yes, Smudger." Aadyot obeyed me but my heart sank. There were two of us and there were many men ahead of us. When we fired our guns then the camp and the ship would hear the sound but would that be a death knell for us?

Our weapons loaded, we moved a little closer to the men. I counted more than a hundred and that that meant there were others I could not see. Their backs were to us. There were a few blue uniforms but most were dressed in the Holkar uniforms we had seen at the previous attacks. I stopped when we were fifty yards from them. I chose the place to halt as there was a branch from a tree that came out at right angles and was quite low down. It made a good place to rest my musket and would afford some protection from the balls that would be sent back in our direction. "We use this to fight." Aadyot primed his musket and rested it on the branch. I aimed at the back of the French officer and said, "We fire and keep firing until…"

"It has been an honour to serve with you, Smudger."

"And you but let us leave our goodbyes for a time when all hope is lost. When the rest of the platoon hear the firing they will come."

"Yes, Chosen Man."

"Fire!"

I did not see where the ball went for I was too busy reloading. Balls flew back at us. I fired again as did Aadyot. After three volleys I also heard, in the distance, the sound of muskets from the camp. I recognised the India Pattern Musket. I kept loading and firing as balls shredded the leaves above our heads. I also heard balls smacking into the tree branch that protected us. Suddenly there was the sound of a series of cracks, deafening booms and whines from the river. I knew what it was. The Indiaman had fired a broadside.

A ship's broadside, even a small one was something of a blunt weapon. They would be firing blind in the jungle and the balls could hit friend as well as foe. We were in as much danger as the enemy. "Get down."

We ducked behind the tree branch. A ship's broadside would scythe through trees, undergrowth and bodies with equal ease. I heard the screams of men and the sound of wood being shredded. The air was filled with an unearthly noise not to mention the stink of massive charges that made our muskets seem puny. I had witnessed such a broadside from a ship. Now I understood the terror it inspired in those at the receiving end. The captain sent four broadsides to sweep the trees clear.

When it stopped I did not move. I looked at Aadyot who looked terrified. I gave him what I hoped was a reassuring smile. I reloaded my weapon. When there was silence I raised my head. All that lay before me were the dead men who had been killed by the small broadside and the trees that had been scythed down. There was now a new clearing in the jungle. I realised that the ship must have used grape and ball. The captain was taking no chances. We moved towards the enemy with muskets at the ready but the ones we saw were dead. There would be survivors but with their officer dead, I saw his body, they would not stay. I saw that he had a bullet hole in his back but he had no head. I had killed him and then a cannonball had taken his skull. I searched the body for papers but found none. I did discover a golden locket and some coins in his purse as well as a sword. I took them.

I looked up when I heard a laugh. It was Seamus, "Sure, and the lucky little man has survived again. It is good to see you two again."

A grin spread across my face, "And you, too, Seamus."

The ship had sent a boat ashore and by the time we reached the camp, the Peshwa, his wife and the servants were aboard. The next boat would take the bodyguards and the major. He was smoking a cheroot and speaking to Captain Crozier as we approached. I heard him say, "The captain can take the platoon, Dick, but not the horses and not the Peshwa's men."

In my head I was pleading for the captain to take us all on the ship but I knew he would not. "No, Geoffrey. These are brave men," he pointed to the pitifully small number of men who remained, "and they have stayed by the Peshwa. I will not abandon them. As the crow flies we are about fifteen miles from Bombay. We will head there."

Major Tucker shook his head, "And as you are not a crow you will have twenty or thirty miles to travel. There will be more jungle and, I do not doubt, more enemies."

"We will do it. Are you headed to Bombay?"

He shook his head, "Lord Mornington is waiting at the mouth of the river at Bassein. The captain said that his lordship is keen to conclude the negotiations for the alliance."

Captain Crozier held out his hand, "Then I shall say farewell here. I hope that we shall meet again and that we will survive."

The major laughed, "Of that there is no doubt." He turned to me, "And once more I am in your debt, Smith. Had we been caught unawares then all the sacrifices we have made would have been for naught. I would say good luck but you seem to have that in abundance."

"Major, the captain is waiting. Time and tide, Sir." The bosun pointed to the dory.

We watched the major as he headed for the boat, "Look after my horse, eh?"

Captain Crozier shouted back, "Of course."

We watched the major climb aboard and when the dory was hoisted aboard the captain began to turn his ship around. There was enough room for him to do so but I knew he would be glad when he had open water beneath his keel once more. The major waved at us. He was free from the jungle. He would have a bath and would sleep that night between sheets. He would enjoy hot food served on good plates and he would not be at risk of an ambush. We, on the other hand, were far from safe. We had the jungle and, potentially, an army out there intent on causing us harm.

When it was out of sight Captain Crozier was all business. "It is too late in the day to travel now. I want a whole day to reach a road. We will burn the bodies and see what we can salvage. They may have supplies. We will need at least one day and, perhaps two, to reach Bombay."

Corporal Teach said, "Sir, isn't Bombay run by the company?"

"It is, Corporal, but the land around it is far from settled. We will travel as though we are at war. That way we have a chance of surviving."

It was when we were piling the bodies that I realised there were just thirty-eight men left from the original five hundred who had left the hill fort. The price paid for the Peshwa's escape had been a high one. One good thing was that we now had enough horses to mount everyone. The Peshwa's infantry might not be used to horses but they would find the journey much easier on horseback.

It was galling not to head directly for Bombay but to follow the mangrove swamp south until it petered out and became a tangle of streams. The captain now led the little band. We had just six of the original horsemen left; the rest had succumbed to disease or wounds on the road. Unlike the infantry none had deserted. I found that interesting for they were horsemen and they could easily have done so. The havildar who had spoken to us was typical of the men of the Peshwa's horse. The six were our advance guard and scouts. They came from this land and they knew the best route to follow. We were in their hands. The captain had Sergeant Grundy and Corporal Teach at the rear with Seamus and Dai. The rest of us rode at the fore of our column. The infantry who had survived and seen their Peshwa and his wife escape seemed in good humour. They had survived and done what was ordered. They had saved their leader. I heard the banter in their voices as they rode the unfamiliar horses behind us.

It was the end of the day when the road ahead of us erupted in a volley of musket fire. When two horses, bereft of riders, rode in then we knew we had been ambushed. We were not horsemen. We were infantry who were riding horses. The captain ordered us to dismount.

"Ganguly, hold the reins. The rest of you form a line. Smith, order the Peshwa's men to dismount and form lines."

I turned and shouted, "Dismount. Form lines and load your muskets." The captain had not asked me to order that but I knew it would be prudent. The dismounting of the horses was not as successful as one might have hoped and some men fell. Their cries told me that they had been hurt. Even when they were dismounted they appeared to have forgotten how to load weapons. As Sergeant Grundy and his rearguard arrived we barely had forty men in three lines to face whatever was coming down the road towards us. Our platoon all fitted our bayonets. We knew we would need them. The ones with us did not all emulate us. It was fear and, perhaps complacency. They had thought the danger was gone with the departure of the Peshwa. It was not.

Captain Crozier had long since taken to using a musket and he shouted, "Present!"

The French officer who led the infantry down the road had more than twice our numbers. The sprinkling of European faces told me that there were non-commissioned officers with the men of Holkar. They had a line ten men wide and the column appeared to be a long one. There had to have been more than one band of soldiers seeking us. Perhaps these thought the Peshwa was still with us. The red coats of the East India Company might have led them to believe that.

This encounter would be decided by the quality of the two officers who led the two groups and by those wearing either red or blue. The rest would just be numbers. They halted just eighty paces from us but Captain Crozier knew our weakness and he needed every advantage. Even as they raised their muskets to fire he gave the order for us to fire. "Front rank, fire!"

Some of the second rank fired prematurely.

The captain shouted, "Second rank, fire!" We dropped to one knee to reload but I saw that some of the Peshwa's infantry were slow to do so. They still stood and obscured the aim of the men behind.

I heard the French officer give the command to fire and he had his front ranks all fire. The Charleville musket was not as good as ours but I saw men fall. Some were the ones who had reloaded from a standing position and others were in our second rank.

"Third rank, fire."

The muskets of the third rank were not as effective as the front rank. If we had enjoyed the luxury of time then Corporal Neville would have stood with the second rank and Sergeant Grundy the third.

The enemy fired one more volley and then I heard the French command to charge. We all stood. The last thing we needed was to take a charge when kneeling. As we stood the captain shouted, "Fire!"

Forty muskets did not open fire. Men had fallen. The third rank had not reloaded and some of the second rank were still struggling. Just half of our muskets fired but, as the balls hit the enemy I saw the French officer clutch his shoulder. He was wounded. Then the column struck us. They had the advantage of weight of numbers but they had bodies strewn before them. As luck or perhaps it was our accuracy with the musket, would have it, the platoon had more bodies before us. I parried the bayonet away with contemptuous ease and even as the bayonet slid along my leather belt I was driving my blade deep into the man. I twisted the blade to pull it from his body and he screamed. I knew that speed of hands was all important and after pulling the weapon back I lunged at the head of the next man. I was taller than he was and had a longer reach. I was gambling that my bayonet would strike him before he gutted me. I won the bet and my bayonet pierced his eye.

I was in the middle of a sea of metal as bayonets lunged, flashed and stabbed. I saw the shining of a sword and knew that Captain Crozier had drawn that weapon. I suddenly remembered the brace of pistols hanging around my neck. When the next man to attack me tripped I rammed my musket's blade into his back and then, leaving the musket there, drew and cocked the two pistols. Both fired a big ball and while they were not accurate at more than twenty or thirty paces I was just ten paces from the next men racing to gut me. When I fired one pistol the man I struck had almost reached me. The ball smashed his skull and as brains and bones showered the men behind so the ball carried on to hit another man, making a large hole in his shoulder. My second pistol was just as effective. I let the two pistols hang from their lanyards as I picked up the musket and looked for another enemy. My two pistols had cleared a space and that allowed me to turn to the side where Bob Cathcart was fighting two men. I drove my bayonet into the side of one of the attacking men allowing Bob to stab the other. The two of us then went to the aid of Eddie Lowe. On the other side of me, George and John Williams had taken advantage of the hole I had created and the five of us saw our chance.

Eddie shouted, "Charge!" We ran towards the French sergeant who was trying to rally the flagging attackers. He raised his musket and pulled the trigger. He had not reloaded and as Bob drove his bayonet into his stomach the rest of us hacked and slashed at the men he had commanded. Their leader gone and their spirit broken, they ran.

Captain Crozier was taking no chances and he shouted, "Stand to!"

The five of us halted. We looked down at the French sergeant. The moustache apart he was the double of Sergeant Grundy. He gave a sad smile and with a sigh, died. He was serving his country but was far from home. I saw the dead officer. He had been hit by one musket ball but it was the second to his head that had killed him. The third Frenchman was nowhere to be seen.

The five of us looked at each other. Bob shook his head and said, "Eddie, you are a mad bugger. Why the charge?"

He shrugged, "I was fed up with being the one on the receiving end. Besides, you daft buggers all followed me."

George gave him a playful pat to the back of the head, "You might be mad but the Devil's Dozen looks after its own."

We turned and looked. Less than twenty of the men who had followed the Peshwa survived. We saw that Ben Neville and the sergeant had been wounded. Tom and Jack were tending to their wounds while Corporal Teach was looking after a wounded havildar. He was the only non-commissioned officer left.

Captain Crozier said, "You five lunatics, go and gather the horses and then see if the road to Bombay is clear."

Grinning, I said, "Sir."

I went to Aadyot who handed Froggy's reins to me. I mounted and while I waited for the other four reloaded my pistols. I was Chosen Man and I waved my arm to lead the other four up the road. We found three horses grazing at the side of the road and the bodies of the last of the Peshwa's horsemen lay on the road. They had been almost cut in two by the volley. Two horses were also dead. We could do nothing for the dead.

"Bring those three horses with us."

That the others obeyed showed just how far I had come. We rode up the road and I saw the last of the ambushers heading into the trees. They were going to take shelter in the mangrove swamp. The road to Bombay was clear. We returned to the captain and reported what we had discovered.

The wounded men made an early camp necessary and we had men's bodies to burn. After taking weapons from the dead we piled their corpses on dead wood and burned them so that the wind would take the smell way from us. We cooked horsemeat on open fires and had not only a good meal but also a night free from insects. The smoke from the funeral pyre had that effect. The next day our depleted and bloodied column headed up the road to Bombay. We reached it at noon. The men who had been there for the Peshwa looked broken. I had no idea what would happen to them. It was not that we did not care, we did, but our platoon had done the job as ordered and more. We were all proud of what we had achieved. That we had been used was nothing new but we now had a reputation and the welcome in Bombay reflected that success.

Epilogue

While we recovered in Bombay and waited for a ship to take us back to Madras, we heard that the Peshwa had signed a treaty with Lord Mornington. Captain Crozier was wined and dined by the resident and when he returned to the barracks he told us the main points of the treaty.

"There will be a British force of six thousand troops permanently stationed with the Peshwa." He nodded, "That means all those forts we took will be repaired and manned by British soldiers."

Sergeant Grundy laughed, "That will keep him safe and make sure he does nothing daft!"

"And, the East India Company will make money for any territorial districts yielding two million six hundred thousand rupees are to be paid to the East India Company."

Sergeant Grundy laughed again, we had been issued our rum ration and he was enjoying it, "Even better. The Peshwa is going to have to pay for the soldiers who are watching him. You have to hand it to Lord Mornington, he knows how to negotiate."

The captain nodded and, as he listed the points, held up fingers, "The Peshwa can't enter into any other treaty without first consulting the Company. He cannot declare war without first consulting the Company. Any territorial claims made by him would be subject to the arbitration of the Company. He has to renounce his claim over Surat and Baroda. There will be a British resident at Poona."

Sergeant Grundy said, "So, in effect the land ruled by the Marathas is now East India Company land with this Peshwa as a figurehead."

"You have it in one, Sergeant, and he must also exclude all Europeans from his service as well as conducting his foreign relations in consultation with the British. His hands are tied. The French, Portuguese and Russians will have to leave Maratha land."

Seamus poured himself more rum, "And what do we get out of this, Sir? I mean, we all know that but for us the Peshwa would be dead on the road to Bassein."

"What do you expect to get, Hogan? We are company men. We serve the company. We did our duty and we did it well."

We drank in silence until Aadyot, who was normally silent, spoke, "Gwalior, Nagpore and Indore, not to mention Bhonsla and Berar will not endure such conditions. Daulat Rao Scindia will not accept losing his independence. There will be a war." He pointed, "And it will be in the land of Scindia."

My heart sank. Scindia was close to Oudh. It meant I would be far from the sea and any hope of flight would be gone. My treasure was growing but I had no chance to enjoy my riches. I would have to continue as a soldier of the East India Company.

Seamus must have seen the look on my face. He put a huge arm around my shoulder, "Look on the bright side, Smudger. You are a Chosen Man. The next step is corporal!"

I smiled, "Thank you, Seamus, I have risen far enough as it is."

Captain Crozier nodded, "Hogan is right, Smith. You may have begun life as a thief but you are a natural soldier. You have found your feet in the perfect place."

I realised that, in a way he was right. I was comfortable with these warriors and, for the first time in my life, I had friends. I would just play the cards I had been dealt and see what came from them.

The End

Glossary

Bombay - Mumbai
Bring 'em near - telescope
Calcutta - Kolkata
Havildar - a sergeant
HCS - Honourable Company ship
Jangheas - short jodhpurs worn by native infantry
Peshwa - Prime Minister of the Maratha lands
Squits - diarrhoea.
Tiddly oggy - sailor slang for the sea
Ubhaya-Lokadheeshwara - King of the Two Worlds

Historical References

The East India Company ruled large parts of India and had three Presidencies: Madras, Bombay and Calcutta. The British Government, however, had imposed their own Governor General on the company, which meant that while most of the soldiers who fought in the battles I describe were company soldiers, the British Government sent British troops. The Duke of York's campaign in the Low Countries had not gone well and India was a place where Britain could not only defend British controlled land but enjoy victories over the French. There were European soldiers and native soldiers, generally referred to as sepoys. They had cavalry and artillery arms but the bulk of the troops were infantry. The Europeans were not, in the main, considered to be good soldiers. The fictitious section I describe, a sort of nineteenth century Dirty Dozen, are better than most of those who were in the company ranks.

I made up the missionary incident but I am a storyteller and I wanted to give my hero the chance to redeem himself after a life of crime.

The main events in the book: the Battle of Malavelli, and the letters to the Nizam are historical facts. The Resident in Madras did intercept letters that indicated the French were trying to add Hyderabad as an ally. Despite his junior rank, Sir Arthur Wellesley was the de facto commander of the army led by General Hunter when Mysore was invaded. His brother, the Governor General, was with the army and that may have contributed. The 33rd made an uphill bayonet charge against many times their number. They were led in the charge by Colonel Wellesley.

Bully beef eventually became the name for tinned corned beef but in the nineteenth century it was a corruption of the French word, bouilli. It means boiled meat. The French, and the English often served the liquor that cooked the beef as a sort of soup and then the beef as a main course. Soldiers were not so fussy and they tended to eat it all as a stew. Root vegetables and barley would make it more of a meal. As canning was not yet commercially available, they had to make do with salted meat.

The conspiracy to allow the Forlorn Hope to attack when there were no defenders was true. Even more amazing was that British officers climbed the glacis the night before the assault and there met with Mir Sadiq. The premature explosion of the gunpowder also happened. Mir Sadiq and his co-conspirators sent the men on watch to eat their noonday meal. That they did so beggars belief.

I have taken just a couple of liberties with the death of the Tiger of Mysore. A first-hand account of the finding of the body is as follows, "Benjamin Sydenham described the body as: wounded a little above the right ear, and the ball lodged in the left cheek, he had also three wounds in the body, he was in stature about 5 ft 8 in and not very fair, he was rather corpulent, had a short neck and high shoulders, but his wrists and ankles were small and delicate. He had large full eyes, with small arched eyebrows and very small whiskers. His appearance denoted him to be above the Common Stamp. And his countenance expressed a mixture of haughtiness and resolution. He was dressed in a fine white linen jacket, chintz drawers, a crimson cloth round his waist with a red silk belt and pouch across his body and head. He had lost his turban and there were no weapons of defence about him." I made up the presence of Colonel Pohlmann who did exist and was one of the men Arthur Wellesley will fight at Assaye.

The warlord Dhondia Wagh existed and his oath to stain his moustache with the blood of his enemies is true. When he defeated him Sir Arthur had the blood smeared head displayed to show, I think, the barbarity of the warlord but he also took as his ward Dhondia Wagh's four-year-old son. He had him educated and maintained. They were different times.

The word Peshwa can appear to be confusing. It was the title of the Prime Minister of the Maratha States but it was also the name of the area within the Maratha confederation where the Peshwa resided. Baji Rao was the last ruler to use the title.

The hunting of the Peshwa by his enemies is interesting. As they controlled Poona then it should have been simplicity itself for them to capture the man who haemorrhaged soldiers. As far as I can discover he made it to the ship without British help. There must have been some British help as the ship waiting to rescue the Peshwa was British. I have used the Devil's Dozen. The ship waiting to take the Peshwa to Bassein is documented and even though Bombay is quite close to Bassein, the negotiations were signed in Bassein. The treaty bore its name. I do not know why Lord Mornington made it so. As with all my stories when I cannot find concrete evidence I use my little grey cells to come up with a solution. The platoon being used as escorts is one such example.

The story will continue. As Aadyot suggested war would come from this treaty and the road to Waterloo will begin for Sir Arthur Wellesley at Assaye in 1803. The Devil's Dozen will be there and Bill Smith's journey will continue.

Books used in the research

- The Military History Book
- Armies of the East India Company 1750-1850, Reid and Embleton
- The first Anglo-Sikh War 1845-46, Thompson and Noon
- Wellington's Infantry (1), Fosten
- Wellington's Regiments - Ian Fletcher
- Wellington's Military Machine - Haythornwaite
- The Napoleonic Source Book - Haythornwaite
- Nelson's Navy - Brian Lavery
- Assaye 1803 - Millar and Dennis

Griff Hosker February 2025

Other books by Griff Hosker

If you enjoyed reading this book, then why not read another one by the author?

Ancient History

Roman Rebellion
(The Roman Republic 100 BC-60 BC)
Legionary

The Sword of Cartimandua Series
(Germania and Britannia 50 A.D. – 128 A.D.)
Ulpius Felix- Roman Warrior (prequel)
The Sword of Cartimandua
The Horse Warriors
Invasion Caledonia
Roman Retreat
Revolt of the Red Witch
Druid's Gold
Trajan's Hunters
The Last Frontier
Hero of Rome
Roman Hawk
Roman Treachery
Roman Wall
Roman Courage

The Wolf Brethren series
(Britain in the late 6th Century)
Saxon Dawn
Saxon Revenge
Saxon England
Saxon Blood
Saxon Slayer
Saxon Slaughter
Saxon Bane

Saxon Fall: Rise of the Warlord
Saxon Throne
Saxon Sword

Medieval History

The Dragon Heart Series
Viking Slave *
Viking Warrior *
Viking Jarl *
Viking Kingdom *
Viking Wolf *
Viking War*
Viking Sword
Viking Wrath
Viking Raid
Viking Legend
Viking Vengeance
Viking Dragon
Viking Treasure
Viking Enemy
Viking Witch
Viking Blood
Viking Weregeld
Viking Storm
Viking Warband
Viking Shadow
Viking Legacy
Viking Clan
Viking Bravery

Norseman
Norse Warrior*

The Norman Genesis Series
Hrolf the Viking *
Horseman *
The Battle for a Home *
Revenge of the Franks *

The Tiger and the Thief

The Land of the Northmen
Ragnvald Hrolfsson
Brothers in Blood
Lord of Rouen
Drekar in the Seine
Duke of Normandy
The Duke and the King

Danelaw
(England and Denmark in the 11th Century)
Dragon Sword *
Oathsword *
Bloodsword *
Danish Sword*
The Sword of Cnut*

New World Series
Blood on the Blade *
Across the Seas *
The Savage Wilderness *
The Bear and the Wolf *
Erik The Navigator *
Erik's Clan *
The Last Viking*
The Vengeance Trail *

The Conquest Series
(Normandy and England 1050-1100)
Hastings*
Conquest*
Rebellion

The Aelfraed Series
(Britain and Byzantium 1050 A.D. - 1085 A.D.)
Housecarl *
Outlaw *
Varangian *

The Reconquista Chronicles

(Spain in the 11th Century)
Castilian Knight *
El Campeador *
The Lord of Valencia *

The Anarchy Series
(England 1120-1180)
English Knight *
Knight of the Empress *
Northern Knight *
Baron of the North *
Earl *
King Henry's Champion *
The King is Dead *
Warlord of the North*
Enemy at the Gate*
The Fallen Crown*
Warlord's War*
Kingmaker*
Henry II
Crusader
The Welsh Marches
Irish War
Poisonous Plots
The Princes' Revolt
Earl Marshal
The Perfect Knight

Border Knight
(1182-1300)
Sword for Hire *
Return of the Knight *
Baron's War *
Magna Carta *
Welsh Wars *
Henry III *
The Bloody Border *
Baron's Crusade*
Sentinel of the North*

The Tiger and the Thief

War in the West*
Debt of Honour*
The Blood of the Warlord
The Fettered King
de Montfort's Crown
The Ripples of Rebellion

Sir John Hawkwood Series
(France and Italy 1339- 1387)
Crécy: The Age of the Archer *
Man At Arms *
The White Company *
Leader of Men *
Tuscan Warlord *
Condottiere*
Legacy*

Lord Edward's Archer
Lord Edward's Archer *
King in Waiting *
An Archer's Crusade *
Targets of Treachery *
The Great Cause *
Wallace's War *
The Hunt*
The Prince and the Archer*

Struggle for a Crown
(1360- 1485)
Blood on the Crown *
To Murder a King *
The Throne *
King Henry IV *
The Road to Agincourt *
St Crispin's Day *
The Battle for France *
The Last Knight *
Queen's Knight *
The Knight's Tale *

Tales from the Sword I
(Short stories from the Medieval period)

Tudor Warrior series
(England and Scotland in the late 15th and early 16th century)
Tudor Warrior *
Tudor Spy *
Flodden*

Conquistador
(England and America in the 16th Century)
Conquistador *
The English Adventurer *

English Mercenary
(The 30 Years War and the English Civil War)
Horse and Pistol*
Captain of Horse

Modern History

East Indiaman Saga
East Indiaman*
The Tiger and the Thief

The Napoleonic Horseman Series
Chasseur à Cheval
Napoleon's Guard
British Light Dragoon
Soldier Spy
1808: The Road to Coruña
Talavera
The Lines of Torres Vedras
Bloody Badajoz
The Road to France
Waterloo

The Lucky Jack American Civil War series

The Tiger and the Thief

Rebel Raiders
Confederate Rangers
The Road to Gettysburg

Soldier of the Queen series
Soldier of the Queen*
Redcoat's Rifle*
Omdurman*
Desert War
An Officer and a Gentleman

The British Ace Series
(World War 1)
1914
1915 Fokker Scourge
1916 Angels over the Somme
1917 Eagles Fall
1918 We will remember them
From Arctic Snow to Desert Sand
Wings over Persia

Combined Operations series
(1940-1951)
Commando *
Raider *
Behind Enemy Lines*
Dieppe
Toehold in Europe
Sword Beach
Breakout
The Battle for Antwerp
King Tiger
Beyond the Rhine
Korea
Korean Winter

Tales from the Sword II
(Short stories from the Modern period)

Books marked thus *, are also available in the audio format.
For more information on all of the books then please visit the
author's website at www.griffhosker.com where there is a link to
contact him or visit his Facebook page: Griff Hosker at Sword
Books or follow him on Twitter: @HoskerGriff or Sword Books
@swordbooksltd
If you wish to be on the mailing list then contact the author
through his website: www.griffhosker.com

Printed in Dunstable, United Kingdom

63720458R00143